#1 *New York Times* Bestselling Author

LAUREN

By Any Other Name

a novel

**What she doesn't know about
love could fill a book.**

BOOK
ENDS

ADVANCE PRAISE FOR

By Any Other Name

"Reading Lauren Kate's *By Any Other Name* is like watching a Nora Ephron movie. It makes the day seem brighter, the world seem more hopeful, and happiness seem possible for everyone. This book is a buoyant celebration of love."
—Jill Santopolo, author of *The Light We Lost* and *More Than Words*

"I devoured this book in one sitting. Delightful, optimistic, and with a perfect dash of bookishness, *By Any Other Name* is the rom-com the world needs right now."
—Julie Buxbaum, author of *Tell Me Three Things*

"A smart imaginative rom-com that had me turning the pages."   —Abby Jimenez, author of *Life's Too Short*

"A behind-the-scenes look at publishing that feels both realistic and totally fun—I wish I could read Noa Callaway's books in real life! It's a joy to watch Lanie get the courage to go after what she wants, and the supporting characters (like her hilarious best friends and her irreverent grandmother) leap off the page. An incredibly romantic love story that's full of surprises, *By Any Other Name* is perfect for anyone who dreams of happily-ever-afters."
—Kerry Winfrey, author of *Waiting for Tom Hanks*

By Any Other Name

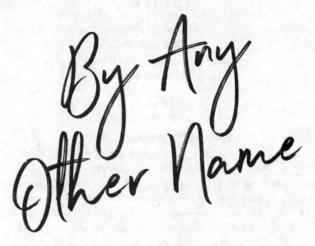

By Any Other Name

Lauren Kate

G. P. Putnam's Sons
New York

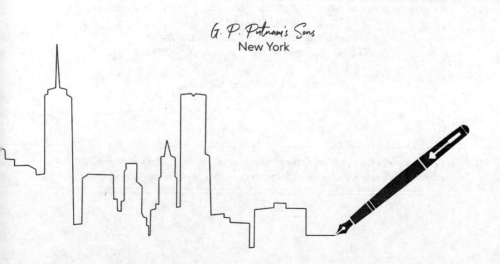

PUTNAM
— EST. 1838 —

G. P. PUTNAM'S SONS
Publishers Since 1838
An imprint of Penguin Random House LLC
penguinrandomhouse.com

Library of Congress Cataloging-in-Publication Data

Names: Kate, Lauren, author.
Title: By any other name / Lauren Kate.
Description: New York: G. P. Putnam's Sons, [2022]
Identifiers: LCCN 2021044069 (print) | LCCN 2021044070 (ebook) |
ISBN 9780735212541 (trade paperback) | ISBN 9780735212565 (ebook)
Subjects: LCGFT: Romance fiction.
Classification: LCC PS3611.A78828 B9 2021 (print) | LCC PS3611.A78828 (ebook) |
DDC 813/.6—dc23
LC record available at https://lccn.loc.gov/2021044069
LC ebook record available at https://lccn.loc.gov/2021044070

Printed in the United States of America
1st Printing

Book design by Ashley Tucker

For Elizabeth Nusbaum Epstein, my BD

Those you love come at you like lightning

—Dorianne Laux, "To Kiss Frank . . ."

By Any Other Name

Chapter One

"PEONY PRESS, THIS IS LANIE BLOOM—" I SAY, BARELY getting the phone to my ear before the voice on the other end cuts me off.

"Hallelujah-you're-still-at-your-desk!"

It's Meg, our senior publicist, and my closest friend at work. She's calling from the Hotel Shivani, where, four hours from now, we'll be hosting a blowout wedding-themed book launch for Noa Callaway—our biggest author and the writer who taught me about love when my mom couldn't. Noa Callaway's books changed my life.

If experience is any guide, we're just slightly overdue for all our best-laid plans to go up in flames.

"No sign of the signed books. And no fucking pun intended. Can you see if they were sent to the office by mistake," Meg says, a mile a minute. "I need time to arrange them into a five-tiered, heart-shaped wedding cake—"

See? Best-laid plans.

"Meg, when's the last time you breathed?" I ask. "Do you need to push your button?"

"How can you manage to sound pervy *and* like my mother? Okay, okay, I'm pushing my button."

It's a trick her therapist taught her, an imaginary elevator button Meg can press in the hollow of her throat to carry herself down a few levels. I picture her in her all-black ensemble and stylishly giant glasses, standing in the center of the hotel ballroom downtown with assistants buzzing all around, hurrying to transform the modernist SoHo event space into a quaint destination wedding on the Amalfi Coast. I see her closing her eyes and touching the hollow of her throat. She exhales into the phone.

"I think it worked," she says.

I smile. "I'll track down the books. Anything else before I head over?"

"Not unless you play the harp," Meg moans.

"What happened to the harpist?"

We'd paid a premium to hire the principal from the New York Phil to pluck Pachelbel's Canon as guests arrive tonight.

"The flu happened," Meg says. "She offered to send her friend who plays the oboe, but that doesn't exactly scream Italian wedding . . . does it?"

"No oboe," I say, my pulse quickening.

These are just problems. As with the first draft of a book, there's always a solution. We just have to find it and make the revision. I'm good at this. It's my job as senior editor.

"I made a playlist when I was editing the book," I offer to Meg. "Dusty Springfield. Etta James. Billie Eilish."

"Bless you. I'll have someone copy it when you get down here. You'll need your phone for your speech, right?"

A flutter of nerves spreads through my chest. Tonight is the first time I'll be taking the stage before an audience at a Noa Callaway launch. Usually, my boss makes the speeches, but Alix is on maternity leave, so the spotlight will be on me.

"Lanie, I gotta go," Meg says, a new burst of panic in her voice. "Apparently we're also missing two hundred dollars' worth of cake balloons. And now they're saying, because it's Valentine's goddamned eve, they're too busy to make any more—"

The line goes dead.

In the hours before a big Noa Callaway event, we sometimes forget that we're not performing an emergency appendectomy.

I think this is because, well, the first rule of a Noa Callaway book launch is . . . Noa Callaway won't be there.

Noa Callaway is our powerhouse author, with forty million books in print around the world. She is also the rare publishing phenomenon who doesn't do publicity. You can't google Noa's author photo nor contact her online. You'll never read a *T* magazine piece about the antique telescope in her Fifth Avenue penthouse. She declines all invitations for champagne whenever her books hit the list, though she lives 3.4 miles from our office. In fact, the only soul I know who's actually met Noa Callaway is my boss, Noa's editor, Alix de Rue.

And yet, you *know* Noa Callaway. You've seen her window displays in airports. Your aunt's book club is reading her right now. Even if you're the type who prefers *The Times Literary Supplement* over *The New York Times Book Review*, at the very least, you've Netflix and chilled *Fifty Ways to Break Up Mom and Dad.* (That's Noa's third novel but first movie adaptation, meme-famous for *that* scene with the turkey baster.) Over the past ten years, Noa Callaway's heart-opening love stories have become so culturally pervasive that if they haven't made you laugh, *and* cry, *and* feel less alone in a cruel and oblivious world, then you should probably check to see whether you're dead inside.

With no public face behind Noa Callaway's name, those of us in the business of publishing her novels feel a special pressure to go the extra mile. It makes us do crazy things. Like drop two grand on helium balloons filled with floating angel food cake.

Meg assured me that when our guests pop these balloons at the end of my toast this evening, the shower of cake and edible confetti will be worth every penny that came out of my group's budget.

Assuming they haven't gone missing.

"Zany Lanie." Joe from our mailroom pops his head inside my office and gives me an air fist bump.

"Joe, my bro," I quip back automatically, as I've been doing every day for the past seven years. "Hey, perfect timing—have you seen four big boxes of signed books arrive from Noa Callaway's office?"

"Sorry." He shakes his head. "Just this for you."

As Joe sets down a stack of mail on my desk, I fire off a

diplomatic text to Noa Callaway's longtime assistant, and my occasional nemesis, Terry.

Terry is seventy, steel-haired, tanklike, and ever ready to shut down any request that might interfere with Noa's process. Meg and I call her the Terrier because she barks but rarely bites. It's always iffy whether simple things—like getting Noa to sign a couple hundred books for an event—will actually get done.

It will be a travesty if our guests go home tonight without a copy of Noa's new book. I can feel them out there, two hundred and sixty-six Noa Callaway fans, all along the Northeast Corridor, from Pawtucket, Rhode Island, to Wynnewood, Pennsylvania. They are taking off work two hours early, confirming babysitters, venmoing dog walkers. They are dropboxing Monday's presentation and rummaging through drawers for unripped tights while toddlers cling to their legs. In a dozen different ways, these intrepid ladies are getting shit done so they can take a night for themselves. So they can train to the Hotel Shivani and be among the first to get their hands on *Two Hundred and Sixty-Six Vows*.

I think it's Noa's best book yet.

The story takes place at a destination wedding over Valentine's Day weekend. On a whim, the bride invites the full wedding party to stand up and renew their own vows—to a spouse, to a friend, to a pet, to the universe . . . with disastrous results. It's moving and funny, meta and of-the-moment, the way Noa's books always are.

The fact that the novel ends with a steamy scene on a

Positano beach is just one more reason I know Noa Callaway and I are psychically connected. Family legend has it that my mother was conceived on a beach in Positano, and while that might not seem like information most kids would cherish knowing, I was raised in part by my grandmother, who defines the term *sex-positive*.

I've always wanted to visit Positano. *Vows* makes me feel almost like I have.

I check my phone for a response from Terry about the signed books. Nothing. I can't let Noa's readers down tonight. Especially because *Two Hundred and Sixty-Six Vows* may be the last Noa Callaway book they get to read for a while. . . .

Our biggest author is four months late delivering her next manuscript. Four unprecedented months late.

After a decade of delivering a book each year, the prolific Noa Callaway suddenly seems to have no plans of turning in her next draft. My attempts to get past Terry and connect with Noa have been fruitless. It's only a matter of time before our production department expects me to turn over a tightly edited—and nonexistent—manuscript.

But that's a panic attack for another day. Alix is due back from maternity leave next week, and the pressure will be on.

I'm flipping through my mail, waiting impatiently for Terry's response, knowing I need to get down to the venue—when my hands find a little brown box in the middle of the mail Joe delivered. It's no bigger than a deck of cards. My distracted mind recognizes the return address and I gasp.

It's the Valentine's gift I had handmade for my fiancé, Ryan. I unwrap the paper, slide open the box, and smile.

The polished wood square is pale and smooth, about the size and thickness of a credit card. It unfolds like an accordion, revealing three panels. In fine calligraphy is The List I made long ago. It's all the attributes I wanted to find in the person I'd fall in love with. It's my Ninety-Nine Things List, and Ryan checks off every one.

I've been told that most girls learn about love from their moms. But the summer I turned ten and my brother, David, was twelve, my mom was diagnosed with Hodgkin's lymphoma. She went fast, which everyone says is a mercy, but it isn't. It just about killed my oncologist father that even he couldn't save her.

My mom was a pharmacoepidemiologist on the board of the National Academy of Medicine. She used to fly all over the world, sharing stages with Melinda Gates and Tony Fauci, giving speeches on infectious diseases at the CDC and WHO. She was brilliant but also warm and funny. She could be tough, but she also knew how to make everyone feel special, seen.

She died on a Tuesday. It was raining out the hospital window, and her hand seemed smaller than mine. I held it as she razzed me for the last time.

"Just don't be a dermatologist."

(When you're born into generations of doctors, you make jokes about imagined medical hierarchies.)

"I hear there's good money in it," I said. "And the hours."

"Can't beat the hours." She smiled at me. Her eyes were the same blue as mine, everybody said. We used to have the same thick, straight brown hair, too, but in so many ways, my mom didn't look like my mom anymore.

"Lanie?" Her voice had gone softer and yet more intense. "Promise me," she said. "Promise to find someone you really, really love."

My mother liked overachievers. And she seemed to be asking, with her final words, for me to overachieve in love. But how? When your mom dies and you are young, the worst part is that you know there's all this stuff you'll need to know, and now who's going to teach you?

It wasn't until college that I was introduced to the writer who would teach me about love: Noa Callaway.

One day after class, I came back to my dorm, and the tissues were flying on my roommate Dara's side of the room where she and her friends were hunched together.

Dara held a half-eaten Toblerone out to me and waved a book in my direction. "Have you read this yet?"

I shook my head without glancing at the book, because Dara and I did not have the same reading tastes. I was pre-med like my brother and obsessing over my organic chemistry reader so I could move back to Atlanta and become a doctor like everyone else in my family. Dara was majoring in sociology, but her shelves were stuffed with paperbacks with cursive fonts.

"This book is the only thing that got Andrea over Todd," she said.

I looked at Dara's friend Andrea, who fell face-first into another girl's lap.

"I'm crying because it's so beautiful," Andrea sobbed.

When Dara and her friends left in search of lattes, I felt the gold foil letters of the book's title staring me down from across the room. I picked it up and held it in my hand.

Ninety-Nine Things I'm Going to Love About You by Noa Callaway.

I don't know why, but the title made me think of my mother's last words. Her plea that I find someone I really, really loved. Was she sending me a message over the transom?

I opened the book and started reading, and a funny thing happened: I couldn't put it down.

Ninety-Nine Things is the story of Cara Kenna, a young woman struggling to survive a divorce. There's a suicide attempt and a stint in a psych ward, but the tone is so brightly funny, I'd commit myself if it meant I could hang out with her.

In the hospital, Cara has only time to kill, and she does so by reading the ninety-nine romance novels in the psych ward library. At first, she's cynical, but then, despite herself, she finds a line she likes. She writes it down. She says it aloud. Soon she's writing down her favorite line from every book. By the day of her release, she has ninety-nine things to hope for in a future love affair.

I read the book in one sitting. I was buzzing all over. I looked at the chemistry homework I had to do and felt something inside me had changed.

Ninety-Nine Things held all the words I'd been looking for since my mother died. It spelled out how to really, really love. With humor, with heart, and with bravery. It made me want to find that love myself.

At the back of the book, where the author's bio usually is, the publisher included three blank pages, lined and numbered from one to ninety-nine.

Okay, Mom, I'd thought, sitting down to get to work. I wasn't sure which of Dara's friends this book had belonged to, but it was now undeniably, cosmically mine.

The beauty of such a large list was that it allowed me to weave between weird and brave, between superficial and marrow-deep and deal-breaker serious. In between *Enthusiastic about staying up all night discussing potential past lives* and *Answers the phone when his mother calls*, I'd written: *Doesn't own clogs, unless he's a chef or Dutch*. At the very end, number ninety-nine, I wrote, *Doesn't die*. I felt my mom was with me, between the lines of that list. I felt if I could pursue this kind of love, then she'd be proud of me, wherever she was.

I don't know that I ever *really* thought I'd find a guy who embodied my whole list. It was more the exercise of committing to paper love's wondrous possibilities.

But then . . . I met Ryan, and everything—well, all ninety-nine things—just clicked. He's perfect for me. Scratch that. He's perfect, period.

I fold up the wooden panels, tuck my gift back into the box. I can't wait to give this to him tomorrow on Valentine's Day.

My phone buzzes. A barrage of texts illuminates the screen. Two from Ryan, on his way up from D.C. He's the legislative director for Virginia senator Marshall Ayers, and on alternate Fridays, their office closes early, so he takes the 1:13 train to New York.

The articles he's texted—one review of a movie we both want to see, and one press piece for some legislation he's been drafting about voters' rights—are quickly shuffled to the bottom of my screen as my launch prep team blows me up.

The cake balloon crisis is still unfolding, and there are fifteen dramatic messages in the text thread to prove it. Two dozen balloons, at six dollars apiece, are missing from the order my assistant, Aude, picked up this morning. Calls to the bakery have been made. Refunds have been demanded.

At last, the message I've been waiting for appears. It's Terry.

Stuck in traffic. Signed books in my possession. Stop freaking out.

I flip the bird at Terry's patronizing message, but I also feel relief spread through my bones. I text Meg the good news, slide Ryan's gift into my tote bag, and google the bakery to see whether I might stop in and solve Balloon-Gate on my way downtown.

Out my window, as the sun shimmies over the river, and it begins, very lightly, to snow, I feel a sense of calm. I love my fiancé. I love my job. Noa Callaway's launches are celebrations of all that love put together. Tonight, two hundred and sixty-six women will go home happy with their new books. I think that my mom would be proud.

Everything's going to be fine.

Chapter Two

HALF AN HOUR LATER, STEPPING OUT OF THE SNOW AND into the warm and buttery bakery, I glimpse our balloons at the back.

At Dominique Ansel now, I chime in on the text thread. Reclaiming lost balloons!

On my phone, Meg dashes back:

Lanie, you really don't have to do that.

I know this is less about the errand being below my pay grade and more about the fact that Meg suspects—not without reason—that I shouldn't be trusted around objects so fragile. I *have* run through more computers and Kindles and photocopiers (yes, I actually slaughtered two photocopiers in my seven years at Peony) than the rest of the fourth floor combined. If you need someone to spill a big glass of water as soon as you sit down at an important agent lunch, I'm your gal. It's a good thing I'm confident in my skills as an editor, because the whole publicity department still makes fun of the day I tried to help them mix a batch of sangria for a bookseller award celebration. The punch called for three cups of sugar, and I added salt. The containers looked the same. While people walked around gagging, I made matters worse by adding more salt. No one's ever let me live it down.

But I'm here, and I have two hands and a good feeling about today. When my assistant, Aude, chimes in, texting crisp, clear instructions for the balloons, I know the team is strapped at the venue. They need me. It seals the deal.

> Balloons under your name. Keep in protective plastic wrap until arrival on-site!!!! Please, Lanie. Inconvenience cost charged back to your card. Ask for Jerome.

Jerome is behind the counter, his name tag prominent on his starched white shirt. He's reading Proust and looks less than enthused when I sidle up in front of him. I notice his tip jar is low.

"Hi, I'm Lanie Bloom. Here for the balloons." I gesture behind him at the floating bouquet on the other side of the kitchen's glass wall.

"No." Back to his book Jerome goes. "Those are for someone else."

"Aude Azaiz? She's my assistant."

Now Jerome looks up. "Ms. Azaiz works for you?" There's shock in his voice, and honestly, I can't blame him. With her boy-short black hair, silver skull nose piercing, and punctuating French Tunisian accent, Aude might be the world's most intimidating twenty-three-year-old. Meg and I marvel at her outfits, the necklines of dresses that rise asymmetrically above her chin. We covet her rotation of leather jackets in surprising colors like marigold. When we order lunch to the office, Aude sends our food back for the slightest infraction—mayonnaise when she asked for aioli, improperly emulsified dressing, the wrong kind of crab in a California roll. Nobody fucks with her.

The mere mention of Aude's name has Jerome behind the glass retrieving the balloons. When he brings them out, they're lovely, gauzy gold, and sheer enough to suggest the sliver of angel food inside. But before he bequeaths them, he nods at my outstretched hands.

"One graze of that hangnail will pop them," he says.

Hastily I gnaw off a thumbnail.

"Your breath will pop them," he says, "and the pastry chef can make no more today. So—" Jerome mimes sucking in his breath, a snide look in his eyes.

I'm about to ask who hurt him as a little boy when he surprises me.

"Ms. Azaiz . . ." His face has gone slightly splotchy. His tone has dropped its scathe. "Is she . . . attached to anyone?"

I grin at Jerome and slip a ten-dollar bill in his tip jar. "Quite single."

That's the thing about romance. Its prospect can make even the most curmudgeonly blush. And though I'm fairly certain Aude would eat Jerome for breakfast in between bites of croissant, I'm always happy to be proven wrong when it comes to things like this.

Jerome nods, his mood elevated. "The reimbursement—back to the same card?"

"Actually," I say, thinking of Meg and Aude and the rest of our launch team, the long hours they've put into tonight. "Can I get that in pastries to go?"

⚜

"Lanie arrives!" Aude calls over her shoulder as I step out of the elevator onto the sleek white-tiled hallway of the Hotel Shivani's twelfth floor.

Even though Aude quit smoking last year, she greets everyone as if she's just stamped out a cigarette. She glides forward to relieve me of the balloons.

"Shit, these are so fragile," she says. We both exhale once they're in her well-manicured hands.

"Lanie!" Meg says, rushing toward me, pushing her glasses higher on her nose. "I can't believe you got those."

"Accept the miracle." I pass her the box of pastries, my hands now free to brush the snowflakes from my hair. Meg's going to love the Jerome anecdote, but I'll save it for a calmer moment. "Get in the zone with a scone."

"Scone zone," Meg repeats, taking a bite and chewing morosely.

"What's the word on the signed books?" I ask.

Finally, Meg smiles, and I know Terry delivered.

"Come on," Meg says, "I'll show you."

We maze through tables draped in golden cloth, past Aude schooling a group of publicists on how to fill satchels of rice for the table setting, and how not to wedge white candles into the wicker Chianti bottle centerpieces.

"Look at that chip in the taper! Stand back, I will do it myself."

There's a white aisle for guests to walk down with their books and a photo booth with rotating Amalfi Coast backdrops. Cases of prosecco and Campari chill on ice. Twinkle lights have been strung from the ceiling, drawing the eye toward the red ranunculus altar in the center of the room. Behind it, Styrofoam boulders form an oceanfront Italian bluff. Out the window, snow falls on the Hudson.

"This is all so perfect," I tell Meg, who's tying the last of the cake balloons to the last of the chairs. "Like Cupid exploded."

"It's a mood," Meg says.

"Should the confetti be scattered or, like, placed?" Meg's assistant calls.

I'm about to say "scattered," because how does one place confetti, when Meg says: "Placed so that it appears to be scattered."

I take out my phone to snap a picture of the space. I can't get it all in the frame but I find a sparkly angle. I'm about to send it to my boss when I remember her baby's ear infection. Alix has been in and out of urgent care the past few nights, and I don't want to wake her if she's napping.

Meg leads me to the back of the room, where she gestures grandly at a white stack of Noa's new books, hot off the press and arranged in the shape of a wedding cake.

"Ta-da!"

"You did all this in thirty minutes?" I high-five Meg. "Looks like those hours of Magna-Tiles with the Boss paid off." The Boss is what I call Meg's three-year-old, Harrison, though her one-year-old, Stella, is gunning for the title, too.

She nods. "Master taught me well."

Gingerly I lift a book off the top of the tower and run my fingers over the embossed type. I've had a hand in every aspect of *Two Hundred and Sixty-Six Vows*, and it's a rush to hold a finished copy before it's officially out in the world. I open to the title page and see Noa Callaway's florid signature scrawled in fountain pen. It makes me smile to picture Noa signing these from her fancy Fifth Avenue penthouse.

"Sorry I missed the book drop-off," I say. "Was the Terrier rabid?"

"Actually, she was in a good mood," Meg says. "She even wondered whether there was anything else we needed."

"No way."

"I asked if she'd give Tommy his monthly hand job."

"God bless Terry," I say, side-glancing Meg. "It's not really that bad with Tommy?"

"Talk to me when you've been married for eight years."

"Sounds like y'all need a date night. Any interesting Valentine's plans?"

Meg sighs. "My mom is taking the kids to some Chinese New Year thing."

"There you go."

"Tommy and I will probably spend the day at home, wearing charcoal masks and scrolling on our phones from different rooms. I'm honestly looking forward to it. Sometimes we'll forward each other a funny tweet. And that's what passes for romance in the Wang household."

"Meg, you need to get laid. Not Twitter-laid. Same room, actual-sex-laid. Promise me."

She rolls her eyes. "What about you? Please say a quickie with Ryan on the subway so I'll have something to fantasize about."

I'm grinning, and I know it's annoying, but I can't help it. "We have no plans. Maybe a walk in the park, a wander into some antiques stores, brunch somewhere we've never been—"

Meg waves me off. "If it's not pornographic, I don't really need to know. I'm going to remind you of this when you're married and trying to pretend Valentine's Day doesn't exist. Speaking of marriage," she says, more cheerily, giving me a nudge. "Did ya pick a date yet?"

She knows we haven't, and she knows I find it maddening that Every Single Person asks this question.

"No, but I *did* choose your bridesmaid dress. Get ready to look smashing in mauve."

Meg blinks at me. She's thirty-four and was born way over weddings. "Good thing I love you."

"I'm joking. You fell hard for that."

"It's this room! Heart-shaped confetti is seeping into my brain." Meg rubs her temples. "I'll wear whatever you want, whenever you decide you want it." She leans against me and together we survey the room. "I bet for an extra grand, we could keep these tables another day and throw your wedding right here. Save you a lot of hassle."

I laugh, but it comes out forced. Meg doesn't notice. She's asking for my phone and trying to flag down Aude to copy my playlist. I hand the phone to her and she disappears, leaving me alone at the altar.

I try to picture Ryan waiting for me beneath these ranunculus and twinkle lights—or even at a real oceanfront destination, like we've discussed a couple times. I can't see it. And after a moment of trying, tears sting my eyes.

I move to the window, where no one can see me wipe them away. Every time I think of our wedding—I get stuck.

For some reason the idea of getting married, of taking the big next step in my life, sends my heart back to the child I was when I lost my mom. When I think of a wedding without her in the pictures, I find that I can't pick a date—or a venue, or a dress, or a cake, or a first song to dance to with my dad. Because she won't be there to experience it.

Aude finds me at the window. She's holding out my buzzing phone.

It's probably Ryan. When he gets to Penn Station, he always checks in about dinner, which is always Italian takeout from Vito's on nights I'm working late. I'm trying to push away thoughts of my mother, to focus on whether baked ziti or eggplant parm will hit the spot around ten, but when I glance at my phone, it's not his name on the screen.

It's Frank, executive assistant to our president and publisher, Sue Reese.

Can you meet with Sue at 4:30?

I blink at the message. It's four-fifteen right now.

My chest tightens. In all the years I've worked at Peony, Sue's calendar has been meticulously organized weeks in advance. She doesn't do impromptu.

Something's up. Something big.

Chapter Three

SUE'S ASSISTANT, FRANK, IS THE KIND OF MAN WHO always offers you hot tea with a great big smile when you arrive for a meeting, then frowns when you take him up on it. Generally, I make a habit of trying not to annoy Frank, but today I'm so nervous that I accidentally blurt out "yes."

"Hmph," Frank says, rising from his desk with the kettle.

"Do you know what this meeting is about?" I ask, following him to the kitchen.

Frank has been Sue's assistant for over twenty years, ever since she founded Peony in the late nineties. I've seen him rattle off a thousand facts about Sue into the phone, right off the top of his head—her passport number, her mother-in-law's favorite flowers, the date of her last gynecological exam.

"I don't *think* you're getting fired," he calls over his shoulder, "but I've been wrong before."

"Thanks."

"You don't take milk or sugar or anything, right?" he asks, his tone directing me toward the right answer.

I shake my head.

"The toughest people take it straight." He hands me the mug, then says more brightly, "Go on in. She'll be right with you."

I open the door to our publisher's corner office and step tentatively inside. Sue's spa—as Meg and I call it—is the only office at Peony that doesn't look like a romance publishing office. Every other employee has some variation of wall-to-wall bookshelves crammed with loudly colored spines, but Sue's office is entirely white. The white desk is devoid of papers, the white leather chairs are smooth as cream, and the white modernist coat rack harbors three white cardigans, each one with some expensive flourish, like pale pink leather elbow patches.

The only pops of color come from three large hanging ferns and three framed photographs of sons who look like mini-Sues but with braces. I've never met Sue's kids before, but I have seen her water her plants, and her surprising devotion to them lets me know she's a really good mom.

I'm doing this square breathing trick Meg taught me, trying to stay calm as I settle into Sue's white guest cloud, when a man pops up from behind Sue's desk. We scream at the same time.

"Rufus, what the hell?" I hiss. I can hiss at him because he's my friend. It's a love hiss. "What are you doing here?"

"Um, my job?" he says, rolling out his neck, which is always sore because he over-Pilates because he has the long-standing, unrequited hots for Brent, the instructor at Pilates World.

"Well, get out! Come back later. I have a meeting."

"Sue's printer broke," he says, fiddling with some cables in a way that makes me suspect he won't be done anytime soon. "Just because I've had to resurrect your hard drive from the underworld—is it three times now?—does not mean I don't also perform valuable IT for the rest of this company."

"In my defense—"

"Oh, I dare you." He shakes his head in pity.

"Mercury was in retrograde!"

"Permanently?" He laughs. "Why are you hissing so much?"

"I hiss when I'm nervous," I hiss, glancing out the open door. "Frank used the word *fired.*"

Rufus rolls his big brown eyes, which reassures me. A little. He thinks this is absurd. Then again, he doesn't know about Noa Callaway's egregiously missed deadline.

"Why would *you* get fired?" Rufus pauses. "Do you think anyone else saw you stealing those office supplies last month?"

"It was a box of tissues!" More hissing. I can't not at this point. "I had bronchitis!"

"Lanie." Sue sweeps into the office, passing me to hang up her white cardigan—this one has a kind of corset look going on at the back, which only Sue could make look classy.

"Good as new, Sue," Rufus proclaims, setting Sue's printer back on its shelf below her desk.

"Always with the words I like to hear, Rufus," Sue says, taking a seat across from me on her white couch.

"I'll just be going." He says the words *I* want to hear, mouthing *good luck* to me as he closes the door.

"How are you?" Sue asks me once we're alone.

"Good. Fine."

With her pearls and capsule uniform, with her silver-blond, chin length hair always looking like it's just been dry-barred, Sue is so put together that even after all these years, it can strike fear into my heart to look at her. Once, the two of us were escorting an author to an event at a mall in a Westchester suburb. We had an hour to kill before the signing, and Sue bought me a fancy spatula at Williams Sonoma, telling me I'd never make a French rolled omelet without it. I feel like she can look at me and sense that, two years later, I have never swatted a fly without it.

"How are things shaping up for the launch?"

"Brilliantly." I take out my phone to show her the photo I'd taken earlier for Alix. This picture is worth a thousand of the words I'm too nervous now to say.

"I wish I could make it," Sue says.

"We'll splash the launch all over social media. It'll be like you were there."

Sue smiles cryptically at the image going black on my cell phone before looking directly at me. The smile fades.

"Listen, Lanie," she begins, "what I'm about to say isn't going to be easy for you."

I hold my breath, gripping my armrests. If she fires me, I honestly don't know what I'll do. Ryan tells me all the time how many jobs there are out there that I'd be great at, but that's because he wants me to move to D.C. I don't want another job. I want this one.

Sue opens a folder on her lap, flips through a few pages. Torturing me.

"Shoot. It's not here." She rises and goes to the door, sounding slightly piqued. "Frank? The document?"

There's scuffling outside and Frank's apologetic murmurs. While Sue waits at the door, I look away, as from a surgeon about to amputate one of my limbs. I face her oversized windows and watch the snow falling on the café awning across the street.

And of course, this is the view I'd have while getting fired. That café is the place where I got this job, seven years ago.

I was twenty-two, just out of college, and wildly optimistic. The week before graduation I had come across a job posting online:

Editorial Assistant, Peony Press.

By then, I was an English minor, but for all intents and purposes, still pre-med. In an instant, my plans to move home and spend the summer studying for the MCAT? Poof. Gone. This was a sign. I was never meant to be a doctor. I was on this earth to bring more stories like *Ninety-Nine Things* into the world.

I took a Greyhound up to New York. I slept on friends' parents' couches in various boroughs, and waitressed at a Greek diner while I waited for Peony Press to call.

They didn't. Nor did any of the other publishers where I applied for jobs.

By September, my couch prospects and my dad's patience ran out in the form of a plane ticket home. The day before my flight back to Atlanta, a visitor arrived in Queens. I stood on my friend Ravi's mom's fire escape, squinting into hazy sun at what appeared to be my grandmother.

Lest any cookie-baking, tissue-up-the-sleeve images form in your mind, let me set you straight: My bubby Dora is a fighter. She survived Auschwitz, and after her family immigrated to America, she became one of three women in her graduating class at Yale School of Medicine. When she gave me The Talk in eighth grade, it was a weekend-long celebration, culminating in popcorn and a screening of *Dangerous Liaisons*. For as long as I can remember BD has drunk exclusively from a coffee mug that reads BADASS MOTHERFUCKER.

"Which way is this Peony Press?" she called up to me on the fire escape.

"That depends. Do you have a bomb?"

"Darling, I'm wearing Chanel. It doesn't really go." My grandmother jerked a thumb at the idling taxi behind her. "I've got this very handsome gentleman waiting to take us there, so please come down. We'll wave goodbye to the one that got away, I'll buy you a martini, and tomorrow, I'll take you home."

We sat for hours at the café across the street from Peony's office. She told me the same stories that never got old about my mom when she'd been twenty-two. She was adding new details, things I didn't know about the time Mom skipped her graduation to see Prince on his Purple Rain tour—when I realized there was something I had never asked my grandmother.

"BD." I brought out my old copy of *Ninety-Nine Things* from my canvas bag. I'd kept it with me, like a totem, ever since I'd come to New York. "Do you remember what Mom said to me right before she died?"

"You could fill a book with all the things I don't remember, honey," she said, but with that little wink that let me know she *did* remember, only she wanted me to tell the tale.

"She said she wanted me to find someone I really, really loved. But she didn't say how. Or when. I just can't figure out if I'm going about it—my life—in the right way."

"If I could solve the mystery for you, I would," she said, patting my cheek, "but then, what the hell would the fun of life be?"

I knew she was right, annoying as it was. BD took a picture of me holding the book, with the Peony office through the window in the background.

"One day," she said, "in the comfort of your unknowable future, you'll look at this picture, and you'll be glad we took it today."

And that was when Alix de Rue stepped into the café for a decaf cappuccino.

I recognized her from the photograph accompanying the only interview I'd found online related to Noa Callaway. She was five feet tall in kitten heels with a short blond bob, glossy lips, and a giant purple scarf. I nudged BD.

"That's the one who got away."

"The editor?" BD gasped. "Go talk to her."

"Hell no."

"If you don't, I will," BD said. She was one large dirty martini in. "I'd hate to see you lose the job to me."

I downed the cold rest of my coffee and stood up. "You're right. That would suck."

I moved toward the bar, heart suddenly pounding. "Miss De Rue?" I offered my hand. "I'm Lanie Bloom. I'm sorry to bother you, but I'm a huge fan of Noa Callaway."

"Me, too," she said and smiled at me briefly before returning to her laptop.

I took a breath. "The editorial assistant position—"

"Has been filled."

"Oh." Even though I already sensed this, even though I'd never even gotten a form email back from HR, I felt my heart collapse like a detonated building.

"Did your new assistant do *this?*" BD asked, suddenly behind me, thrusting my copy of *Ninety-Nine Things* under Alix de Rue's nose. It was opened to the back pages where I'd written out my list.

I could have sunk into a puddle of shame watching Alix de Rue read what I'd written about Scorpios in the sack. When I'd made this list, I'd felt free. Now I thought about my mother and wondered whether she would be embarrassed.

"I told Noa readers would fill this out," Alix said, more softly now, touching the page with cuticle-bitten fingertips.

"This book changed my life," I confessed as Alix handed

it back. "I guess I don't have much to show for it yet, unemployed and begging strangers for jobs at cafés with my drunk grandmother—"

"*Tipsy*," BD corrected me.

"But someday . . ." I said to Alix, with a little laugh, attempting levity.

"My new assistant hates 'love stories,'" Alix said. "He's someone's nephew from our parent company and I was asked to give him a trial period."

"Is that so?" BD asked, giving me a vaudeville wink.

Alix narrowed her eyes and seemed to take all of me in at once: my atrociously heavy tote bag, my scuffed white tennis shoes, the eight pounds I'd lost that summer from worry and walking and late-night discounted bodega salad bars, my slightly greasy, too-long bangs, my college girl's jean jacket, and my desperate, romantic hope that my dream might not actually be absurd.

"What I love about love stories is their bravery," I said.

"What other writers do you love? Not only Noa Callaway?"

"Elin Hilderbrand. André Aciman. Zadie Smith. Sophie Kinsella. Madeline Miller. Christina Lauren—" They tumbled from me. I might never have stopped if Alix hadn't waved me off.

"All right, all right." She laughed. "Good."

"But most deeply"—I held Noa Callaway's book to my chest—"her."

Alix took a ream of papers from her leather bag. She riffled through them and eventually handed me a thick stack bound by a rubber band. She slapped a business card on top.

"Read this tonight. Email me your thoughts tomorrow."

⚜

Now—seven years, twenty-nine thousand paper jams, two apartments, three promotions, one inherited tortoise, eighteen flings ranging from scorching to moronic, two world-ending highlights mishaps, and eight bestselling novels later—is it all coming to a sudden, screeching end?

Sue walks back to her white chair, holding an ominous stack of papers. She uncrosses and recrosses her legs.

"Lanie," she says. "Alix isn't coming back."

As I probe deep for a poker face, I feel shock spreading over my features. This is not what I'd prepared myself for.

"She's decided to stay home with Leo."

I'd known Alix was anxious about coming back to work, about putting her son into day care—but she loves this job. Sorrow weighs in my limbs. Alix is my mentor and my friend. Alix is my advocate at Peony. I want to talk to her, to hear this news in her words, but as I sit across from Sue, I become aware of the quizzical look on her face. She hasn't brought me here only to deliver this news. There's also my fate to attend to. Collateral damage.

"We need to talk about Noa Callaway," Sue says.

"The manuscript." I nod, my stomach twisting.

"Where is it?" Sue asks.

"It . . . well, it's . . . I don't know."

"It's four months late, Lanie."

"Yes, it is." And now Alix won't be coming back to rescue it.

Sue tilts her head, looks hard at me. "One might expect author and editor to be on their third round of revisions by now."

"That's true, one might. But with Alix's leave, and, well, Noa's process has always been unique—"

"Noa has never delivered late. Not once. These books determine our budget. They *are* our budget. Noa Callaway delivering on time allows you to sign up that little . . . what was it, the debut?"

"*The Beginning of a Beautiful*," I say. My most recent acquisition, won in a hard-fought auction, is a queer *Casablanca* reboot by a debut author from Morocco.

"I know, Sue. I know how important Noa's deadlines are to the whole company."

"And yet," she says, "you haven't been able to get Noa to deliver."

"She's working on it," I say. "We emailed this morning and . . ."

But what had Noa and I emailed about this morning? Not the manuscript in question. Our emails are like banter between old friends. I have long played the yin to Alix's yang— and until Alix left for maternity leave, everyone seemed comfortable with that. I love my emails with Noa. She makes me laugh. She writes things to me I know her readers would trade years of their lives to read. But no one ever will. They're just for me.

This morning, I'd sent Noa a link to the cake balloons for her launch, and she'd responded with a GIF of a woman being lifted off into the Manhattan skyline by a vast bouquet of balloons.

Let me know what time you'll be passing by. I'll wave you onward from my window. Wonder where you'll land. . . .

I know Noa lives at 800 Fifth Avenue, and I am guilty of having scoped out the building while jogging once or twice. I can see her there, at her luxury window, a pair of binoculars pressed to her eyes. I like to picture her looking something like a young Anjelica Huston.

Noa's working title for this next book is *Thirty-Eight Obituaries*—we'll have to change that, but the premise is great. It's going to be about a young journalist who lands her first job at her dream newspaper, only to find it's in the obituary department. The hook, as Alix pitched it to me, is that the protagonist's first assignment is to prepare the obituary for a young, hard-living enfant-terrible sculptor. In case he dies doing one of his increasingly dangerous artistic stunts, they'll have the obit ready to go. Cue the unexpected love story.

It's so on-brand Noa Callaway that it seems like it should write itself. So what is going *on* with Noa that she can't finish it?

I suddenly wonder whether Alix knew something was wrong with this next book. It was due before she went on maternity leave. Was part of her decision not to come back . . . her anticipation of a Noa Callaway catastrophe?

"When Alix left on maternity leave," Sue says, "she told me she had faith in you, Lanie. I can understand that during her absence, you've been in a holding pattern with Noa. But now—"

I meet Sue's eyes because this feels like the moment she's going to lower the boom. I think of my favorite Noa Callaway line, from her third novel, *Fifty Ways to Break Up Mom and Dad*:

Life's greatest mystery is whether we shall die bravely.

If my career is about to die, I'd like to meet its end bravely. But I don't feel brave. I feel terrified, like I'm losing my balance at the end of a plank.

"I need you," Sue says, "to take over."

"Take over," I say slowly. "Noa Callaway?"

Am I not fired? Apparently, I'm not fired.

Sue looks at the photos of her sons, at her ferns. Then at me, and she sighs.

"As you know, Noa is . . . difficult."

I feel her waiting for me to agree. I haven't met Noa personally, nor spoken to her by phone, but from the interactions we've had, I consider her eccentricities to be like those of any genius. She can be cryptic and occasionally short via email, but more frequently, there's a sparkle to our correspondence that sets it apart.

When we worked together on her sixth book, *Twenty-One Games with a Stranger*—about two rival gamers who hate each other in their waking lives but slowly fall in love in their dreams—Alix wanted to cut a scene where the characters play chess at a gaming convention. She said it was out of step with the techie aesthetic that was working in the rest of the book.

I learned to play chess from BD the summer my mother died, and I sensed that the chess scene in Noa's draft was a metaphor for the larger romantic relationship. The interplay of strategy and patience. In my notes to Alix, I spelled out how Noa might drive this point home with a few light edits. It was the first time Alix copied and pasted a paragraph of mine directly into one of her editorial letters. The day after Alix sent the letter off, I got an invitation to play online chess from Noa Callaway. She didn't have to mention that she'd sensed my influence in the letter. We've been playing ever since.

"Given the circumstances," Sue says, "it makes sense to promote you. *Provisionally.*"

I blink.

"Tomorrow you'll become Peony's youngest editorial director. *Provisionally.*"

"Sue," I whisper. That's a *big* promotion. "Thank you!"

"Don't thank me yet," Sue says. "This is only a trial. Three months. If you can't get a number-one-*New-York-Times*-bestseller-worthy manuscript out of Noa by then, I'll find someone who can."

"I can do it," I say without thinking. I have no idea how, but I'll find a way.

If I can't get Noa to deliver a great book, it's not just our fiscal year that will suffer. It's my whole career. It's the *Casablanca* reboot. It's the paranormal ballet romance written by the sweetest seventy-year-old former dancer with an unparalleled gift for hot sex scenes. It's the #ownvoices imprint Aude and I dreamed of launching next year. "I won't let you down, Sue."

"Good." Sue slides me the stack of papers. "Sign here."

"What's this?" I ask as I realize exactly what it is. A detailed non-disclosure agreement.

"Just a precaution," Sue says.

"Oh my god," I say as it hits me. "Wait, I'm not actually going to *meet* Noa Callaway? Noa never meets anyone in person."

"Let's keep it that way." Sue's smile is stiff and a little too wide. "Focus on the book, Lanie. Get Noa Callaway to deliver. And buckle your seat belt. You may be in for some turbulence."

Chapter Four

AT SEVEN O'CLOCK, AT THE TAIL END OF THE LAUNCH'S cocktail hour, I'm waiting in the greenroom at the Hotel Shivani, halfway recovered from my meeting with Sue. My speech is memorized. I had to write it a month ago so it could be vetted by Alix, by Terry, and, ostensibly by Noa—though she never remarked on it to me. All I have to change is the line about me standing *in* for Noa's editor to say I *am* Noa's editor. That should be easy enough.

Dearly beloved, we are gathered here today . . .

In wedding-style metaphors, my speech is meant to take the reader through the full journey of our work on the book. From the dramatic way Noa delivers manuscripts—via hard copy, in a metal briefcase, delivered by Brinks messenger—which can feel akin to a blind date. To the courtship phase of the editorial process—the bumps along the way being the best parts. I'll pause for a laugh when I share Noa's top contender for this book's title: *Twelve Divorce Filings*. I swear, I thought she was going to die on that hill.

My phone buzzes.

HAVE FUN TONIGHT!!! Ryan texts.

I know he set an alarm reminder on his phone to write to me just when I'm about to take the stage, when my nerves are peaking and I can use encouragement. Then comes a follow-up: Can't wait to see you after. And a third: Don't be Bill Murray.

I roll my eyes, but I'm laughing. This is his way of saying *Stay on script*. From all the D.C. cocktail parties he's dragged me to, Ryan has observed that I am either exceptionally articulate . . . or a total bumbling disaster. He says that I'm a land of extremes, just coasts, no middle ground.

Ready to rock, I text back, stepping out of the greenroom and into the candlelit party.

The hall is filled with the sound of women loving the same thing. These are my people, this is my crowd. I take the stage and stand beneath the altar, proud of Meg and her team and the stunning party they've brought to life. Proud of Noa and this dazzling book. And damn it, proud of myself. I reach for the mic, adjust it. Emotion swells in my chest. I wish my mom could see me.

I look out at these wonderful, passionate women, all two hundred and sixty-six of them, and am overcome by my new responsibility.

Then the feeling veers toward panic—that Noa Callaway will never write another book, that the disaster is unfolding on my watch—and suddenly I can't see. The guests are a sea of red. There's a droning in my ears. The speech has vanished from my brain.

I am either going to faint or throw up.

I fumble for my phone. I'll simply open up the speech. But the facial recognition isn't working, and I can't hold the mic and the phone and my effing cake balloon *and* type in my password all at once. I'm going to have to abandon it.

And say what?

I open my mouth and a squeak emerges. My eyes fall on Meg in the front row, who is gaping at me, ferociously mouthing the words *good evening*.

"Good evening!" I belt out.

Meg palms her forehead and gives me a thumbs-up. At least my voice seems to have returned.

"I'm Lanie Bloom, and I'm Noa's editor."

The whispers throw me, and I remember that the rest of the office doesn't know about my promotion. There's true shock on Meg's face, which she masks with a wild grin when we lock eyes. The words sound normal to our guests. Still, I shiver saying them.

Then, from the back of the room, I hear a single pair of hands clapping. The applause spreads forward, growing in volume. Aude whistles between her teeth. This buys me some time, and it refocuses my attention on who these readers are, on how much we have in common. I decide to speak from the heart.

"I'm also a fan of Noa's. In fact, Noa's books are the reason I became an editor. I've never stopped feeling honored to work on them. When I look out at you tonight, I know I'm

among friends. That's the Noa Callaway effect." Another
cheer rises from the group, and my eyes follow the sound to
a young woman I recognize from previous events. She's with
her whole crew, as usual, and more than a few of them have
Noa Callaway quotes tattooed on some part of their bodies.
This is a good sign.

"Let's give a round of applause to the Callababes from
Providence"—I gesture toward them—"who met at Noa's
very first book launch ten years ago and have stayed friends
ever since. Can you believe these ladies train down together
for every Noa Callaway launch?"

The room indulges me with applause, and I suspect the
Callababes' numbers will increase tonight, another Noa Callaway effect. Everyone's invited to the fandom.

"I want to thank the book clubs, the bloggers and book-
stagrammers, and the amazing mother-daughter Facebook
group having that competition tonight to see who can finish
reading the novel first. Screw school, amiright?"

A group of teenage girls back me up: "Hell yeah!"

"I want to thank those of you who came solo. You may
have arrived alone, but trust me, you'll go home with new
friends, whether you like it or not." I scan the room as people
laugh. My eyes land on a man's silhouette near the back exit.
For a second, I wonder if it's Ryan, here to surprise me.

But this man is taller than Ryan. He's trimmer, too, less
muscular. His thick, dark hair is longer, wavier. He's standing
with his arms crossed over his chest. He's not our typical de-
mographic, and I almost move on, but I don't, because just
then, he steps into the light, and I can see his face. There's

something playful in his eyes. He looks . . . intrigued. By me? By my groping improvisation? Does he see that I'm hanging on by a thread?

Instead of simply absorbing this and moving on, I swerve into what Ryan calls the Carpool-Lanie; if I'm going down, I'm taking someone down with me.

"I want to thank the lone guy at the back, for getting the signed book for his wife. I'm going to go out on a limb and guess that she works nights, and you're getting laid at sunrise when she finds her signed book on her pillow. Man of the Year, everybody."

The audience gives a few wolf whistles, and I glance back to see whether the man is laughing. But he's moved from his spot. I lose sight of him in the crowd. I tell myself his wife would laugh if she were here.

"I've been told not to improvise these speeches," I say. "And look at me now, going full Bill Murray on you." I take a breath. "I think what I'm trying to say is what a relief it is to feel connected instead of alone. That's what we're all hoping for when we pick up a novel. Isn't it? Noa's stories bond us with forty million other readers, all around the world, and yet, somehow, they feel as intimate as a conversation. When I read Noa's stories, I feel that no one has ever understood me so well. She's my friend. I know she's your friend as well. Let's raise a glass to Noa, and to the brilliant *Two Hundred and Sixty-Six Vows*."

At this moment, the very last line of my speech comes at me. It was one of Terry's edits, and it's perfect for this crowd. "Let us renew our vows as readers. Would you all please reach

for your balloon, and find your pin?" I take my own balloon
and hold the pin aloft. "Repeat after me: With this cake, I
thee read."

"With this cake," the crowd responds, "I thee read!"

And then, around the room, comes the percussion of two
hundred and sixty-six balloons being popped. Everyone
cheers as the edible confetti rains down.

After my speech, guests gather around Meg's marvelous
book cake to grab a signed copy. I mingle with some ladies
from White Plains, then join Aude behind the table to pass
out more books. It's the time of night when people start
dreading their commutes, and I know we need to move them
out efficiently, back to their lives and obligations.

I'm handing out swag—engraved champagne flutes and
tote bags featuring the book cover—when I look up and see
the man I'd called out in my toast.

"Hey, Man of the Year." I hand him a book. "Thanks for
playing along."

Up close, his green eyes ambush me. "Glad to be of service."

His voice is lower than I expected.

"I hope your wife thanks you sufficiently."

He opens his mouth then closes it.

"Girlfriend?" I offer.

"No. It's not . . ."

When he trails off, I feel bad, knowing I've overstepped.
We sometimes get a few gay men at Noa's events, but I'm
definitely sensing straight here. Then it hits me. "Oh, I'm
sorry, you must be press."

I'd forgotten that a journalist from *New York* magazine had RSVPed. Meg had been thrilled about the coverage, and now I've probably ruined his enthusiasm to write about our event.

"Be sure to mention what a fool I made of myself?"

He shakes his head. "You'd fly away with the story."

In my mind I see Noa's GIF of the woman riding the balloons into the distance. "On a cake balloon."

"Speaking of, is this one spoken for? I didn't get any." Meg appears beside us, popping the very last balloon and snatching the cake like a pro. I wonder if Meg notices that the confetti seems to fall in slow motion around me and the man whose name I haven't caught.

"This is Meg, our publicist," I tell him. "You probably spoke about the piece."

Meg looks at me, confused. She shakes her head. "Doris came from *New York* mag. She left already, but they got a good picture of you onstage."

"Oh," I say and turn back to the mystery man. "I keep projecting mistaken identities onto you."

He's still gazing at me as though we share a secret, and something about it is awkward, and something about it is spellbinding. Even though I'm aware we're holding up the line, I extend my hand.

"I'm Lanie," I say.

"I know," he says, raising an eyebrow, which makes me rack my brain for a memory of meeting him sometime before. No. I'd remember him. He has the kind of face you don't forget.

"You introduced yourself onstage," he says, and both of us laugh. Mine is nervous.

"Ross," he says, then puts his hand in mine.

"Nice to meet you."

"I'm not so sure," he replies. But his smile takes out the sting. It's a good smile, nice teeth, smooth lips just barely parted.

Holding his hand, a little spark shivers through me. I gulp, realizing I am attracted to this man.

I pull my hand and gaze away from his.

"Enjoy the book," I say, watching him take my words as a cue to go.

"Oh. Sure." He waves, and begins to back away. "I will, thanks."

That's when I realize he's going home without a book.

Chapter Five

SOME PEOPLE USE THEIR COMMUTES TO CATCH UP ON group text chains or true crime podcasts. I am a secret M-train fantasizer. It's not always sexual, but a solid sixty percent of what passes through my mind while hurtling underground between our office in Washington Square and my apartment in midtown east could get me arrested in certain states.

Tonight it begins with Ryan on the couch, watching basketball and scrolling through *The Economist* app while he waits for me. Act Two has me entering the apartment, tossing off my trench coat—having shimmied out of my dress in the hallway, a trick my friend Lindsay taught me in college. I straddle Ryan wordlessly. Reunion sex ensues. Act Three opens on the chilled bottle of prosecco, consumed au naturel.

Ryan and I met in traffic. I love this, and not just because it gives me a lifetime fast pass out of tedious small talk at parties. (No one wants to hear about your awful commute, but if traffic be the food of love, play on!) I love it because the way

I met Ryan feels like the way two characters in an epic love story might meet.

It was a steamy summer morning in Washington, D.C., about three years ago. I was in town for a conference. I'd left plenty of time to get from my Georgetown hotel to the Walter E. Washington Convention Center, where I would speak on a panel about feminist romance. But a bus broke down on M Street, with my taxi directly behind it.

Ryan's first sight of me was a stream of curse words flowing from the window of my taxi. He was on a vintage Triumph Bonneville motorcycle, idling next to me.

"In a hurry?" he said.

Looking back, I liked his voice right away: steady with a hint of teasing.

"I'm supposed to be at the convention center in negative five minutes."

"Then you'd better hop on."

I laughed, then really looked at him for the first time. I've always had a thing for bikers. It's actually an item on my Ninety-Nine Things list. Not the greasy, aggressive kind. Think Steve McQueen in *The Great Escape*. Ryan fell squarely into the latter category. He was wearing a nice suit and shoes that gleamed with fresh polish. He had clean fingernails, sexy hands. Then he lifted the visor and I saw his eyes. I was a goner. Even if I'd needed a lift to Louisville, Ryan's brown eyes would have gotten me out of that cab.

Check another item on my list.

"You can wear my helmet," he said, like he knew he had me.

"I don't normally do things like this," I said, chucking a five at the cabbie and opening my door.

"Maybe we should make a habit of it," he said. "I'm Ryan."

"I'm Lanie."

I put the helmet on as cars honked all around us. If I'd been with Meg or Rufus we'd have flipped them off en masse, but I stood there patiently as Ryan fastened the helmet's clasp, feeling his fingers at my chin.

"Don't worry about them," he said close to my ear, nodding at the honkers. "In a few seconds they'll all be in the rearview mirror."

᭙

It's ten-fifteen by the time I slip my key into the lock of my fifth-floor walk-up apartment. I've lived here for six years but have only had the place to myself for the past three, after my roommate moved to Boston, and I could finally (barely) cover the rent on my own. I hired a company to knock down the temporary wall in the living room that had served as my roommate's old room, and restored the apartment to its one-bedroom glory.

Tonight, when I open the door, a blast of heat engulfs me. I throw up my hands to ward off flames. I sniff for smoke, but all I get is Vito's garlic knots.

I step inside, and there is Ryan in my kitchen, shirtless and half-submerged in a heap of hoses and hardware, which looks like it used to be my dishwasher. At the sound of my boots, his head pops up, and he gives me the wide grin that makes my dry cleaner fan herself with her pad of receipts.

Ryan played tennis at Princeton, so if you've seen Nadal change shirts after a match, the comparison would not be hyperbolic. His muscles are so defined they have etymologies.

I've never been drawn to muscles before, but on Ryan, it's part of the whole package. He's solid inside and out. He's the youngest LD on Capitol Hill, leader of his local Big Brothers program, captain of the intramural soccer team, *and* he happily offers to babysit his niece and nephew. He has never—not once in three years—not called me when he said he would, nor left me to wonder about his intentions. When he wants something, he gets it. In that way, we're alike.

Ryan has presidential aspirations. Legitimate ones. When he told me this on our fifth date, laying out the path for the next twenty years of his professional life as we sat at the ceviche bar on West Fourth, it startled me, but then I figured Michelle probably wasn't troubleshooting how to be FLOTUS on her fifth date with Barack, so I might as well enjoy my scallops and take life as it came.

"Hi, honey," he says.

"Don't move a muscle." I reach for my phone to document this. "How have we never done a Christmaskuh card showcasing your abs? 'Give me a *pec* under the mistletoe' in a brushed script font. Or, if you turned around, we could do '*Lats* of love this holiday season.'"

"Awful." Ryan laughs, his brown eyes crinkling, his Greek-statue triceps flexing as he twists my cheap wrench. He rises and comes to me, lifting me threshold-crossing style. We kiss. "But if it's a holiday card, we're supposed to be together."

"But then I'd block your twenty-four-pack."

"People would still know it's there," he says and kisses me again.

I tap his chest. "By any chance, is there something besides your bod making it so ungodly hot in here?"

Ryan sets me down, leans handsomely against the stove and tucks his thumbs in the waistband of his jeans. "Do you want the good news or the bad news first?"

"I always want bad news first," I say, setting down my many tote bags. I leave the house with one and somehow manage to come home every day with four. "What kind of person can absorb good news knowing bad news lurks around the corner?"

"All right," he says. "The bad news is I broke your radiator while fixing your dishwasher. The good news is I fixed your dishwasher." He tugs at my sleeve. "Take your coat off. Stay awhile."

I'd love to throw off my trench, but I am fully nude beneath it, and this hot flash is not the opening salvo I'd envisioned for our passionate tryst tonight. I lean around him to survey the disaster that is my kitchen. So much for my three-act fantasy.

"Dishwasher sure looks fixed," I joke. "While you're lining up renovation projects, do you think you can fix my headboard tomorrow? I was hoping we could do some damage to it tonight."

"I mean," he says, pointing at the hoses, "the rattle's fixed.

Or it will be by the time I put it back together. But that's the easy part."

"Sure." My dishwasher has rattled during the rinse cycle since before I moved in, and it's never really bothered me. It's one of the quirks of New York apartment living I feel one must come to love. If it's acting up while I'm having a dinner party, two thwacks does the trick, but most of the time I run the dishwasher on my way to bed and sleep right through the cacophony.

Ryan is a light sleeper. He finds the rattle uncharming. He finds most of my apartment's quirks uncharming, and is working his way through their solutions.

"Where's Alice?" I glance over Ryan's shoulder at the small dog bed where my tortoise usually hangs out. Alice is eighty-six years old and very opinionated, especially about climate. I inherited her from my neighbor across the hall, Mrs. Park, when she moved to Florida. Alice and Ryan do not get along.

Ryan lifts a shoulder. "I think she went that way about an hour ago." He gestures toward the bathroom.

I find Alice under my sink, where the pipe drips. "Good thing he hasn't fixed the drip yet," I whisper.

"Tortoises like heat," Ryan says as I carry her back into the kitchen. "They're cold-blooded."

"Not Alice," I say, adding ice to her water and setting out some cold cubes of orange from the fridge. "She's sensitive. She thinks she's a dog."

"Maybe our next pet could be an actual dog? My brother just got a goldendoodle and—"

"Do not talk about Alice like she's already gone. She could outlive you!"

He laughs. "How was the Valentine's dance?" Ryan is always ever so slightly mistaken about what's going on at my work. But tonight, I don't correct him. To split hairs over the fact that the party's theme was *Vows* not *Valentines* would open the vault of Wedding Conversations.

Namely ours. Ryan doesn't understand why I start sweating when we talk venues. In his mind, we are two exceptionally capable decision makers, and, with the help of a professional planner, should be able to pull off this event with ease. He wishes—like everyone else wishes—that we could just set a date.

I pull the bottle of prosecco from my bag. Ryan clocks the fancy label and raises an eyebrow, intrigued.

"Now do *you* want the bad news or the good news first?" I ask.

He's at my mirrored bar cart, where I keep BD's champagne flutes. "What kind of lunatic wants the bad news first when there's prosecco losing its chill?"

"You've got a point, pop that bottle, but still, I have to go in order. I'll make it quick." I duck as Ryan sends the cork ricocheting around my tiny kitchen. He splashes some foam into my glass.

"The bad news is, Alix isn't coming back from maternity leave."

"They fired her?" Ryan shakes his head. "She could file a discrimination—"

"No, no," I cut him off. "It was her choice. To stay with her baby."

"Makes sense," Ryan says. "That's what my sister-in-law did after the twins. A lot of women—"

"Ryan," I say, putting my glass down and resting both hands on his shoulders. "What would you say if I told you that you are looking at the brand-new editorial director of Peony Press?"

Ryan blinks. It takes him a moment to realize that a response is in order. "I'd say, um, wow. That is unexpected . . . *by* amazing. Are you serious?"

"No, I'm fucking with you," I deadpan. "Of course I'm serious!" I fling my arms around him, excited. "When Sue told me, I thought I was getting fired."

Ryan laughs. "You work your ass off for them. They had no choice but to promote you." He pulls away from my embrace, clinks my glass, and takes a deep gulp.

I don't drink. I feel myself shaking my head. His logic doesn't feel quite right.

I do work hard, and that's the side Ryan sees—the weekend afternoons when I'm editing, when it's impossible to shake me out of storyland. But productivity isn't what I want to be recognized for. I don't put in long hours to edit more manuscripts at a faster rate than my colleagues. Manuscripts aren't candy on a conveyor belt in *I Love Lucy*.

Editing is intuitive, alchemical. When I dive into an author's first draft, I'm diving for the story I think she always wanted to tell, for a future book that readers around the world can pick up and find magic in.

"So, you accepted?" he says. "The promotion?"

"In what world would I *not* accept this promotion?" I say. "This my dream job, and years sooner than I would have dreamed of getting it. I'm taking over Noa Callaway!"

"Ah, the diva," he says, turning his muscled back to me as he rebuilds my dishwasher.

I clear my throat. "The astonishingly brilliant, reason-I'm-in-publishing, demander-of-non-disclosure-agreement, four-months-past-her-deadline diva. Yes."

"You're obsessed with her," is what Ryan says, and I can't tell if he means this as an insult. He openly idolizes the senator he works for—so, is this simply, in Ryan's mind, a statement of fact?

When Ryan meets someone he admires on the Hill, he buys their biography and becomes a disciple of their history and habits. I've never needed to know who lay behind the curtain. It is enough for me to share the same planet as Noa Callaway's fabulous heroines.

Around our office there are competing theories about Noa Callaway's true identity. Most imagine a fiftyish woman with teenage daughters, ergo worldliness with a youthful pulse. Aude said she heard from another assistant that the pseudonym comprised twin sisters who lived on either coast and swapped chapters by email. I have lunched with agents who said over Scandinavian gravlax they had credible intelligence that Noa is a forty-six-year-old gay man writing from a yacht off Fire Island, then begged me with their eyes to confirm that it was true.

I think about Sue's warning—to keep our working relation-

ship email-only—and something inside me resists. It's my job
to get Noa to deliver. If she's truly struggling, and all I can do
is email her, am I being set up to fail?

"Also," I say to Ryan, "my promotion is provisional."

Now he looks at me. "How do you mean?"

"I mean Sue said if I don't get a number-one-*New-York-Times*-bestseller-worthy manuscript out of Noa in three
months . . ."

I glance at him, waiting for him to complete my sentence
with a confident, *You'll do it.* He doesn't. He's back to focusing
on the dishwasher. That's when I realize he hasn't even said
congratulations.

"Hey," I say, walking over to him, gently taking the wrench
from his hands and tapping the side of his head. "What's going on in there?"

Ryan wipes his hands on his jeans. "I'm proud of you,
Lanie."

He glances at my left hand, the empty finger where my
ring will finally sit once its resizing is finished at the end of
the month.

"But?" I say, even though I think I know. I need to hear it
from him.

"We said after the holidays, we'd start planning the wedding," he says. "Then, you got all swept up in that launch
party. Now that's over, and there's this."

I sigh. Even though I think we're moving at a perfectly
reasonable pace—we only got engaged in October—it often
feels like Ryan thinks we should be married and pregnant by

now. There have been a few arguments—not big blowouts, but enough to leave me tired whenever I think about it.

"Ryan," I say softly.

"I'm worried this promotion will drop *us* down to the bottom of your list of priorities," he says. "Our wedding. And everything else."

Everything else. The words come quickly, quietly, almost spoken under his breath. Ryan and I have agreed that after the wedding I'll join him in D.C. But the logistics of that move, and what they'll mean for me and my career, have yet to crystallize. I can tell that Ryan's thinking my promotion doesn't do our plans to cohabitate any favors.

Then there's the religion question, whether I'll convert to Christianity. It's important to Ryan that whatever future kids we have share the same religion as both their parents. I'm not particularly religious, but neither have I managed to get on board with converting. It feels wrong to change myself so we can become some WASPy united front on a future campaign trail. What is this, 1956? Even more than that, I can't imagine telling BD that I'm not a Jew anymore and neither will her great-grandchildren be.

These are big questions, ones we've both gotten skilled at sweeping under the rug since our engagement. It never feels like a good time to tackle them. Tonight I'm too tired—and too elated—to even entertain possible answers. So I tell Ryan the thing that always makes me feel better when I worry about the hows of our future.

"You're my Ninety-Nine Things," I say, taking his hands.

The fact that Ryan is so indisputably perfect for me matters a lot in my book. But he doesn't smile like he usually does.

I turn to the prosecco for help. I put both our glasses back in both of our hands. I meet Ryan on his level, which is a practical, plan-making level. "What do you say the next time we're in D.C., we go look at those wedding venues your mom wanted to show us?"

"Really?" he says.

I nod. "And in the meantime, tonight, can we please just drink to my good news? This is me begging you to drink excellent prosecco."

Ryan smiles his gorgeous politician smile, the one that says *I'm on your side*. He raises his glass. "Congratulations, baby. Tell me everything Sue said."

So I do, flopping on the couch with my prosecco while Ryan tinkers with my dishwasher. As I finish recounting my meeting with Sue and go on to tell him about the launch, I can't help remembering that handshake with Ross at the end, the intensity of his eyes, the thrill that passed through me.

⚜

A glass of prosecco later, Ryan has not only restored my dishwasher, he's nearly got the radiator valve sorted, too. We're both in our underwear now and thoughts of Ross's handshake are long gone. Ryan's grunts and curses have decreased to once every three minutes, and I feel a space for conversation opening.

"Shall we discuss plans for tomorrow?" I ask.

Ryan doesn't look up from his work. "Plan One is to enjoy our vastly improved quality of life, now that you have a working dishwasher. And a revamped radiator."

"That rattle was my lullaby. You'd better hope I'll be able to sleep through the silence."

"I'm thinking you, me, that couch, pizza delivery, *with* jalapenos because I love you, and the new Scorsese. Is that a perfect Saturday, or what?"

"It's Valentine's Day!" I cry, more fiercely than intended. I've always been pretty lackadaisical about the holiday, but maybe I'm a bit worked up because this is the first year that Valentine's Day has fallen on a weekend, which means it's the first one we've actually gotten to spend together.

"I'm joking." Ryan grins. "You should have seen your face when I said *Scorsese*."

I throw a pillow at him. "I hate Scorsese. It's like, would it kill him to put a woman in a film before Act Two—"

"Lanie," he cuts me off, sensing a diatribe. "I've got a whole day planned, capped off by a very fine dinner at your favorite, Peter Luger. I made the reservation months ago." He glances at me, and I know I haven't reacted with the desired level of enthusiasm. "Lanie?"

We've celebrated our last four special occasions at Peter Luger, but if I mention that, it'll be: *It's an institution!* or *I thought you loved their creamed spinach*, which I do, above all vegetables on earth, but I don't feel like defending creamed spinach tonight. The routines we've fallen into sometimes make me feel restless and claustrophobic, like a windup toy stuck in a corner.

"Do you ever worry that we act like old married people who are neither old nor married?" I ask.

And I think he's going to say: *No, because there's no one else I want to be old and married with, which is why I proposed to you.*

But Ryan surprises me, like he does sometimes. He picks me up, tosses me over his shoulder, and barrels toward the bedroom, making me yelp with delight.

"You ever seen an old married guy do this?" He tosses me on the duvet, and I'm hungry to get my hands on him.

❧

By dusk on Valentine's Day, we've had brunch at our favorite spot, Parker & Quinn, which I love for their DIY mimosa bar (four kinds of juice!) and Ryan loves because he gets to watch the Wizards beat the Bulls. He's taken me to a midtown tennis shop for a racquet so that his couples goal of playing doubles in D.C. can finally be reached. I, in turn, have dragged him to the Guggenheim because I can't get enough of Helen Frankenthaler's *Canal.*

As we leave the museum we've still got an hour until dinner, so I suggest a walk back through the park.

We approach the Gapstow Bridge at Sixty-Second Street, which has been a touchstone of my jogging route since before I got the job at Peony, back when I was lost and broke and alone, begging the universe to reveal my destiny. The stone bridge looks like it was torn out of a fantasy novel, slate gray and mossy, crossing the north edge of the Pond. Beyond it rises one of the most stunning views of the Manhattan skyline, glittering in the gloaming. It's a place where I've never felt like I could ask for too much, so long as I was willing to work to make it happen.

I stop at the center of the bridge, take Ryan's hand to make sure he stops, too. "This might be my favorite place in all of New York."

"It's beautiful," he says, tugging my hand a little, glancing up at the sky. "Should we get going? Looks like it's going to rain again."

"Wait. I was going to save this for tonight, but the moment feels right right now." I open my purse and take out my small gift wrapped in tissue.

As Ryan unwraps the gift, I feel a growing anticipation. I'm practically bouncing on my heels by the time he parts the wooden panels.

"Your list," he says. "From the book."

"Yeah. From the book."

"Doesn't own clogs. Check. You do know I'm not a grocery list, right? I'm, like, a real guy?"

"Don't you think it's amazing that I had this unreasonably long and meticulous plan for love—and I found a man who meets every single one of my requirements?"

"Uh-uh, I found you," he says and kisses me.

I show him how to put his gift in his wallet, and I like the way it looks there. "Now even when we're apart, you'll know why I love you." We're stepping off the bridge when I stop. "Wait, it's Saturday."

"All day long."

"They should be here."

"Who?"

"Edward and Elizabeth." I scan the grass below the bridge, as I did so many times on my Saturday evening jogs. But the couple I'm looking for is nowhere to be seen.

Their names aren't really Edward and Elizabeth. Or maybe they are—I've never actually met them. But I used to see them here each week. For as long as I've lived in New York, they have mattered to me.

"The picnickers," I tell Ryan, hoping he remembers. Early in our relationship, I told him how this couple walks to the same spot in Central Park every Saturday night and feasts on an elegant picnic at the water's edge, on the north side of the Pond.

"Is that them?" Ryan points at an elderly pair approaching on the path.

I rise on my toes, follow his gaze, optimistic.

"No." I shake my head. Not even close.

It's been years since I've been in Central Park on a Saturday at dusk. Probably since I started dating Ryan. A cold feeling of futility settles over me as I consider that one or both parties of my couples crush might not still be alive.

Ryan puts his arms around me. I think he can tell I'm disappointed. We're about to kiss when thunder claps and the sky cracks open with rain. I want to linger, to ignore the storm and our dinner plans, to stay here kissing until Edward and Elizabeth appear. They never let the weather stop them. I've seen them picnic with a battery-powered heat lamp in a snowstorm.

But Ryan takes off his coat and drapes it over my head. He tugs on my hand.

"We'd better make a run for it or we'll never get a cab," he shouts over the downpour.

He's right, I know, but leaving like this, before I see Edward and Elizabeth, feels every kind of wrong.

Chapter Six

ON MY FIRST DAY AT PEONY, I WALKED IN ON ALIX SMOK-
ing weed behind her desk.

"I am so sorry!" I'd cried, backing away and vowing to
knock louder next time, wondering if I should leave the cover
materials I'd come to drop off—or abort the mission entirely.

"Come in, come in," she told me, coughing as she sprayed
fig-scented diffuser. "I don't usually do this, but I have a call
with Callaway this morning."

Noa had just turned in the first draft of her third novel,
Fifty Ways to Break Up Mom and Dad. I'd devoured the
manuscript—and pored over Alix's eighteen-page, single-
spaced editorial letter like an archeologist examining the
Dead Sea Scrolls.

The book centers on a couple in their twenties who plan
a romantic getaway to New York . . . only to have it crashed
by his mom and her dad. Things get worse when the young
couple discovers that not only did their parents used to date,

both are single again. Much to their children's despair, the old flame hasn't gone out. So the younger couple hatches a plan to turn their parents off each other through a series of schemes masked as vacation adventures. A culinary competition, tickets to Broadway, kayaking on the Hudson, etc. But every moment of the young couple's trip only brings their parents closer.

The hang-gliding scene in the second half contains a line that's long stayed with me. Just before they run off the cliff, the main character's mother says:

"Life's greatest mystery is whether we shall die bravely."

I cried the first time I read that scene. Out of all the Noa Callaway aphorisms that have touched me over the years, that was the one I most wished I could have shared with my mom.

I would have loved to know whether she felt brave at the end.

In Alix's editorial letter, she waged a scorched-earth campaign on the novel's second act. I agreed with her suggestions, but if I had to account for all those cuts I was asking a bestselling author to make? I'd be getting high behind my desk, too.

"It's going to be a great book," I said to Alix.

"It better be, for what we paid for it," she said, pinching out her joint with her fingers. "This draft is twenty thousand words longer than it needs to be, but if I know Noa, it's going to be like I'm auctioning off the crown jewels when I suggest we lose one word."

I couldn't make out the precise threats and accusations shouted through the walls that morning, but after two hours on the phone with Noa, Alix emerged on her way to a very long lunch. She asked me to email Noa's assistant to arrange the messenger to deliver the edited manuscript in hard copy.

I wrote to Terry and introduced myself. I cc'ed Alix and Noa as directed, though Alix told me Noa never got involved in logistics. I couldn't help fangirling a little and mentioning the fact that the love interest's last name, Drenthe, happened also to be my middle name. How reading this manuscript was the first time that my middle name hadn't struck me as a punishment. I was not expecting an email back from Noa herself two minutes later.

Dear Drenthe,

Welcome to the hell of working with yours truly!

I should be able to peel myself off the floor long enough to receive your package around one this afternoon.

I have never labored over anything the way I labored over my five-line response to Noa Callaway:

Noa,

The rowboat fight scene is one of my favorites. Not just in this draft. In any novel I've ever read. But I agree with Alix that it's not serving this story. Maybe it's the opening scene of your next book?

If ever you need someone to grieve the darlings

that must be cut, email me. They'll get a moment of silence over here.

To my unending amazement, throughout the next week, I got an email from Noa every day, with the subject lines: *Cut Darling #1, 2, 3*, and so on. Each contained a single line, a paragraph, or a plotline on the chopping block.

I called BD and read some of them aloud to her, relaying to Noa all the places where my grandmother had laughed. I climbed out on my fire escape and voice-recorded myself shouting lines of interior monologue into the Second Avenue traffic. I scrawled in Sharpie one extravagantly beautiful description of a woman's hair on the sole of my Converse, then I walked all over Brooklyn that weekend, taking a picture for Noa of how the line had gotten its day.

You're making this more fun than it has any right to be, she'd emailed me back at midnight.

Even after the book went to print, even years and several books later, sometimes I'll still get an email about something Noa hates having to cut: the tiny pink flowers in her basil pot, half an inch of hair, a man in line for a taxi, her mother's dinner after a fall broke her arm.

The day *Fifty Ways to Break Up Mom and Dad* was published, a dozen white tulips were delivered to my office in a mason jar, with a note saying *These also had to be cut.*

We've worked together on seven books since then, and our process has been the same: Alix gets the ranting and resistance; I find ways to make Noa's revision process less painful. I'm like the fun uncle to Alix's single mom.

Only now . . . Alix is gone, and where does that leave Noa and me?

Yesterday, Terry called to set up a face-to-face meeting with Noa. I was so shocked, I'd agreed to the suggested time immediately, without thinking about my own calendar. Then I had to cancel last minute on Ryan's senator's birthday in D.C. He isn't thrilled, but I'll figure out a way to make it up to him next week.

I know this meeting goes against Sue's wishes, but in what world could I say no to meeting Noa Callaway? I figure what Sue doesn't know won't hurt her. Besides, the meeting wasn't *my* idea. I'm just the one over here thrilled about it.

I pull up Terry's email on my phone for the four-hundredth time. I'm supposed to meet Noa at four o'clock in front of the chess house in Central Park. She'll be looking for me.

This information set my mind whirling, because even though my face is a Google search away, I can't imagine Noa Callaway stalking me online. Still, I wasn't going to question Terry on *how* Noa would identify me. I'm wearing BD's vintage Fendi skirt suit—dressed down with Converse, knit tights, and a scarf Aude gave me for my birthday. To be on the safe side, I brought a copy of *Two Hundred and Sixty-Six Vows*, which I'm carrying face out.

I've always wanted to play at the chess house, with its shaded arch of benches and stone tables in front of the red-brick building. I've suggested it to Ryan on a few warm Sunday afternoons, but he doesn't have the patience for the game.

The February sky is clear and crisp. Turning west onto the path at Sixty-Fifth Street, I hear the chess players before I see them. For a gang of largely retired women, they swear like sailors and slap their timers like bongos. BD would fit right in.

"You gonna take my bishop before we die, Marjorie?" a player asks from one table.

"No way, Betty, I'm not falling for your Siberian trap," her opponent says.

There must be a dozen players, ranging from sixty to eighty, rotating around four boards. My eyes and intuition scan the group, eliminating half of them. I *know* Noa Callaway, and she's not the diminutive Russian lady with lipstick on her teeth. I'm trying to make eye contact with a platinum blond boomer with diamond-rimmed bifocals at the tip of a Roman nose, but she's focused on advancing her queen and not looking up. Which, honestly, is so Noa Callaway of her.

I draw closer. If I can just catch her eye, then I'll know. I can take five seconds to acclimate to the reality of her. Then I'll be good. I can focus on not fucking up this meeting, on being professional instead of an adoring fan. But before she notices my approach, my gaze is disrupted by her opponent, who is looking right at me.

I freeze when I realize I know him. It's Ross, from the launch party. Man of the Year. Edible confetti shower sharer. Thrower of lightning bolts through my body.

Look away. You have one job.

He smiles at me, a sly expression on his face. I see they're in the endgame, and that Ross's queenside pawn majority is rolling.

"Hi," he says.

"Hi." My cheeks ignite. I'm not dressed for lightning storms today.

"Checkmate, bitch!" the woman says all of a sudden. If she isn't Noa Callaway, I give up. But when she looks at me, the blankness in her gaze hits me hard.

I raise my book and say her name, but she doesn't hear me. She's calling to the other women in the group.

"I finally beat Ross!" She pumps her fists as women rise and swarm the table. Everyone needs proof. When they get it, Diamond Bifocals disappears in hugs.

"Want to play?" Ross says, gesturing for me to sit down.

"I'm sorry. I'm supposed to meet someone."

His smile pulls me close, then drops me with how quickly it vanishes. I turn my gaze away, make myself available to Noa Callaway.

"Lanie," Ross says.

"Excuse me," I say, waving an apology as I back away. "It was nice to see you again."

"Lanie." His voice commands my attention.

And then—my stomach sinks. Because I get it. It's like the force of gravity has doubled. That's how heavy I feel as Ross and I regard each other for a long and silent while.

"You?" My legs feel shaky. I drop onto the bench.

"Yeah."

"Oh my god."

Noa Callaway has an Adam's apple. Noa Callaway has *chest hair*. Noa Callaway has a deep voice and a firm handshake. By all estimation, Noa Callaway has other firm things, too.

The years of emails, the online chess games? All this time, it's been *him?*

I think of reading *Ninety-Nine Things* furtively in my college dorm room. The way that story spun my life in an entirely new direction, toward this version of me, right here, right now. I think of my Ninety-Nine Things list, snug in Ryan's wallet, the man it led me to.

"I'm sorry," I say. "I can't seem to catch my breath." The scarf is too tight around my neck. I gulp from the water bottle in my bag. I close my eyes and try to speak. "How . . . how could I not have known?"

"I could have sworn you did know," he says.

"Why would you think that?" I hear the anger rising in my voice.

His lips part. His eyes widen. He's like a zookeeper realizing the grizzly is about to attack.

"The other night, at the launch," he says. "I was worried that seeing me was what threw you off onstage."

"*Threw me off?*" Could he be more tone-deaf? "I was thinking about the *readers*, about my obligation to deliver Noa Callaway's next book to them. I was genuinely overcome with fondness for those women. Not that you'd know anything about being genuine." I clap a hand over my mouth, then let it slide down to my heart. "Your fans will lose it if they find out who you really are."

His eyes dart around the park, then lock on mine. "Why would they find out? Isn't it in everyone's best interest to keep this between us?"

"They *trusted* you."

It's less embarrassing than saying *I trusted you.*

A silence follows. He seems completely unaffected by the idea that he's betraying millions of readers, and that I am now complicit. How is it possible that the book that changed my life—that convinced me Ryan is the one!—was written by an *asshole?*

"I've always wondered where you learned to play chess," he says, pointing at the board between us.

"My grandmother taught me," I say, distracted.

"Did your grandmother dress you, too?" he asks, taking in my Fendi suit.

I stand, heart pulsing, barely able to restrain my rage. It's a good thing the chessboard is inlaid upon the table; otherwise I'd slam it on his head so hard it'd knock his next three novels out of him.

I straighten my blazer. "Yes. It was hers. And it's fabulous. And the Noa Callaway I was led to believe existed would appreciate its timeless elegance."

He stands up, too, which makes me move more quickly, stuffing my book and scarf and water bottle back into my bag.

"This isn't going well," he says.

How dare he. My idol has been desecrated. The very reason I got into publishing pulled out from underneath me. Everything I loved about love is in question. And *he* thinks it's not going well? I turn on my heel and speed walk away.

"Lanie." He follows me past the chess house.

I don't know where I plan on going. I'd like to run very far away from here. I'd like to buy six pints of ice cream and hide under my duvet for the rest of my life. I'd like to enter a wormhole where my longtime hero is the inspiring woman I always imagined—not this guy.

I think of Sue forecasting turbulence. This is more like dual engine failure.

"You need me," Ross says as we pass the Dairy, children running out around us, clutching new souvenirs. I stop in my tracks.

"What?" I hear myself. I sound demonic. And I feel even darker inside.

"You need me. This book," he says.

He's right. If I don't want to get fired, I do need him, and I need to coax his next book out of him. Peony needs him. All the other decent human beings I work with need him. That means they need me not to quit right now.

He looks over my head as he delivers his next gem. "Don't conflate art and artist. If you're concerned about my readers, then focus on my books, not me. I'm not the origin of my books' meaning. Society is the only author."

"Oh, give me a break." I start walking again, calling over my shoulder, "People love cheap clothes, too, but hey, who cares about sweatshops, right?"

"That's my point!" he persists. "'The birth of the reader must be at the cost of the death of the Author.'"

I ball my fists in rage. I've loved the essay Ross is quoting ever since I read it in Intro to Literary Criticism in college. But at this moment, in this rage, "The Death of the Author" begins to take on a new, more tempting and literal light.

"Roland Barthes did not toil in relative obscurity," I say,

"just to give some spoiled millionaire permission to be a prick."

He laughs, throwing back his head as we exit the park and wait for the light at Fifth Avenue. "See? Now we're having fun."

I wonder if he's a legitimate sociopath. Would he be having so much fun if his entire career felt as tenuous as mine does now? Why *doesn't* it feel that way to him? The light turns green.

"I need to go," I say. I practically sprint across the street.

If I could only run back in time and never read a Noa Callaway book. But then where would I be?

The fucker is running after me.

"Maybe you should ask yourself why my gender is so disturbing to you," he shouts. "Isn't it aggressively heteronormative to assume I have to be a woman?"

"Goodbye, Ross," I shout back.

"Lanie, please," he says, surprising me.

I stop. I turn around. His tone and expression are more earnest than they'd been a moment before. I find this more unbearable than when he was being a pseudointellectual jerk. How can this be so uncomfortable? When there were two computers and the comforting labyrinth of the internet between us, Noa Callaway and I had such amazing chemistry.

"Will you come up?" he asks. We're standing beneath a building's awning, and he points at the door. "This is me."

"I know. I've only been sending you packages here for seven years." I glance up at the building, which I've speculated about so many times, imagining a very different Noa Callaway inhabiting its penthouse.

There's no chance I'm going up there. I've been disillusioned enough for one afternoon. I need space from this man to figure out what the hell I'm going to do about him.

"No, thanks," I say.

"Don't you think we should talk about the book?"

His words jar me into seeing how far astray we are from any semblance of professionalism. This was all supposed to go so differently. And it's not entirely his fault. Maybe only ninety-five percent. I take a deep breath, let it out. I think of everyone depending on me to deliver the new Noa Callaway book.

"I'm listening," I say. "I don't need to be in your penthouse to listen."

"Fine," he says.

"So? Talk."

"Wow. You know, you're different in person."

"You did not just say that," I say, shaking my head. "Are you finishing the draft, or what?"

He doesn't answer right away.

I fill the silence. "We're going to need a better title than *Thirty-Eight Obituaries.*"

"Oh, that," he says, scratching his chin. "Yeah, I scrapped that idea. Didn't I tell you?"

No, he failed to mention that. Among a few other key details he's left out of our email exchanges. And just like that, my promotion goes from provisional to phantasmal.

"What's wrong with the obituaries concept?" I say. Our sales team had loved the idea. Sue had loved it, too.

He shrugs. "Too New York–centric. I want to do something fresh."

"All your books are New York–centric!" I want to scream but manage to keep my voice to an angry whisper. We are standing on the street in the middle of Manhattan, after all, and his identity is a secret to everyone but unlucky me. "That's your brand. It's what your readers *like* about you. It's why *Vogue* called you the 'Queen of Gotham Love.' Remember?"

For years I've admired how Noa's books aren't just love stories between a couple, they're also love letters to the city I adore. Even *Vows*, with its Italian wedding scenes, started off with a magical proposal on the Staten Island Ferry.

"I've used the city up," he says. "Run out of landmarks for the characters to kiss in front of."

I roll my eyes because of course he'd reduce the poignant love in so many Noa Callaway books to cliché.

"And in its place, you're planning to write . . . what?"

"I've got some irons in the fire."

"Oh god."

He's lying. Everything about him screams he hasn't typed a word.

"You look worried," he says. "Everything's going to be fine."

"For you."

"For us. We're a team now, Lanie."

I've got to get out of here before I get arrested for assault. But I can't let him know how much he's gotten under my skin.

"Look . . ." I want to say *Ross*, but it no longer fits. "What should I even call you, now that we've . . ." I trail off. It's wrong to use the word *met* about a person I thought I knew. I had shown myself to Noa Callaway in my emails. I had allowed my life to be brightened by hers.

His.

"My real name is Noah Ross," he says. "Most people call me Ross, but none of them know what I write. Why don't we stick with Noah?"

"Okay, Noah." I cross my arms, level my gaze at him. "You've got two hours."

"To do what?" His laugh sounds dubious.

"To send me what you've got. Your . . . irons in the fire."

Noah looks at me like I've suggested we get matching neck tattoos. "You know that's not how I work."

"It is now." I hope he can't see my knees shaking. "Your manuscript is four months late. I'm not going to get fired because you're tired of success. So organize your ideas and send them to me. You said we're a team now. Well, my team wins."

Chapter Seven

I AM IN A FUNK NOT EVEN TAYLOR SWIFT CAN PENETRATE. I yank out my earbuds and kill my playlist, breathing frost as I jog along the river.

After the disaster of meeting Noah Ross, I knew I had to keep moving. I think more clearly when I'm not standing still, and there was no way I was going to sit idly by the rest of the evening, checking my email and waiting to see what he'd send.

I went home just long enough to hang up BD's Fendi suit, feed Alice, and grab my running shoes.

Now, I appeal to the pavement of Manhattan, to the fading blue sky with its high cirrus clouds, to the lights coming on across the river and the steam rising out of subway grates and the pickle-scented air by the bodega, to the noise and the hustle and the mingle of eight million dreams—please, help me figure this one out.

How is the question looping through my mind for the first

cold couple of miles. How does a guy like Noah Ross write women, write love so well?

At the launch, he had said he wasn't married, no girlfriend, so I can't credit a woman in the background. Then again, who knows if he was lying to me about being single, too.

Not that I care. I'm just genuinely confused. How did he convince me, surely one of his most careful readers, that there was a deep, true, feminine intuition behind his stories? How did *his* take on love come to be what shaped my own?

I cringe, thinking of my list. My Ninety-Nine Things. Tenderly crafted a decade ago on my dorm room bed.

When I picture cynical Noah Ross coming up with the premise of *Ninety-Nine Things I'm Going to Love About You*, I have to stop running because I think I might be sick. Seagulls scatter as I lean over the railing on East River Esplanade, gulping air to catch my breath. Wind lashes my face as the river rolls by beneath me, undisturbed.

And then, I wonder—

If I hadn't taken that book so seriously, if I hadn't committed my own list to paper, carried it around with me all these years . . . would I have fallen so hard and fast for Ryan when we met? Would I be as sure that he's the one?

Stop it, I tell myself, and run west, away from the river. Just because Noa Calloway is a lie doesn't mean my relationship is. It doesn't mean love isn't real and true.

This is not about Ryan. This is about my career.

And the man who might wreck it.

If I let him. Which I'm not going to do.

Usually, I'd be reaching out to my people about now. Ryan, first and foremost. And a half-second later, BD, then Rufus and Meg. But as my fingers itch to send a series of SOS texts to each of them, I see that non-disclosure agreement in my mind.

I'd signed it in Sue's office like an idiot. I can't tell anyone the truth about Noa Callaway.

Suddenly, I feel my torment focus into a single vector: Sue.

Peony's president and publisher sat there as I signed the NDA, and told me to buckle up. I feel betrayed by her, her poise and calm and cardigans. To be fair, I don't think she's ever actually met Noah, so she may not know his particular shade of self-obsessed. But surely, she knows he's a man. Why doesn't it present a crisis of conscience for her?

Silly Lanie. Naïve Lanie.

Money.

That's why.

But what about Alix? If I am a good boss and a mentor to Aude it's because Alix taught me how to be good. Why didn't Noah's identity ever seem to bother her? I've tried calling Alix, but her mailbox was full, and my emails have gone unanswered. So I'm left to wonder:

Is it different because Alix discovered him? Signed his first novel with Peony? What if she crafted his pseudonym herself? Is *this* why she really gave her notice—to finally make peace with The Lie?

I need to talk to Sue. There's got to be another, more honest way to publish these books. Something between unmasking Noah for the asshole he is and perpetuating a fabrication to millions around the world.

But the thought of going into Sue's office, making any such request with no manuscript to show for my provisionally promoted self . . . it would be tantamount to asking Sue to fire me.

I need ammunition. I need a watertight concept from Noah and a delivery date I can hold his ass to. Then, I can think about next steps.

I begin to sprint. My legs and arms pump with sudden optimism. My muscles burn as I enter Central Park.

I didn't know I was headed here until I stop to catch my breath and find myself in the center of the Gapstow Bridge. I put my hands on the stone railing and let it center me. I take in the big, beautiful city in the dusk.

Pink clouds stretch across the sky like spun sugar. There's still snow on the north side of the Pond. In the distance, windows glitter gold as the sun sets, a shining fence around the park.

Used the city up. I roll my eyes, recalling Noah's words. It isn't possible. I don't believe him. Something else is going on with Noah, something I can't see. Whatever it is, I'm not going to let it wreck my life. I'm going to pull one more book out of him. Then I'll figure out what to do about his pseudonym.

I'm glowering into the distance, contemplating how I'll do this, when two approaching figures sharpen in my view. It's getting dark, but I can still see them. Something about the way they move is familiar.

Of course. It's Saturday night, Edward and Elizabeth's

picnic hour. And here they are—not gone like I'd feared. My heart lifts.

She is slight with cropped, silvery hair and a smart trench coat. He is scarcely taller than her, in professorial glasses and thick-soled orthopedic shoes. When he smiles, he's a dashingly handsome older man.

They're older. But it's them.

Elizabeth has her arm threaded through the same picnic basket, but she's added a cane since I last saw her. Edward, as usual, bears a tiny folding table and two chairs. I watch as he helps her step up onto the grass. It's damp from the morning's rain, but as usual, they have come prepared. As Edward unfolds the table and chairs, Elizabeth lays out a white tablecloth, carefully smoothing it down. He lights candles. She produces a box of fried chicken, a jar of pickles, and a bottle of wine. The whole scene is impossibly charming, but the best part is when they sit down and take each other's hands across the table. For a while, they just talk, and though I long to, I've never drawn near enough to eavesdrop.

I'm so glad to see them. It feels like a sign from the universe that not everything has gone to hell.

I take out my phone and snap a quick picture of the couple in profile, of their glowing candlelit picnic. I'm about to send it to Ryan, because this will be us one day.

But then I imagine him at his senator's birthday dinner in D.C., the one I was supposed to attend. How he might not be pleased to get this photo.

I put my phone away. I blow a kiss to Edward and Elizabeth, then jog toward home in the New York night.

❧

"I'm about to tell you something," I say to BD the next morning over brunch at an Ethiopian restaurant in Hell's Kitchen. "But first I need to swear you to secrecy."

BD puts down her menu and smiles. "*This* is why I need to come to New York more often. Do you know the last time your father or your brother started off a conversation half so well? I think Hillary's husband was in office."

BD's in town for just a few hours, passing through the city on a road trip with a group of friends she calls the League of Widows. This afternoon, they're on their way to Niagara Falls.

I was up all night debating whether I should say what I'm about to say. But if I hadn't canceled my D.C. weekend with Ryan to meet with Noa Callaway, then I wouldn't have gotten to see BD at all. So in a way, it feels like it was meant to be that my grandmother is here when I need her most.

"You joke, but—" I say.

"I joke, but I'm dead serious. In the way only an octogenarian can be. You can trust me with your confidence, Elaine."

"Thank you." My eyes fill with tears.

BD scoots her chair around the table to be nearer to me. She holds my hands. Hers are always cold and smooth, and she wears about eighteen thousand very nice rings.

"Honey. Is it Ryan?"

"What? No. Everything's fine with Ryan," I say. "It's . . . Noa Callaway. I met Noa Callaway."

I swallow and meet my grandmother's wide eyes. BD has

been a fan of Noa's almost as long as I have, ever since I bought her *Ninety-Nine Things* a decade ago in large print.

"She's a he," I say and hang my head. "A man. And not the good kind."

"Well, that's a third-degree doozy." BD tosses her napkin on the table, as if she's just lost her appetite.

I, on the other hand, have started stress-eating. I grab a huge wedge of injera and sweep up a mound of spicy chicken doro wat.

"Okay, where do we begin?" she says.

"We could begin with the fact that the whole reason I got into publishing is because of Noa Callaway, and it turns out she's a lie," I say with my mouth full. "Now I'm an accomplice, and Peony is profiting off the misconception that our biggest author is a woman."

"Go back, go back." BD waves her hand. "Let's work our way up to moral depravity—"

"But morally, I am violating the trust of millions of readers! Can I even call myself a feminist?"

My grandmother pats my arm. "I don't think Gloria Steinem is coming to take your card away just yet," she says, then pauses to think. "Another way of looking at what happened is the classic you-met-your-hero, Lanie. Why don't you slow down and tell me about it?"

"Ugh," I say, as the memory flows back into my mind. "His real name is Noah Ross. He's a mid-thirties narcissist with a smug smile and a completely reckless disregard for the fact that he's four months late on his next manuscript. He doesn't seem to grasp that even if it doesn't matter to *him* whether he writes another book, it matters to a whole lot of other people. It matters to me."

"What makes you so sure he's *not* working on this book?"

"Because yesterday I told him to send me what he had so far." I push back from the table. "Radio silence."

"So." BD raps her long nails on the table. "Noa Callaway is a putz, and he's got writer's block, just in time for your provisional promotion. This is not good."

"I keep coming back to the moment when I finally understood who he was. We were at the chess house in Central Park. And this *thing* passed between us. It was like both of us knew everything was about to change—and not for the better."

"So, you weren't the only one nervous about the reveal?"

"He wasn't nervous," I say. "He was ice-cold. He brought me to a location that meant something to us both—you know, our online chess games?"

"Legendary," she concedes.

"And then he played me like a fiddle."

"A pawn would be a more apt metaphor, here, Editor."

"Whatever! He also mocked my suit!"

BD's brows shoot up. "The Fendi?"

I nod, daring BD to defend him now. "Characterizing, wouldn't you say?" I sigh. "I wore it because I think I was expecting him to be more like . . . you. Less like . . . himself. Honestly, it's hard for me to remember now who or what I'd been expecting. Oh, BD, why couldn't it have been you?"

"Well, I'm flattered, but I can't say I'm surprised."

"Really?" I say, amazed. "You've read all Noa's books.

You're honestly telling me you suspected Noa Callaway had a . . . you know . . ."

"You can say *penis* to your grandmother, Lanie."

"Oh jeez. Fine. *Penis.*"

"*Manhood*," BD says.

"*Dick.*" I put my head on the table. She runs her nails along my shoulder like she did when I was little, and it helps.

"All I'm suggesting is," she says, "there's a reason he's been hiding behind a pseudonym."

"I wish I knew what that reason was," I say, lifting my head off the table. "It might make him seem more human. Less like the Great Red Spot of Jupiter settling permanently over my life. Then again, knowing my luck, I'd probably discover things about him that would only make me hate him more. Can you believe, he actually asked me why it bothers me to find out he's a man?"

"Did you have an answer?"

I sigh. "It made me think of something Ryan said once, at a work party I brought him to. About how the whole point of fiction is that it's a lie." I grimace, remembering. "It didn't score huge points with Sue. But you know, Ryan's bookshelves are crammed with biographies of Great Men. He and his friends all quote from the same texts. They read them like technical manuals, how-to guides to Become Great. I think it lets them fantasize that someday, the story of their lives will be interesting enough for other men to want to read."

BD laughs, nodding.

"Wouldn't it rock *his* sense of self," I say, "if *Profiles in Courage* turned out to be a hoax?"

"Have you told him?" BD says.

"I mean, the odds are JFK had a ghostwriter, but—"

"I mean about Noa Callaway," BD says. "Have you talked to Ryan about it?"

"BD," I sputter, feeling myself overdoing a display of shock. "My NDA! I can't tell anyone . . ."

She gives me her *I'm-just-going-to-wait-for-you-to-get-there* look.

"I told *you* because I need advice, because I trust you," I say. Still getting the look. "And because . . ." I pause. "I already know what Ryan would say."

She tilts her head, takes a tiny sip of her coffee. "What would Ryan say?"

"First, he'd call Noah an asshole. Then he'd seize the opportunity to say that maybe this isn't my dream job anymore. Before I knew it, we'd be talking about the improbability of my working remotely from D.C. Hypothetical children and their hypothetical Halloween carnivals, which I'd be missing because of my hypothetical commute. And then he'd go, 'Maybe a fresh start in D.C. is what you need.'"

I thought I'd just done a pretty good impersonation of Ryan, but BD isn't laughing. She's staring at me, concerned.

I raise my shoulders. "That's why I figured I would start with you."

BD and Ryan have met only once, at a big family reunion where all of my extended Atlanta relatives vied for Ryan's attention, thereby guaranteeing that none got quite enough. It's a goal of mine for my grandmother and my fiancé to bond before the wedding, but it hasn't happened yet. She knows him, but she doesn't *know* him, and I'd better clarify some details of our dynamic so she doesn't get the wrong idea.

"BD, what I mean is—"

"You know, your grandfather wrote terrible poetry," she interrupts. "He once wrote a series of haikus called *Foreplay.*"

I glance around. "I missed the segue in the conversation."

"Believe me, he was good at many things. The man could read an X-ray like it was a nursery rhyme," she says. "He made the lightest pierogi you ever ate. And when it came to a sensual massage, your grandfather had hands like a—"

"Okay, BD!" I say, laughing. "I get it, but what's the point?"

"That no one person can fulfill every single one of another person's needs. Which is why book clubs and grandmothers exist. I'm sure Irwin would have liked a more enthusiastic audience for his efforts in verse. Whereas I would have preferred the poetry of his fingers to the poetry of his . . . poetry. I would have liked him to pick up a novel once in a blue moon. There was this wonderful couples book club at the JCC we never got to join." She takes my hand. "I do wish you could have known him."

"Me, too," I say, and give her hand a squeeze. Irwin died before I was born.

"My point is no marriage gets it *all* right, honey, but I hope that in choosing Ryan, you have found someone you can turn to when you have a problem, when you really need a steady heart."

"Of course," I say, too quickly. "And I will tell Ryan. At some point. When I have a better handle on what I'm going to do."

"When's that going to be?" she asks. "It won't get easier to tell Ryan, especially if you have more interactions with Noah."

"I'm screwed, okay?" I say, surrendering dramatically. "Did I mention Noah told me he's *used up* New York, that there's nothing fresh for him to write about? Why did he have to choose *now* to get writer's block?"

"Very selfish of him." BD nods as the waiter clears our plates. "This is supposed to be your moment to shine."

"I don't know what to do." I reach for the bill in the middle of the table, because it's one way to seize control, and because if I lose my job, I won't be able to treat BD to lunch for long. "How would Mom have dealt with this?"

"Your mother believed in the hair of the dog. She'd look for a way to solve this problem according to its nature." BD takes out her golden snakehead compact mirror and reapplies some bright magenta lipstick. She looks at herself in the mirror, seeming pleased. "What about *Fifty Ways to Break Up Mom and Dad*?" she asks after a moment.

"What about it?" I say.

I think about my favorite scene, where the characters go hang gliding. The moment just before they run off the cliff.

Life's greatest mystery is whether we shall die bravely.

I read this scene aloud to Ryan once. I was just about to tell him how it made me think about my mother, when he'd teased me—"So suicide is sexy now? That's the message?"

But that wasn't the message at all, and everyone in *Fifty Ways* made it down the fictional cliff in one piece. The message, as I understood it, was that some people can look into the abyss without losing sight of themselves or what they love. Without being too scared about what lies on the other side.

Maybe my mom's last words to me *were* an act of bravery. She wasn't worried that I was too young to handle them. She trusted me enough to make a leap.

Did she also trust that when the time came for me to make my own leap, I'd be able to feel her with me? Is that moment now?

"Are you saying Noah Ross is my abyss?" I ask BD.

"Maybe," she says. "I'm also saying the man needs a taste of his own medicine. No one 'uses up' this city, and if he thinks he's the lone ranger who's done it, he's got another think coming. You might have to be his tour guide on this adventure. It just might take you fifty ways."

"What do you mean? We go hang gliding over the Hudson? No, thanks."

"I mean take him to the places you take me," she says. "This charming hole-in-the-wall, for example."

"It's the best Ethiopian food in the city."

"And maybe Noa Callaway has never sampled its delicacies or thought about writing of them. He writes about the big tourist attractions. Show him *your* New York."

"I don't know . . ."

"Remember when you took me to the Lithuanian consulate for Užgavėnės a couple years ago? That was fun!"

"I remember you went home with the consulate general's phone number," I say.

"Exactly. I'd even go so far as to call it inspiring."

"I took you there because I love you. Because I wasn't scared you'd mock it or think it was boring. I am not showing that man *my* New York."

"You know it's a good idea, though," BD says, sipping the last of her coffee.

"He probably does need to get out from behind his desk more often," I acknowledge. "At the park, he had the look of someone who hasn't seen the sun in a month."

"See?"

"I could ask Terry to take to him to some new places," I say. "I wish I could get overtime approved for Aude to do it. She'd have him whipped into shape in a week. . . ."

"Lanie, *you* are Noa Callaway's editor." BD shoulders her Birkin and rises from the table. "If Noa doesn't write this book, Terry and Aude will still have jobs. Will you?"

I worry a hole in the paper tablecloth, not liking where this conversation is headed. Not able to stop it, either.

"Fine," I say, standing up. "I will consider proposing a visit to someplace in New York that Noah Ross has likely overlooked."

BD links an arm through mine as we leave the restaurant. "I foresee success."

We step back into the city for the pleasant stroll up to Lincoln Center, where she'll meet her League of Widows.

"I'm glad you're so confident," I say as we wait for a crosstown bus to pass. "Should I remind you that in *Fifty*

Ways, the plan backfired horribly? They were supposed to break up their parents. They ended up breaking up themselves, climactically—at their parents' wedding."

"Yes, but that was fictional kismet," BD says and winks at me. "You are my real, live granddaughter, whom I'm proud of and believe in. You are going to rise to this occasion like a Tinder date with a pocket full of Viagra."

"BD!" I groan. "I'm going to have to work so hard to erase that mental image."

"I'm sorry, doll, but I couldn't resist."

Chapter Eight

ON TUESDAY, I WORK FROM HOME, OSTENSIBLY TO EDIT
the third draft of the paranormal ballet manuscript. But
really, I am busting my ass to clean my apartment, from worn
floorboards to art deco crown-molded ceiling. I may be a
mess, but my apartment doesn't have to be.

I've mopped and I've dusted. I've taken a toothbrush to
my grout. I've fluffed every pillow and gone through two
bottles of Windex. My toilet bowl is sparkling, and the inside
of my refrigerator is now scrubbed of last week's experiment
in wilted arugula. I even bought one of those vacuum robots,
which is presently chasing poor Alice around my living room
and will probably give her tortoise nightmares.

All this because I had the superb idea of inviting Noah
Ross over for an editorial powwow.

We can go ahead and blame Terry, who nixed five in a row
of my perfectly good ideas for cafés, bistros, and teahouses
around the city where the two of us might discreetly meet.

Too busy, said Terry, or too loud, or too near the publishers' lunch circuit (it was on Eleventh Avenue, please!). She rejected one place because they only serve two-percent milk.

Terry was pushing for Noa's Fifth Avenue penthouse—*less hassle for him*, was the phrase actually employed—but after last weekend at the chess house, I learned my lesson about meeting Noah on his turf.

Thus I boldly threw my hat-sized apartment into the ring. And I guess Terry couldn't come up with any objections that wouldn't have sounded prohibitively rude, so she ended up agreeing. I'd felt vindicated hanging up the phone.

Ten seconds later, the cleaning panic set in.

My goal is to make my apartment a completely neutral site, where the water stains on my windowsill and the lopsided lampshade in the entry hall won't distract us from focusing on Noa Callaway's next book.

The trouble is, I'm realizing how much in my apartment speaks volumes about me. Volumes that I don't want Noah Ross to hear. My vintage bar cart, for example, boasting BD's blown glass cocktail shaker, martini set, and the collection of bespoke vermouths left over from the New Year's Eve party when Rufus and I went a little too nuts on Negronis. I stare at it now for ten minutes, wondering if its prominent place in my living room says *your editor knows how to have fun* or *your editor knows how to black out on a Monday night*. I wheel it all the rattling way into my bedroom before I realize that if, on the off chance, Noah Ross were to open my bedroom door, thinking it was the bathroom, it would be way worse for him to see my bedside speakeasy.

Then there's my bookshelf. My carefully curated pride and joy, whose space is so limited I feel it keeps me honest. But now I'm wondering: Is it serious enough? Is it light enough? Is it diverse enough? Is it classic enough? Are Noa Callaway's books prominent enough? Are they *too* prominent?

Noah is going to be looking at this shelf and forming opinions about it, about me. We're book people. It's what we do. Should I try to make room for the copy of *War and Peace* I use as a doorstop in my closet?

"I know it looks like I'm losing my mind," I say to Alice, who is glaring at the robot vacuum from the safety of her dog bed. "But sometimes, this is what being a boss looks like."

Noah is supposed to arrive at three o'clock, when the south-facing windows of my living room let in their softest light. By two-fifty, I've changed out of sweats and into a white peasant blouse and what Meg calls my "adult jeans," because they need to be ironed. Though I'm tempted to put on the Fendi suit again, just to fuck with him.

I've got my French press packed with freshly ground espresso, a clean fridge chilling whole milk, *and* almond milk, and damn it, I bought something called oat milk, too—okay, Terry? I've got Pellegrino and a box of pastries from the only bakery in midtown Aude finds edible. All that and a stomach full of nerves.

I don't know whether my Fifty Ways plan is actually going to work, but that's not even on today's menu of worries. To-day is about getting him to agree to try it out.

At two fifty-eight, I position myself at my bedroom window, overlooking the entrance to my building. I may or may not be hiding behind my ficus plant when a black town car slows to a stop on the street below.

"Typical," I mutter, thinking what a *hassle* it must have been for Noah to be chauffeured down here in his town car's heated seats.

But then, the driver comes around to open the back door, and out slides a blond woman in a floor-length rabbit fur coat. She's toting four sweater-vested shih tzus and an extra-long selfie-stick. I'm waiting for Noah to get out after her, for this to be his type. Instead the driver closes the door, waves goodbye to the woman, and the next thing I notice is a commotion on the street corner.

It's Noah Ross, arriving on foot from an unknown direction, staring into his phone—and getting fully entangled in four shih tzu leashes. He hops to get free of one leash then ensnares himself in two more. The woman with the dogs is getting really pissed. The dogs are yapping as she brandishes her selfie-stick at Noah and yanks her leashes so violently he almost bites it on the pavement.

Here I'd been so nervous to host a man currently getting tag-teamed by four specks of fur in argyle. I smile to myself and enjoy the show.

Until my buzzer rings.

Then I scramble to the phone in the hallway, pick it up, and jam my finger on the pound sign to unlock the downstairs door. After that comes the hardest part: the wait for him to walk up five flights of stairs.

I use the time to take a final look around my apartment. At the last moment, my gaze falls on the framed photograph of Ryan and me at the Nationals game on the night we got engaged. We're grinning, cheek to cheek, and he's holding up my hand to show the ring, which was too small to get over my knuckle so it sits jammed midway down my finger. I hate how I look in the picture: deer-in-the-headlights with mascara all the way down to my chin from crying. But Ryan had the photo enlarged, matted, and framed, so it hangs on the wall near the window. The look on my face is so intimate that suddenly I know I can't bear for Noah Ross to see it. I snatch it off the wall just as my doorbell rings.

"Be right there!" I shout, frantically looking for a place to stash the frame. The lower shelf of my coffee table is an understated mausoleum of old magazines. I wedge the frame between some old *Cosmo*s and *New Yorker*s then steel myself to let Noah in.

You can do this. BD believes in you.

"Hello!" I say, forcing brightness into my voice as I swing open my door.

And there he is. His hair is damp from a shower, and he's dressed up in a linen collared shirt, dark blue slacks, and stylish brown leather brogues. His pea coat is draped over his arm—no one can do a five-floor walk-up wearing that much wool.

I just saw him downstairs through my window, but it's startling to face him at close range. I still have trouble believing that *he* is Noa Callaway. I'm still, to be honest, pretty mad about it. He looks flushed, a little off, and I remind myself he's just climbed seventy-eight stairs and been accosted by shih tzus, so I give him a moment's grace.

"What can I get you to drink?" I say.

He steps through my doorway as if into an active volcano. "This is . . . your apartment?"

"Home sweet home," I say.

We both survey the scene of my one-bedroom pre-war walk-up. Lovingly furnished with estate-sale finds and BD's hand-me-downs and lived in for six years by yours truly.

"I didn't realize the address Terry gave me was your home," Noah says, determined to harp on this.

"Where did you assume I had invited you?"

"*I* don't make assumptions," he says.

"How benevolent," I say and let him stew in whatever he's trying to insinuate about my apartment. I refuse to apologize for the state of my living quarters, even as I can't help wishing I'd made room for *War and Peace* on the bookshelf.

I become aware of an acute discomfort in Noah. He's stuck in the doorway and doesn't seem to know what to do.

"There's a hook behind you for your coat," I say, and then we fumble over who will hang it up.

"Espresso?" I say. I'm eager to leave the hallway and make it to my slightly more spacious kitchen. "I'm fresh out of two-percent milk, but I have whole, or almond, or . . . oatmeal, I think." I glance at him. "That was a joke? Terry mentioned some issue with two-percent, oh never mind . . ."

He's looking at me blankly.

"I can just make the espresso and—"

"No, thanks," Noah says. He walks past my kitchen and into the living room. He sinks down on the couch and looks, for a moment, almost normal there. Then he ruins it with a snarky, "It's not like this is going to take long, is it?"

"You're in a charming mood," I call from the kitchen, making myself a stupid espresso because I paid eleven dollars for it at Blue Bottle. Then I hear my words on playback and I wince. "What I mean is, no, I won't waste your time."

Espresso in hand, I meet him in the living room. As I reach for my notes, there comes a rustling from underneath the coffee table. Noah jumps about a foot off the couch.

"What was that?" he says.

"I have a tortoise. Alice. It was probably her," I explain. "Do pets bother you?"

"No. It's fine. I just ran into some aggressive dogs outside your apartment. Made me jumpy."

I bite back a laugh. "That must have been scary."

Noah's peering under the coffee table as Alice pokes her head out. She appraises him discerningly, in the form of her trademark slow blink. An actual smile lights up his face.

"Hello, Alice," he says, his voice exuding a friendliness apparently reserved for reptiles.

"It can take her a couple decades to warm up to new people," I say, but then Alice blows my mind by taking one step and then another in Noah's direction.

Unfortunately, her advance disrupts the equilibrium of all

the crap I've shoved under the coffee table. And out slides the framed picture of newly engaged Ryan and me. It clatters to my hardwood floor.

Noah picks up the frame, and I die a slow death watching him study it closely. He glances at me, then at the photo again. At last, he tilts his head to see under the coffee table.

"Is this where you keep all your ex-boyfriends?"

"He is not my ex-boyfriend—"

"Oh, right." He points at my hand in the photograph. "The ring. Ex-*fiancé*?"

"Don't worry about him!" I say and snatch the picture from his hands.

"Sorry," Noah says. "Occupational hazard."

I'm angry that he's seen what I look like when I cry, guilty that I'd shoved Ryan under the coffee table for this asshole. I return the photo to its place on the wall.

Noah watches all of this with great interest, eyebrows annoyingly raised, and by the time I get back to my chair across the couch from him, Alice is sitting in his lap.

"We've bonded," he announces, giving her a pat on the head in the one place she will accept affection.

I rub my temples, trying to focus. "Do you know why I asked you here today?"

"Because I didn't turn in my homework on Saturday?" he says.

I narrow my eyes at him. "Because I know you don't have a book."

"I told you—"

"Yeah, yeah." I wave him off. "Irons in the fire. Look,

what I need is for you to have an actual idea that I can sell to Sue."

He opens his mouth to argue. I'm not having it.

"To that end," I continue, "I thought about what you said the other day. About having run out of New York City landmarks for your characters to kiss in front of? And so, I have prepared a list of landmarks you have never written about, and may have never considered." I hold up my notebook. "You're going to look at my list. You're going to cross off the places you've been to. Then, one by one, we're going to visit the places left on the list until you find something worth writing about."

"Lanie—"

"Talk to the list." I set it down in front of him.

Fifty overlooked New York City landmarks. They are numbered in order of my personal preference, but all of them are gems. At the top, in an effort to inject a touch of playfulness, I've written the header *Fifty Ways to Break Up Noah and His Writer's Block*.

"Do you have a pen?" he asks, stone faced and unappreciative of my good humor.

I hand over my pen. Noah crosses something out. I lean forward, watch as he retitles the page: *Fifty Ways to Break Up Lanie and Her Anxiety*.

"Just some light edits," he says.

I want to tell him that my anxiety and his writer's block are not mutually exclusive, that they are, in fact, in every way intertwined. But I hang back, because now he's actually reading the list.

I'd spent most of Sunday drafting it after my brunch with BD. I had scoured the internet. I had paged through four old diaries. I had texted friends for help jogging my memory about the city's little wonders that we've stumbled upon over the years.

To Rufus: Remind me how we scaled the back of the Pepsi-Cola sign in Gantry Plaza after that BBQ in Astoria?

He'd written back: All I remember is it involved a stolen fire ladder and a whole lot of Tanqueray.

To Meg: Does your mom-friend still live in that romantic little enclave on the UWS? Intel on how a girl might get access to the garden for an hour?

She'd written back: You mean Pomander Walk? That mom and I had a falling-out over gluten allergies. But the bish needs my help planning the school's spring fundraiser, so lemme see what I can do.

My friends are used to these kinds of inquiries by now. They've stopped asking why and simply trust they'll someday see the results in the pages of a book.

In this case, I really, really hope they will.

"What do you think?" I ask Noah when I can wait no longer.

"I think I made a good impression Saturday," he says. "You really want to hang out with me. Fifty times."

I grit my teeth. "More like I want to keep my job. For fifty years."

"You're serious about this?" He meets my eyes then shakes his head in disbelief. "Then I'd really better think of something, or there's a lot of suffering in our future."

My eyes flash. "What is so wrong with this list?"

"The Austrian Cultural Forum? You want to spend a Saturday with me at the Austrian Cultural Forum?"

"It's an architectural marvel! Twenty-four stories high and just twenty-five feet wide!"

"Well, bravo to the architect," he says. "But just because the two of us stand before this marvel doesn't mean a book idea will fall into my head."

"Why are you pretending that the concept of inspiration is so foreign to you?" I snap at him. "You've written ten books. Surely you know by now that writers go out in the world, look around, and get ideas?"

"Not like this," he says. "I can save us both a lot of torture by stating now: It's not going to work."

"You know what else isn't working?" I say. "Whatever you've been doing. You're four months late and have nothing to show for it." I sigh. "Please. Don't leave Peony hanging like this. People are counting on you. You might not care about that, but I do. . . ."

I trail off because to say more feels futile. Why should he care about what I care about? He doesn't owe me anything, even if he did spend the last seven years email-masquerading as my friend. It was only that, a masquerade.

He's quiet for a moment, his eyes moving over my list. Alice rests her chin on his forearm, which is her most endearing gesture. I notice Noah glancing down at her, his lips nearly twitching to a smile. Suddenly, Noah picks up the pen. I hold my breath as he crosses out a few items on my list. Then a few more.

The Marilyn Monroe subway grate—gone. I can live with that. Though it could have been fun to gender bend the flashing scene from *The Seven Year Itch*.

The Liberty Pole at city hall—also out. I'd thought maybe a jury duty meet-cute, but okay.

But when he crosses out Pomander Walk, I can't keep quiet. Meg made up with Mama Gluten Free to get me those keys.

"Pomander Walk is magical," I argue. "It's this romantic pedestrian-only secret alley on the Upper West Side. It feels like you're in a Dickens novel—"

"I know," he says curtly. "I've seen it. I'm not writing *Great Expectations*."

"You're not generating them, either," I mutter.

"Could you not hover over me while I do this?" he asks.

I back off and move to the window to give him space. Even though I wasn't hovering, merely trying to help.

Truthfully, it's nicer at the window, getting away from the gravitational pull of Noah's negativity. I gaze outside at the bright afternoon, watching one of the red CitySights buses lumber down my block. This line of hop-on-hop-off bus tours passes my apartment an average of five times a day. A speaker blasts the same recorded spiel each time. Like everyone else on East Forty-Ninth Street, I have it memorized. I could recite it in my sleep.

"Katharine Hepburn lived for more than sixty years in this Turtle Bay brownstone . . ." I say along with the recorded speech.

"Did you just do the tour bus monologue?" Noah snickers from the couch.

"No," I say. "Okay, yes. I didn't realize I said it out loud. When you've lived someplace for seven years, you sort of become one with its soundtrack." I glance at him, wondering if he knows what the hell I'm talking about. It's probably quiet as a tomb in his penthouse thirty-four stories above Central Park.

"Do the M50 bus," he says.

Without thinking, I deliver a serviceable impression of rusty brakes, rumbling hydraulics, and the drone of the accessibility ramp being lowered. Then I remember Noah Ross is staring at me, and I get embarrassed and go silent.

I've clearly embarrassed him, too, because he doesn't even acknowledge my attempt at being a bus. He only stares at me, then changes the subject: "So Katharine Hepburn lived here?"

"She lived across the street, which is why it costs about ten grand more a month to live over there. I went to look at her brownstone once, when it was listed. A friend got me into a pocket open house. It was really nice. You could picture her there, having toast and tea and giving Spencer Tracy the business."

"You like Katharine Hepburn?" he says.

"She's Katharine Hepburn." What more is there to say?

"What's your favorite of her movies?"

"*Adam's Rib*," I say, hoping that film's battle-of-the-sexes theme isn't lost on him. "*Bringing Up Baby* is great, too. What's your favorite?"

He's looking at me funny, just refusing to hold up his end of the conversation.

"Wait." My heart lifts. "Are you getting a book idea?"

He rolls his eyes and shakes his head. "No, Lanie, you did not just solve everything by reciting a tour bus speech."

"You say that like it would be a bad thing. . . ."

"This may come as a surprise to you," he says, "but I would like to write another book. I'm here, aren't I? I am even entertaining this absurd proposal of yours." He shakes my list at me.

"Oh, you are entertaining it? Because I thought you were just crossing shit out."

"I've narrowed it down to five . . . experiences I am open to having with you."

"Five out of fifty?" I say. "My houseplants have better odds of survival, and my houseplants live a dismal life."

"Five items have made the cut," Noah says, "*if* you can agree to my conditions."

I feel my brows knit together. "Conditions?"

"Why don't you sit back down and I'll explain?"

"Thanks for the invitation," I say, sitting back down in my own pink tweed recliner. He is so irritating. "Talk."

"I can agree to the following," Noah says, consulting the page. "The medieval gardens at the Cloisters; the Minetta Brook in the West Village; Seven Thousand Oaks in Chelsea; Breezy Point in Queens; and Poe Cottage in the Bronx."

These are fine selections. I signal my approval with a slight nod. "And your conditions?"

"We're going to alternate," he says. "We visit one site from your list. And then one site of my choosing."

No, no, no. My list was carefully selected. Intentional. Productive. I feel confident that if I agree to this condition, Noah Ross is going to make a joke of the endeavor. And I'll end up wasting my time at some depressing outer-borough diner.

"I'll take it seriously," he says. "I promise."

I swallow. I don't really have a choice. "Then I agree."

"Good. Condition number two," he says, "we don't meet here again."

I glance around. "Here, meaning my apartment? What is your problem with my apartment?"

"It's distracting. Can we just agree to meet at the sites from now on?"

"Fine," I say. "Anything else, Highness?"

"One more," he says. "Once we agree on an idea . . . assuming we *can* agree on an idea, you leave me alone to write it. No babysitting. No Fifty Ways to get Noah to Chapter Two lists, et cetera."

I think about my trial promotion, how so many things will have to go right in order for it to become permanent. How hard it will be to trust this man to make them go right. Part of me would love a good long respite from interacting with him. The other part of me is scared he'll fuck it up.

I take a breath and meet his eyes. "We *will* agree on an idea, because we have to. And once we do, *if* you can assure me I'll have a draft in my hands by May fifteenth, you won't hear so much as a peep out of me."

"What about a squeak? Like the brakes of the M50 bus?"

he teases. It's the world's driest tease, like a Vegas showgirl hairstyle from the eighties.

I give him a closed-mouth smile. "Let's just say it'll be like we've never met."

Noah puts out his hand. "Then I think we have a deal."

Chapter Nine

THE FOLLOWING SATURDAY NIGHT, RYAN AND I HAVE managed to snag two barstools at Grand Army in Boerum Hill right after a sold-out Jenny Lewis concert. We're clinking two flutes of rosé champagne as the waiter sets down a dozen oysters on the half shell. The circular bar is cozy and candlelit, the oysters briny and ice-cold. The restaurant is packed, which I find romantic. There's nothing that makes me feel more a part of my city than being holed up at a bar filled with interesting people having sparkling conversations.

To Ryan, on the other hand, crowds equal "trendy," read: overhyped and overpriced. If he walks into a place and there's a mural painted on exposed brick, with a hashtag inviting guests to Instagram their visit, he's basically out. But he did grow up on his dad's boat on the Eastern Shore, which translates to a weakness for fresh oysters.

He takes his with Tabasco and a squeeze of lemon. I'm a

mignonette and horseradish girl. Most nights, this simple tab-
leau would be enough to make me very happy, but I've been
a mess ever since meeting Noa Callaway, and I don't see my
streak ending anytime soon.

I know I told BD I'd tell Ryan, but the truth is, even if I
weren't bound by this NDA, Noa Callaway's identity—his
maleness—would be a hard topic to broach with Ryan. Either
he wouldn't see why Noah's gender is a betrayal of our readers, or it would become leverage in Ryan's case that this may
not be my dream job, that moving to D.C. holds the answer.
And/or his jealousy radar might go up once I told him about
the Fifty Ways plans.

Which would be absurd, of course. Noah and I can barely
stand each other in person.

Also nagging at me: BD's brunch comment about no
marriage getting everything right, but how important it is to
find the person you can turn to no matter what. I know she
meant it gently, lovingly, but it bothers me to consider that
she thinks something might be wrong with my relationship.

Was it just a simpler time back in my grandmother's day?
No, I know I'm selling BD short by even wondering that. She
was married to my grandfather for fifty years. Like everything
else in her life, she worked hard for it. Ryan and I should be
so lucky to have a marriage as solid all our lives.

"You sure you're okay?" he asks, fixing himself a Kuma-
moto. "You've been acting funny all weekend."

"I'm just stressed," I say.

And lying. Also lying. Not a great look on me.

"Work again?" Ryan sighs, putting down the oyster he was about to shoot. "Listen, Lanie, I've been thinking, and I just don't think this is good for you."

My champagne sticks in my throat and I cough. "What do you mean? What's not good for me?"

"This job—if it's not one thing with your work, it's another. A week ago, you were so stressed about meeting the diva that you canceled your trip to D.C. Then, as soon as you did meet her, you transferred all that stress into panic over some arbitrary deadline."

"This deadline is the opposite of arbitrary. It matters to Peony's bottom line. It matters to Noa's readers. It matters to me—"

"Okay, okay," he says. "Point taken."

I'm working myself up—and sensing Ryan shutting down. He's so focused on the oysters, it's like he's trying to make a pearl. Does he *want* me to fail with Noa Callaway? Does he *want* me to get fired?

"I don't know anyone with a demanding job who *doesn't* stress about work," I say. "*You* stress about work all the time."

"That's different," he says and tips the oyster to his lips.

"*How* is it different?" I raise my voice, drawing eyes from the couple next to us at the bar.

"Lanie," Ryan says in his *calm-down* voice. It usually works, but not today.

"Please, enlighten me."

Ryan sighs. "Because we both know the trajectory of my career. It's different from yours. After we get married, you're moving to D.C." He looks at me, like, *What?* "Sometimes I wonder if the reality of that move has even occurred to you. When are you going to tell Sue that you're relocating?"

He knows I've been putting off that conversation. Sue is a tremendous publisher, but she keeps out of her employees' personal lives. She knows that I'm engaged, but I doubt she has any idea Ryan lives in D.C. My trial promotion has not made me any more eager to tell her.

"Best-case scenario," Ryan says, "you're commuting half the week. What are you going to do, sleep on Meg's couch? And what about after we have kids? You complain all the time about this job. Is that really what you want to model for our family—"

"I do not complain all the time!"

"You might not notice it," he says, "but you do. Maybe this isn't your dream job anymore. In D.C., you could have—"

"Don't say it—"

"A fresh start—"

"I will walk if you bring up that job at the Library of the Congress again." I cringe, picturing tasteful archives, tidy shelves, and drawers stretching into organized infinity.

"You told me once you'd love to learn to read Braille!" Ryan says. "And Deborah Ayers is a very connected woman. If you'd been at the party last weekend, you would've met her. All I did was mention that you'll be transitioning to D.C. soon, and she said she'd be more than happy to sit down and discuss your interests."

Before I can groan, Ryan fills my hands with his. They're warm and familiar. I squeeze them, wanting to fold myself

inside him. But something holds me back. It's this feeling that
if I fold myself inside Ryan, I might get lost. Irretrievably.
I've never felt that way before, and it startles me.

"You know what I think you need?" he asks.

"What?"

"A really top-notch couples' massage. I'll book it for us.
Next Friday night, when you come to D.C. It'll knock us both
out, and we'll wake up fresh for the chili cook-off at my parents' country club Saturday morning."

Ryan used to joke with me about his parents' many social
functions, but sometime in the last year he changed. Instead
of laughing with me about the country club's penchant for
taxidermy, he gifted me the exact same sweater I spotted on
two of his friends' girlfriends at the last event.

"I've never been good at getting massages," I say.

"I've never met anyone who's bad at getting massages.
You've never said no to a Ryan-rubdown." He jazz-hands at
me, trying to lighten the mood.

"That's different." I look at him pointedly. "My mind just
whirls. And I always feel like the masseuse can tell that I'm
not being Zen enough."

"This is the best massage inside the Beltway. Everyone
loves it. I promise, you will, too." He runs his fingers through
my hair. It's tangled from walking in the wind after the concert.

"Yeah, okay," I say.

"You don't sound convinced."

"It's just . . . it's a massage. Not some magic spell that's
going to fix our problems."

"*Our* problems?" He shoots me an uneasy look. "I thought we were trying to address *your* stress."

"Ryan," I say, turning toward him.

"I mean, yeah, I noticed you've been distant all week. I guess I should have said something sooner," he says, speaking quickly. "But work's been crazy. Maybe I've been distracted. It happens. We just need to reconnect." He signals to the bartender for another round.

It used to be easy for us to connect. Now, even the couple of days a week when Ryan and I are together, it feels like we're pretty far apart.

I know he's trying to help, and that he can't really do that without knowing the specifics of my problem. A romantic reconnection is probably what we need. Then I could open up to him about Noah.

I turn to him, our knees overlapping under the bar. I touch my forehead to his, aware of how uncomplicatedly romantic we probably look to the table of thirtysomething ladies behind us. I'm often aware of that kind of thing with Ryan, probably because women check him out all the time.

"I've got it," I say. "What about that motorcycle ride through the Appalachians we've always wanted to take?"

It's a trip that doesn't need advance planning, no airplane tickets or hard-to-get hotel reservations. We could go on a whim as soon as Noah gets an idea and retreats into his writing cave. A long springtime weekend on the bike with Ryan, stopping at B and Bs along the way, would be the perfect thing to distract me from wondering what's happening with Noah's word count.

"Or we could rent a camper van?" Ryan says, "Sleep under the stars. It'd be good practice for future family vacations."

"A motorcycle would be amazing," I push. "And it's so us."

He squints. "What do you mean, 'so us'?"

"It's how we met? On your bike? Last summer we went for a joyride every weekend we were in D.C.?" I feel like knocking on his skull to see if he's actually in there.

"You know, just because we met on a motorcycle and rode it a lot last summer doesn't mean we're bound to travel that way exclusively for the rest of our lives."

"I didn't say we're bound to anything—"

"What about our luggage? What if it rains? What if I want to have a few glasses of wine with dinner? Honestly, Lanie, it sounds like more of a headache than it's worth."

"Backpacks instead of roller bags. A couple of those raincoats that fold into little pouches," I say, taking out his catalog of complaints one by one. "And if you want to drink, then I can drive." I nuzzle into his neck. "Think you're man enough to hold on?"

"Since when do you drive a motorcycle?" he asks. "You let your regular driver's license expire when you moved to New York."

"I could learn," I say. "I can get my license in time for a trip. That way you don't have to do all the driving. I could practice on your bike. You could teach me—"

"Actually," Ryan says and clears his throat. "I don't think that's going to happen."

"Why not?"

There's a long pause, where I hear the background noise of the restaurant like the roar of a Roman coliseum.

"I was going to tell you," Ryan finally says. He puts a hand on my thigh in a way that makes me nervous. "I sold my bike, Lanie."

"You *what*?" I gasp. "But you loved that bike . . . *I* loved that bike. *We* loved that bike. Why would you ever sell it?"

"Baby," he says, rubbing my leg. "This friend of a friend offered me twice what the bike is worth. I was thinking about you, and how, when you move in with me, we'll need that garage space for a second car. Maybe a Volvo. Plus, once we have kids, our priorities are going to change. It won't be long before I'm running for office, and a motorcycle is just a liability. I don't want to be 'that biker dude' in the attack ads."

Attack ads? Priorities? I reach for my champagne and guzzle it.

"That bike was the beginning of our story."

"Everything's a story with you," he says.

What about the feeling of freedom each time we hopped on the bike together? What about the wind on our skin? Or the front-row seat to the sights and smells of a city, how everything changes with the seasons? What about those few wonderful weeks each spring when the cherry blossoms bloom?

What about the way the motorcycle drove his mother crazy?

Oh my god.

I cross my arms over my chest. "Did your mother make you do it?"

"Don't start with my mother again." Ryan groans.

"I'm just shocked. I wish you would have talked to me before you sold it."

"Hey," he says, more warmly. "If it's that important to you to have one last hurrah on a motorcycle before we get married, let's rent one and do the Appalachians."

It's his *I-surrender* voice, the hoisting of the little white flag. And this is when I'm supposed to laugh and say *thanks, baby*, and then we'd let the conversation drift to something pleasant. We could start talking about the trip, about making it real. About the route we'd want to take and where we'd stop along the way. This is when I'd pretend Ryan didn't just say some truly alarming things about his expectations of our life.

We've become masters at changing the subject, lightening the mood. Pretending certain realities don't loom in our near future.

But tonight, I don't do the thing we always do. I don't lean in for a kiss or shrug it off. I look him in the eye and say:

"I'm tired of this idea that everything has to change—that *we* have to change—after we get married. It's a wedding, not an apocalypse. Isn't the point to celebrate what we already have?"

"Okay . . . how much have you had to drink?" he says, bumping my shoulder with his. I know he means to be playful, but it feels patronizing.

I rise from the barstool, grab my purse. "I need some air," I say.

Ryan glances around, always aware of appearances. Even

when he doesn't know a single person in this restaurant or this neighborhood. As if everyone is already deciding whether to vote for him. It's maddening.

"Sure," he says when he realizes I'm serious. He throws down a credit card and motions the bartender. "Let's get you some air."

I march outside alone before the bartender runs his card. I have half a mind to hail a cab and head back to my apartment by myself. The thing that stops me scares me.

If I left now, made Ryan meet me back home, I might cool off a little by the time he caught up with me. And we might make up without having the fight we really need to have.

We're overdue.

So I wait on the curb, and I think. About why I love him—so many reasons. Ninety-nine of them. But since learning the truth about Noa Callaway, there's been a voice in my head asking if they're the right reasons. I think about the life each of us wants—so different from the other.

Before I've figured out how to square all this, Ryan comes outside. He's as handsome as ever in his navy bomber jacket and jeans. His eyes twinkle, as if to say, *You're not still mad, are you?*

"Feeling better?" he says, and opens his arms to me.

I step into his embrace, feel his arms close comfortingly around me. For a long time, we say nothing. Tears sting my eyes as I pull back to look at him.

"Why do you love me, Ryan?"

He drops his arms, rubs his face. "Lanie, what are you doing?"

"I'm being honest. It's an honest question."

He shakes his head and turns away, facing the street and the traffic, the cabs stopping and spilling out happily chattering young people, looking for the heart of Saturday night.

"I don't understand what happened to us," Ryan says, not looking at me. "We used to be so happy. The night we got engaged I was ecstatic. Kissing you on that jumbotron, my ring on your finger, I felt so proud that everyone could see we were the perfect couple. Now . . . recently, you act like you're being held at gunpoint just to pick a date for our wedding—"

"I don't think I want to be a perfect couple," I say.

He laughs like this is crazy. "What?"

I take his hands. "I just want to be me. I want you to be you. Complete with all our eccentricities. I want us to write poetry to each other, even if it's bad."

"I don't think I follow. . . ."

I close my eyes. "I wasn't happy that night we got engaged."

"What?" This is a record-scratch moment. Ryan's tone draws eyes from strangers on the street.

"I've been happy in our relationship. I've been mostly very happy. But I wasn't happy the night you proposed."

He squints at me. "You wept! You have that picture on your wall!"

"I didn't weep out of joy," I say.

Ryan thinks. "Okay, yes, I remember you started freaking out about your mom—"

"That was part of it."

"And the other part?" he asks.

"I'm a Dodgers fan."

"Come again?" Ryan asks.

"I'm a Dodgers fan. You know that."

"I know you have an old Dodgers T-shirt. I know you love Vin Scully. But what was I supposed to do, fly you out to a Dodgers game and propose there? It makes no sense to be a fan of a team in a city you've never lived in! You don't even like Los Angeles!"

"I'm a Dodgers fan because of Sandy Koufax," I say. "I've told you that. My mom was four years old the year he sat out game one of the World Series on Yom Kippur. BD told you the story of taking the train across the country with my grandfather to watch Koufax pitch his no-hitter against the Yankees. He's a hero in my family, like he's a hero for most Jewish families in America. You're supposed to remember things like this about the person you want to marry. But that's not even the point."

"What *is* the point?" Ryan asks.

"The fact that I'm a Dodgers fan has almost nothing to do with our relationship. But the Washington Nationals have even *less* to do with our relationship. They're your team, and that's great. I had fun at the game with you. But there's nothing special about them or that stadium to *us*. You could have proposed to me at the bodega where we buy coffee, and it would have meant more. I wasn't happy, Ryan. I was in shock when you proposed. Or should I say, when the *jumbotron* proposed. *It* asked me to marry you. You never even said the words." I sigh. "I could have been anyone in the crowd."

"You're not anyone," he says, his voice cracking. "You're Elaine Bloom and I love you. Uniquely."

"I know that you love me. And I love you. But I don't think we love what our future looks like together. You want me to be all the things you want in a wife. But I'm not a Nationals fan just because I wore your hat that night. I won't be a WASP, even if I convert. I'll never stop being an editor, even if I change jobs. I don't want five kids just because you do. And I hate wedding planning without my mother, not because I need her to pick out my dress, or even to see me wear it that day. I hate it because I know that if I go through with it, I might be getting her last words to me wrong."

"*If you go through with it*," Ryan says, putting his hands on his head. He starts pacing. "Oh my god. You're breaking up with me."

"Yeah," I say softly. Though I didn't know it until now. "Yeah."

I close my eyes. This hurts. I don't want to break up with Ryan. I really don't want to break up with Ryan. But I have to. I have to do it now, even as the rest of my life is already imploding. Because while Ryan is still all of the ninety-nine things I thought I wanted, it turns out that isn't enough.

And though he'd never admit to having a list of his own, I'm not the woman he wants to spend his life with, either. More important, I don't want to become her.

"You deserve—" I start to say.

"Don't tell me what I deserve," he snaps. "I know what I deserve. I also know you're going to regret this. Because you're never going to find someone who will take care of you the way I can take care of you, who will give you the life I would have. And by the time you realize that, it's going to be too late."

"I realize it already, Ryan. It's already too late."

He stares at me as if we've never met before, which is what it feels like to break up with the person you thought you'd love forever.

"Well," he says. "I guess this is goodbye."

He turns and starts down the block. Steam from a subway grate rises up and obscures him from me even further.

I did this, and I can't believe it's happening. I can't believe how fast Ryan is walking away. For much of my life, I've wanted to be a Noa Callaway heroine; I've wanted to fall in love with a Noa Callaway hero. I thought I had found him in Ryan. And now, the only thing I know for sure is I was wrong.

I think of my engagement ring, finally resized and ready for me to pick up at the jewelers. What do I do with it now?

"Wait," I call out, chasing after him. "What about—"

He waves me off, still walking away. "You'll figure it out, Lanie," he calls over his shoulder. "Or you won't. It's not my problem anymore." He turns and gives me a crushing look. "That's the beauty of breaking up. One less problem."

Chapter Ten

THE DIAMOND RING SITS IN ITS OPEN CLAMSHELL BOX in the center of the outdoor table, looking radioactive.

Late last night, when it became clear that my breakup with Ryan was not an oyster-induced hallucination, I'd texted Meg and Rufus:

Maison Pickle. 11 a.m. Emergency Brunch.

The term is a holdover from Meg's and my days as assistants. It basically means there will be an excess of cocktails, complaints, and, in this case, crying. The host of Emergency Brunch need give no advance explanation, but these days, now that Meg has kids, and all of our lives have more responsibilities than they did seven years ago, it is only invoked in dire situations.

I wait for them under a heat lamp on the patio at Maison Pickle on the Upper West Side, a box of tissues in my lap. It's unseasonably warm, the sky blue and flecked with fluffy clouds, but all I see is gray.

It feels like, if I had been even halfway paying attention, I might have seen this coming from a mile away. That's the most embarrassing part. An essential piece of me knew something wasn't right with Ryan for a while now, and I spent a long time trying to shut that piece up.

I'm dreading having to say the word *breakup* aloud to Meg and Rufus, to make the nightmare real. When I see them come up from the train at Eighty-Sixth Street, this dread manifests like a brick over my chest.

As it turns out, I don't have to say anything. My friends take one look at my face—puffy; my hair—greasy; and my freshly resized engagement ring—very much not on my finger— and they know.

"Fuuuuuuuuck, Lanie," Rufus says, planting a kiss on my head as he sinks into the chair next to me.

"We need a bottle of prosecco," Meg calls to the nearest waiter. "And three shots of tequila."

"Damn, mama," Rufus says to her. "Are we going clubbing after this? Because I'll need to change."

"It's called the Kate Moss," Meg says. "You take the shot and sip the bubbles, and it helps, okay?"

"I never argue with Kate Moss," Rufus says, obliging. He takes off his sunglasses and sets them on the table next to his keys, his phone, his sunscreen, and his thirty-dollar lip balm. Meg and I bought him a man bag last Christmas in an attempt to limit the amount of real estate he always takes up on restaurant tables, but he's set in his ways.

"So, what happened?" Meg silences her phone. She does this only for very significant conversations. It makes me feel a grateful swell of love for her.

"We were out last night," I say, my stomach knotting at the memory. "We were having a good time. Like we always do. But then, I don't know, suddenly it became clear that whenever we talk about getting married, it's like the word has two different meanings. One for Ryan, one for me. And when I pushed on that a little, the whole thing just fell apart." I snatch a tissue and blow my nose.

Meg frowns at me, reaching across the table to squeeze my hand. "First of all, weddings are the devil. Planning one is enough to drive the happiest couple bananas. Tommy and I barely made it down the aisle after a feud over our table runners."

"The fuck is a table runner?" Rufus says.

"Don't ask," Meg replies. "I'm still mad we went with maroon. The point is, it's a lot."

"I guess," I say, "but our disconnect was less about the wedding, and more about the marriage. We didn't want the same life. We tried to ignore that for a long time. Stupidly long. Because . . . because . . ."

"Because he was Ninety-Nine Things?" Meg offers.

I drop my head on the table. Over the years, my friends have ribbed me about my list. But lovingly, acceptingly. If Meg and Rufus had any idea what an imposter Noa Callaway is, they'd pity me for real.

"I'm such a fool," I moan.

"Lanie," Rufus says, "plenty of people stay in worse relationships for way more pathetic reasons."

"True," Meg says. "Do you remember Mary, my assistant two assistants ago? And those really long lunch breaks she used to take?"

"She was always very sweaty in the afternoons," Rufus says.

"Well, I found out it was because her boyfriend refused to let her dog out, so she had to run home to Tribeca. Every. Single. Day. *He worked from home!* But she didn't want to leave him because his apartment was rent-controlled."

"Well, my cousin," Rufus says, leaning in and lowering his voice like he always does when he talks about his family, even though they all live on the West Coast, "is dating this dude who makes her call him 'the Terminator' during sex. And she stays because he put her on his gym membership!"

"That's kind of hot?" Meg says, as if trying to imagine it.

"You have a problem," Rufus says to her.

"It has a name," Meg says, closing her eyes. "Dry Spell."

"Meg, you and Tommy *are* allowed to have sex," I say. "Even though you're married."

She groans and leans back in her chair. "Married sex requires so much imagination, it's exhausting."

"Like . . . you start doing it in imaginative places?" I ask. "Fire escape, that kind of thing?"

"No, like I imagine Tommy is my friend's ex-fiancé, and he's calling me the Terminator."

Despite myself, I laugh, and Meg and Rufus cheer at the sound of it.

"Our point is," Rufus says, "you and Ryan are both boneable, successful, decent people. Stone-cold catches. It makes sense that you tried to make it work."

I run my finger over the ring in the box on the table. When the jeweler called this morning to schedule the pickup, I'd laughed so manically into the phone that I definitely freaked him out. I'd swung by the shop on my way to brunch, a now-or-never feeling in my heart. The jeweler had asked me to try it on before I left, but I knew if I did that, I would have started weeping. Which I didn't want to do, not until I was safely and anonymously walking through Central Park.

I know the ring probably fits perfectly. It's beautiful and tragic. I can't bring myself to take it out of the box.

"We would have been really unhappy," I say to Meg and Rufus. It helps to say it aloud.

"Eh, happiness is overrated," Meg says. "The first few years of parenting is like watching the man you used to want to fuck twenty-four/seven be slow-motion Frankensteined into a pastiche of every quality you loathe—"

"Meg," Rufus says, giving her a look. "We are here to instill hope, remember? That there's something better out there?"

"I'm just doing my due diligence," Meg says. "In case the two of them get back together—"

"We won't get back together," I say.

"You sure?" Rufus says.

"Real sure?" Meg asks.

"I'm sure." I stare at them. "What?"

Rufus lets out a low whistle and makes eyes at Meg. "Well, then, we can move into the honesty portion of the brunch."

"What the hell have you been doing until now?" I demand.

Just then, our server appears with an ice bucket of prosecco and a tray of shots. She's peppy and ponytailed, and before she even sets the drinks down, all of us reach for the tequila and take it in a gulp. I gag a little, and also wish I had another.

"Ohmigod, *who* just got engaged?" the server asks, bright as the glaring sun. She glances around at the three of us, trying to make sense of the dynamic. "That ring is *gorgeous*. I want one just like it someday!"

"Take it," I growl at her.

She flinches, glances at Rufus as she fiddles with the foil on the prosecco. "Is she okay?"

"Leave us," Rufus whispers and eases the bottle out of the server's hand.

"Wait, before you go," Meg says, making a stop sign with her hand. "We'll take a large platter of all your pickles, deviled eggs, an order of fried chicken and French toast, and one deluxe French dip."

"Are you pregnant again?" Rufus asks, sizing up Meg.

"Rufus, I just ordered enough alcohol to pickle all three of us. But, this *was* my go-to brunch when I was pregnant, and it is perfection, thank you very much."

As soon as the server walks away, I stare down both my friends. "Start talking. And not about pickles. You hated Ryan? All this time?"

"No, no, we liked him," Rufus says, his tone tactful. "He

was a fabulous boyfriend. Capital F, capital B. Meg and I both appreciated the eye candy, especially that weekend at the Jersey Shore."

"Remember his red bathing suit?" Meg makes a sizzling sound. She's already flushed from the tequila.

"But," Rufus says, "we're . . . glad you're not going to marry him."

"Was it just me," Meg says, "or was he *always* looking for reasons you should quit your job?"

I nod. I sigh. "He started working that angle on our second date."

"And the religion thing?" Rufus says, untwining the wire around the prosecco cork. "You would really have deprived us of your legendary Passover seders?"

"You just like to make fun of my gefilte fish," I say.

"That is not fish. It's just not. Also? Ryan called me Randall every time I saw him," Rufus says. "For three years."

"He did not!" I gasp. "That is deeply un-presidential."

"Yeah, I'm not voting for him," Rufus says, and pops the cork on the bottle. "Opa!"

"So, what are we drinking to?" I ask as he fills my flute.

"To you *not* moving to D.C.," Rufus says.

"To you never being fucking FLOTUS!" Meg says.

"I will drink to that," I say and raise my glass. "No offense, Michelle."

"No offense, Michelle," they echo and drink, too.

We sip our Kate Mosses and watch the city waking up around us, the hot dog vendor setting up on the street corner, the stroller parades of the Upper West Side, the bike messengers banging on windows of careless Uber drivers. We're quiet for a while, and it's nice. I feel scaffolded by my friends.

Then the sun peeks out from behind a cloud, making the 1.5-carat diamond glint.

"What am I going to do about this ring?" I say, wanting to cry again.

"Does he want it back?" Rufus asks.

"Beats me, he won't answer my calls or texts."

"Ryan is so the kind of guy who will not take back the ring," Meg says. "He'll see it as some magnanimous gesture. Very gauche for a politician to take back a ring."

I nod. "You're right. It's annoying."

"Pawn it?" Rufus says. "Like, classy-pawn. I know a guy."

"Of course you do," Meg says.

I shake my head. "That feels wrong. But so does letting it fester in my jewelry box at home."

"I hate to see platinum fester," Meg says.

"You know what I mean. It feels like this . . . sparkling emblem of my three-year-long self-delusion, of my embarrassing inability to navigate the best course for my life."

Rufus giggles. "You get so verbose when you are tipsy." He tops off my prosecco glass. "Quick, what's a four-syllable word for horny?"

We all sit silently with that for a moment.

"I'm stumped," I say.

"Drink more," Rufus urges.

"Lanie," Meg says, "you're a *good* navigator. I mean, look

at you. You have this baller job, editing one of the most famous writers in the world."

"Who also happens to be your literary idol," Rufus adds,
while I nod and muster my cheeriest fake smile.

"You have us, two of the dopest friends in all of New
York," Meg continues, "and you have this little thing called
resilience. Don't laugh, Rufus. I'm being sincere. I've seen it
in you ever since you showed up at Peony at age baby-twenty-
two. It means you're not going to feel this way for long. It
means you'll bounce back stronger than ever. It means that,
ultimately, you'll get what you want. I can look at you and
know you already know that. Tell me you know it?"

I shrug. "I guess. Maybe."

"Someday soon, this ring is just going to be a ring, a piece
of jewelry from a different era of your life. No more, no
less."

It's hard to imagine a time when seeing this ring won't
make me want to hibernate in a cave of regret, but I might as
well make it a goal.

As two servers appear to set down our bounty of brunch,
I close the clamshell and put the ring into my purse, making
room for better things, like thick-sliced, perfectly golden
French toast topped with fried chicken.

"Have you told BD?" Rufus asks, tucking into the French
dip.

Rufus and BD are g-chat friends; they first clicked years
ago over their shared obsession with Apple events. It's un-
fathomable to me how many rounds they can go debating

whether the new generation of iPhone is worth the price increase.

"Not yet," I say. "I want to get my head on straight about it first."

"My nainai always loved it when I broke up with someone," Meg says, a pickle in one hand, prosecco in the other. This is her natural state. "She called it 'clearing the chaff.'"

"Okay, your nainai sounds terrifying," Rufus says, "and BD is not going to say that to Lanie." He looks at me. "But she is probably going to want you to get back into the saddle soon."

I drown the thought of dating in more prosecco. "I don't see how I can do that. Now that my Ninety-Nine Things list failed me, I have no idea where to start with someone new."

Meg snorts. Rufus puts a hand over his mouth.

"What? What are you laughing at?" I say.

"It's called chemistry," Rufus says. "You just get on board with it. It's really not that hard."

"Says the man who has been patiently waiting for Brent from Pilates World to break up with his partner for . . . how many years now?" I ask.

"Because we have chemistry!" Rufus says.

Meg puts her hand over mine. "Listen, Lanie, I'm as type A as the next person at this table, but I think the message is to stop being type A about love. It'll come, and when it does, you'll know."

"Is that what happened with you and Tommy?" I ask. "You really just *knew*?"

"Sure! And look at us now! We're so close, we're like brother and sister." She cackles. "I'm ordering more Kate Mosses and nobody better stop me."

Rufus and I nod, because no complaints here.

Minutes later, just as I'm about to shoot that inadvisable second shot of tequila, something in my periphery makes me stop. I tilt my head and feel my stomach rising to my throat, because I'm almost certain Noah Ross is walking south on Broadway. Right toward Maison Pickle.

He's alone, in dark sunglasses, jeans, and a pea coat. His hair is damp and he looks casual without looking sloppy. He's holding some sort of box in one hand and is certainly coming this way. A bolt of something shoots through me. Is it that lightning thing again? No, this is panic. I have approximately ninety seconds to figure out how to disappear.

A mental inventory takes place: my ratty college sweatshirt, bad hair, swollen eyes. Is it possible I look *so* terrible that he won't recognize me? To be safe, I pull up the hood of my sweatshirt and grab Rufus's sunglasses from his pile, making myself incognito.

My friends' heads snap toward me, quizzical looks on their tipsy faces.

"Where'd you get these? They're amazing," I say, overdoing my enthusiasm.

"Paul Smith," Rufus says slowly. "Remember, you were there?"

"Yes!" I lie, distracted by the advancing figure of Noah Ross. He's walking much too quickly for a Sunday morning. "That was such a fun day. So fun."

"Mmm-hmmm," Rufus says suspiciously. He tries to follow my gaze from behind his shades. "Who are you hiding from?"

"No one!" I slink down in the patio chair until my nose is level with my empty prosecco glass. "I'm just . . . tired. I was up all night. You know, crying." This is true, and yet I do a great job of making it sound like such a lie that now Meg is onto me, too. She spins around in her chair. She turns to look—I swear—right into Noah Ross's eyes.

But just when I'm sure I'm busted, Noah swivels to the right. He opens a door and disappears inside a storefront two doors down. I let out a gigantic sigh.

Rufus snaps his fingers at me. "Begin to make sense," he says. "Now."

I take off Rufus's shades and lower my hood.

"I thought I saw someone I didn't want to see," I say. "No big deal."

"Who?" Meg says, still peering around.

"Uh, her." I point randomly at the nearest woman in view. "I thought she was my old neighbor who got evicted for selling CBD out of her apartment last year."

"That seventy-year-old woman?" Rufus points at an elderly lady crossing the street with a wheeled grocery cart.

"She kept harassing me to put in a good word for her about the security deposit, and . . . you know what? It's boring, and it wasn't even her—"

"You're being sketchy," Meg says.

"Hey, I wasn't the one running a drug ring out of my apartment. Oh shit!" I gasp, because the door Noah disappeared into has now swung open.

And he's walking out.

And coming this way.

And I have wasted the past two minutes lying to my friends, instead of making a plan for his inevitable return to the street.

I grab my phone and jump up from the table. "Rufus, you were right. I really should call BD. Be right back! Don't anyone take my tequila!"

"What is up with her?" I hear Meg say as I dash around the corner of the block. I pull my hood up again and sit on someone's stoop with my phone to my ear, pretending to be on a call. Furtively I watch as Noah comes to stand on the corner of Eighty-Fourth and Broadway. It's definitely him. Same pea coat. Same pomposity.

Well, he's ruined the rest of my life. He might as well ruin Emergency Brunch.

He's still holding that box, which I can now see is some sort of animal kennel. He opens the front of the crate and carefully pulls out . . . a fat black-and-white-spotted rabbit.

He holds the creature up close to his face, both of them facing a redbrick apartment building on the south side of the street. He points at a window, as if he's explaining something important about Upper West Side real estate to the bunny. I watch the rabbit nuzzle Noah's cheek. I am paralyzed with a feeling of incredulity.

Then Noah carefully puts the bunny back inside the crate, closes it up, and turns back the way he came, heading north on Broadway.

Watching him go, I exhale about a month's worth of oxygen. I slump against the stoop and shake my head. What is he doing away from his pristine Fifth Avenue orbit? Why is he spending his Sunday with a rabbit on the Upper West Side? More important, why isn't he writing, or at least attempting to?

And why did the sight of him alarm me so much that I had to literally run away?

Okay, that one is obvious: Because I can't let Meg and Rufus know about Noah. Because of my NDA. And also, if I'm honest, I would still like at least the façade of a professional relationship. I don't know if Noah Ross could look at twelve-hours-post-breakup Lanie and trust me as his editor.

I wish I didn't feel the need to prove myself to him.

Now, I'm working myself up *again* over Noah Ross, and I don't want to. I want to go back to brunch and get drunk with my friends. I round the corner, return to my seat.

"Sorry about that!" I chirp and make my tequila disappear.

"So, what wisdom did BD impart?" Rufus asks, his tone leading.

"Oh, she . . . wasn't home. Got her voicemail."

"It was that guy with the bunny," Meg announces suddenly.

"What? No. What?" I laugh a very weird laugh.

"I recognized him," Meg says. "Took me a minute, but he's that guy from the launch. Man of the Year. You were talking to him at the end of the night."

"Oh yeah," I say, "I remember that guy. He was here?" I look around me. "I didn't see him—"

"Lanie, you're so bad at lying!" Rufus says. "Dig yourself out! Not deeper into the hole!"

"You sparked with that guy," Meg says, eyes narrowed, finger pointing at me.

"What is this, an Anna Kendrick movie? I did not spark with anyone."

The thought makes my fists clench, because Noah and I have done exactly the opposite of spark. But then, I see the commitment in Meg's eyes. I realize that it's going to be much easier to lean into her version of events than it would be to leave open any other possibility why seeing Noah Ross has got me so freaked out.

"A little," I say, holding my proverbial nose.

"Ohhhh," Rufus says, pursing his lips and giving me a knowing nod. "And you think you look like hell today, so you don't want this mystery Man of the Year to see you?"

"Yeah?" I try to go with all of this. At least, the last bit is partly true.

"You know, you actually look really good when you've been crying," Rufus says.

"Really?" I bump his shoulder. "You've failed to mention that on several dozen previous occasions."

"Yeah, but I was always giving you the silent compliment," he says. "It's your eyes. They get super blue."

"Aw, thanks, Ruf." His words remind me of my mother. Her eyes used to do the same thing.

"So . . . go get his number," Rufus singsongs, ushering me out of the chair.

I wave him off. Noah is still just a block away. Too close. "I will do nothing of the kind!"

"At least let us google-stalk him, then?" Meg says, picking up her phone.

"Cease and desist, I beg you both," I say. "I haven't been single a full day yet. Can I get a grace period before I'm thrust back into the meat market?"

"Fine," Meg says, "but only if Ruf and I get to take you out for this inaugural thrusting." She's scrolling through her calendar on her phone. "Okay, Tommy has poker night next weekend, but the following Friday is Mama's Night Out. Oh good, I'm getting my eyebrows threaded that day. Let's not waste it."

"I already know the perfect place, and which overalls I'm going to wear," Rufus says.

They both turn expectantly to me. I'm glad the conversation has veered away from Noah Ross. And also that I have lucked into these generous, funny, nosy, well-accessorized, and occasionally drunk friends.

Who knows, maybe two weeks from now, the thought of going out on the town as a single woman will feel less unthinkable.

I raise my glass, and we all clink. "Kate Mosses, here we come."

Chapter Eleven

ON FRIDAY AFTERNOON, I'VE GOT EIGHTEEN BROWSER windows open on my desktop. I am crafting a compendium for how to visit the Cloisters museum without a hitch. I need Noah to be inspired by the medieval gardens and Netherlandish triptychs, not distracted by the hunt for a bathroom, or annoyed by a closed snack bar at the moment he wants a coffee.

I am finally reaching the state of preparedness where I feel nothing can go wrong. And that's when fate slaps me in the face, in the form of a text from Ryan.

Let me state for the record that I have messaged my ex-fiancé no less than ten times this week. Low-key checking-in texts. *Here-if-you-want-to-talk* texts. *Hope-you're-having-a-good-week-at-work* texts. I'm not trying to harass Ryan, or get back together. But it's weird that we were intimate for three years—and planning to spend the next threescore staying that way—and suddenly, it's like we cut a cord, and we're strangers. It seems to me there should be some sort of wind-down period, a lame-duck session of the relationship. A couple of texts, nothing crazy. But Ryan seems not to share my vision.

Until today, when he actually writes back. Three times in a row.

> Mom was spring-cleaning my place and found some of your things. Mostly clothes, but that robe with all the colors is there. And some award of your mom's. She's hitting Goodwill tomorrow. Wanted to give you a heads-up, in case you want any of it.

And then:

> I'm in Boston for work, or else I'd try to hold her off longer. Sorry.

And then:

> Also, the ring is yours. I gave it to you. Please stop asking if I want it back.

I read and reread the first text: In case I *want* any of it? BD's Missoni robe? My mother's framed and mounted Kenneth Rothman Career Accomplishment Award, basically the Oscar for epidemiologists? I'd brought it down to show Ryan's father once, after we'd had what I thought was a breakthrough conversation about my family. By the time I showed it to Mr. Bosch at a Sunday lunch a couple weekends later, he barely remembered our discussion. I should never have left the plaque at Ryan's.

This means I have to go to D.C. Tonight.

And cancel on Noah Ross tomorrow.

I dial Terry, feeling very put upon. "Terry, this is Lanie Bloom."

"I have caller ID."

"Can I talk to Noah?"

"Noa doesn't do the phone. You know that. Be glad you got me."

"Listen, something's come up, and I need to reschedule our meeting tomorrow. Do you have access to his calendar?"

"I'll pass along the message, and see if Noa would like to reschedule."

"It's not an *if*, Terry—"

"You'll hear from me if Noa does."

I manage to wait until Terry hangs up to start cursing the phone.

⚬

An hour later, I've crammed my work for the weekend into three canvas totes. I've resurrected the old gym bag under my desk—leftover from an expensive lie I once told myself that I should join the spin studio across the street—and am amazed to find that spin-curious Lanie packed the bag with a change of clothes, clean underwear, deodorant, and a toothbrush. My Amtrak tickets and hotel are booked and now I can spend my remaining minutes in the office writing an email to Noah.

Terry has not called me back.

In my first draft of the email, I went on too long and was overly repentant. Then I deleted everything and went the never-apologize-never-explain route. People need to reschedule. It happens. Our agreement is not off because of one conflict. I keep telling myself this, but I'd feel better if Terry called. The email is still sitting in my drafts.

"Alors," Aude says, appearing in my doorway in herringbone pants so high-waisted I think all her ribs are inside. "You should leave if you don't want to miss your train."

"You're right," I say, shutting down my computer. "Merci."

"De rien." She pauses. "How will you get into Ryan's apartment?"

I wave my keychain, which still holds a key to Ryan's brownstone. I'll leave it behind for him when this is done.

"Lanie," Aude says, "when you get there, allot yourself a very short time inside Ryan's home. In and out—two minutes tops. I think it would be best."

"What do you think I'm going to do? Climb inside his hamper to breathe in his laundry?"

Aude looks down. "I once slashed an ex's mattress when I went to pick up my knife block after we broke up."

"See, that wasn't even in my head before, but now . . ."

"In and out," Aude coaches.

"In and out," I say.

She kisses my cheeks and hands me the printout of my

tickets. I'm rounding the corner to the elevator when I almost collide with Meg.

"Hot soup!" she shouts in warning.

"And hello to you, too," I say.

"Oh good, it's you. I was just coming up to bring you this." She holds out a thermos, and when she cracks the lid, I recognize the aroma as her mother's homemade egg drop wonton soup. My weakness. "I meant to bring it to you for lunch, but shit got crazy on the second floor. Are you leaving early?"

"Ryan's mom is going to 'donate' a bunch of my stuff if I don't go get it. Tonight." I give Meg a side-eye that bespeaks my annoyance. "So, you know, I'm taking a fun, spur-of-the-moment trip to D.C."

"Girl," Meg says, her tone empathetic. "Want company? Wait, sorry, I forgot two small humans rely on me to meet their every need. You know I'll be there in spirit. And . . . I wouldn't spend too long on the inside if I were you."

"Did you slash an ex-boyfriend's mattress, too?" I ask.

"There may have been some defecation left in the saddle of a certain NordicTrack."

"Meg, no!"

"Not proud of it," Meg says with a shudder.

"Well, I think we have a winner." I laugh. "I've got to run. Thanks for the soup."

"It's a classic combination," Meg says, waving as I step into the elevator. "Amtrak and egg drop."

"Like tacos and Tuesdays."

❦

On track twelve at Penn Station, I climb the stairs toward my regular spot on the south end of the quiet car. I've taken this train so many times to visit Ryan. I know that at this hour on a Friday, it's always crowded, but I spot a lucky open window seat at one of the four-top tables. There's a jacket, a bottle of water, and a book about the Vietnam War on the rear-facing seat, but the forward-facing side looks open, so I slide in with my things.

As the train pulls away, I settle in, opening my thermos and taking out my tablet. It's loaded with five novel submissions I'm supposed to read by Monday. Usually, I can tell within five pages whether I need to read more, and usually the answer is no. But I already know there's one in here that's promising. A romantic satire by a debut author whose first page had made Aude laugh out loud when she started reading it this morning.

I reread the first page three times before acknowledging that I have no idea what I've just read. I'm more upset than I want to acknowledge about having to clear my things out of Ryan's place. It's like, I know how we got here, but also—*How the hell did we get here?*

I give up on work for now. At least the soup is good.

From the bottom of my bag, I take out my old paperback copy of *Ninety-Nine Things*. I flip to the back of the book. How smug I'd felt three years ago, checking Ryan against my list. Look where it got me. Tears sting my eyes, and when I wipe them away, more come.

"It's meant to be a comedy," a male voice says over my shoulder.

I look up, then flinch at the sight of the very last person I want to see right now.

Noah Ross wears a black sweater and a Mets cap tugged low. He's drinking coffee from a Styrofoam cup. There's a few days' worth of dark stubble on his face, which makes him look rugged yet refined, like if you went camping, he'd cook a gourmet dinner on the fire.

I snap the book closed, put it down like it's a thousand degrees. It embarrasses me to be caught vulnerable by him, and I'm trying to think of a way to gracefully steer this conversation toward a *how-funny-to-have-run-into-you-and-goodbye!*—when he sits down across from me.

I point at the jacket, the water bottle, the book. "I think someone's sitting there."

"*I'm* sitting there, Lanie. It's my stuff. I just went to get some coffee." He waves the steaming cup.

Of course he's sitting here. Because this day was designed to destroy me. I surrender, Day. You win.

"If you don't want to be disturbed," he says, "I'll find another seat."

"No, please," I have no choice but to say. "Unless . . . I'd be bothering you?" I gesture at his book. The thousand-page tome on Vietnam is not what I'd picture Noa Callaway reading in Noa Callaway's spare time. Shakespeare's sonnets, perhaps. Maybe Charlotte Brontë. Not some dense account of international stalemate.

Please. Please. Please say you want to read your book.

"Not at all," he says, resting an elbow on the shared table between us. "This is . . . funny. Isn't it? Running into you after you canceled on tomorrow? Terry gave me your message."

"Really? I wasn't sure, since I never heard back." I don't try too hard to hide my annoyance.

Noah smirks. "I'm sorry. She doesn't like you."

"How can you tell?" I deadpan.

"It's nothing personal. She hated Alix," he says. "Terry thinks my first drafts are perfect. She's my godmother. It comes with the job."

The Terrier is his godmother? I try to find a place to slot this into my understanding of Noah Ross, but I feel ill-equipped. I realize that I know his preferred chess opening (the Sicilian Defense) and his go-to florist (Flowers of the World, West Fifty-Fifth Street), but nothing about his personal life, where he came from.

"Look, I'm sorry to have canceled—" I say.

He waves me off. "It happens. Is everything okay?"

"Yes," I manage, sounding like a robot powering down.

I glance at my copy of *Ninety-Nine Things* between us on the table. Everything about this encounter feels tremendously embarrassing.

"I've just had . . . you know . . . a . . ."

"Bad day?" he says.

I nod. I don't want to get into my personal life with Noah Ross. He's being slightly less noxious than the first two times we met, but still, everything could go wrong at any moment.

He turns toward the window and lifts the jacket he'd slung over the second seat. Beneath it, I recognize the same animal crate I saw him carrying on Sunday on the Upper West Side. I lean forward, and there is the black-and-white rabbit, asleep inside.

"You have a bunny," I remark.

"You have a tortoise," he says, like this is the end of the conversation.

"Wonder who'll win the race," I say, which actually makes him laugh. "Alice was my neighbor's. Mrs. Park. She moved to Florida a few years ago and couldn't have pets at her new place. She asked if I'd take Alice as a favor. I'm really glad she did," I say, smiling at the pleasant thought of Alice. She'll wonder where I am tonight, but she has enough food and water to last until I'm back tomorrow.

I glance at Noah, because now it's his turn to say something about his own unlikely companion.

"This is Javier Bardem," Noah says, looking at the bunny. "He used to be my mother's."

"Your mom sounds like she has good taste in men."

There's a silence intended for him to elaborate. He doesn't. He points at my thermos.

"Is that egg drop soup?"

"It is," I say, feeling my hackles rise. "It was a gift, and it's my favorite, so don't—"

"I was merely going to say, it smells good . . . *all* throughout the car."

"My soup and I will be happy to reseat ourselves somewhere else," I say. Though I wish he'd be the one to leave. I unwisely unpacked three tote bags' worth of stuff onto the table.

"No, stay," he says. "I need you for cover."

"What does that mean?"

"Three words," Noah says, reaching into a brown paper bag. "Tuna. With. Onions." He takes out a paper-wrapped parcel and soon reveals a large and extremely fragrant sandwich. My eyes start watering, again. "They were out of falafel at my favorite deli, so . . . Maybe our aromas will cancel each other out?"

Against my will, I laugh, and I'm shocked when Noah does, too. I raise my thermos and he holds up his sandwich. We lock eyes.

"Cheers," I say, "to enjoying odiferous food in confined public spaces."

I'm chewing a wonton and learning that I just can't be in a bad mood while chewing a wonton. Noah's chewing, too. The train comes out from underground, and we both look out the window awhile at the pink dusk of almost-spring. Would it be too much to ask for us to eat in silence the rest of the three-hour journey? We actually get along when we're not talking.

My phone buzzes. When I look down, I see that Aude has sent me a photo. Of a keychain. My keychain. The one with Ryan's key on it.

Please tell me this isn't yours, she writes. I found it by the elevator bank.

"Oh *no*."

"What's wrong?" Noah asks.

"Nothing."

"You sure? Because you look like you're about to faint."

"You have no idea what I look like when I'm about to faint." But I do feel a little woozy. The image of Iris Bosch dumping my family heirlooms at Goodwill glows in my mind.

"I'm going to D.C. because I need to pick something up," I say. "I need my keys to do it. And Aude just told me I left them at the office." I cup my face, retracing my steps. "I ran into my friend as I was leaving . . . she gave me this egg drop soup . . . and I must have dropped my keys."

"So, it's actually key drop soup."

I look at him, blink. "Oh my god, you just made a joke." It was corny beyond belief, but it was a joke nonetheless.

Noah cocks an eyebrow, smiles. "I do it once a month on the full moon."

"This is a fine time to let me know you actually have a sense of humor in person."

"Business or residence?" Noah asks.

"Huh?"

"This place you need the keys to get into."

"Residence. Why?"

"What kind of windows?"

"I don't know, ones with panes. They slide up? I think."

I watch Noah's hands clasp together. I watch him lean back in his seat as his green eyes scan the ceiling. He's thinking. This is what he looks like when he's thinking. I picture him sitting like this at his desk in his beautiful Fifth Avenue penthouse, probing his mind for answers about characters I have loved.

"I can get you in," he says.

"Uh, what?"

"There's a . . . ninety-eight-percent chance that I can get you in."

Noah must see the way I'm looking at him because for once, he's quick to explain.

"I was raised in a household of women. My mother and two of her friends. Very overprotective."

"What does any of this mean?" I ask.

"I got good at sneaking out of the house."

"That's different from sneaking *in*."

"What kind of alarm system?"

"He never turns it on."

Noah smiles. "Then we're golden."

I squint at his nonchalance. "So, you're going to get off this train with me? And we're going to this empty house? And you're going to break me inside?"

Noah nods. Smiles.

"This is not the Friday night I had envisioned."

"Stick with me, kid," Noah says. And then, he seems to hear his own words, the rapport that they suggest. His cheeks turn pink, and his manner shifts back to stiff. "If I'm going to agree to this, you need to tell me where we're going, and why."

I was afraid of this. But I have no idea how to break into Ryan's place other than a rock through his window, so if I want my heirlooms without a criminal report, Noah Ross might have to call a few shots.

"It's my ex-fiancé's brownstone in Georgetown."

"The guy on the wall? I thought he wasn't your ex-fiancé."

The train rattles around a bend in the tracks. It's gotten

dark outside. I can't believe I'm having this conversation with this man.

"He wasn't," I say. "Until he was. Anyway, he has some of my stuff with sentimental value, and my ex-future-mother-in-law is going to get rid of it tomorrow." I look at him. "Unless you break me in."

⚜

"So," Noah whispers in the dark side yard of Ryan's brownstone at nine o'clock that night, "how did you two meet?"

"Can we maybe wait until we're not committing a felony to have this conversation?" I whisper back, standing on my toes to watch his work. He's got the screwdriver tool of his Swiss Army knife extended and is slowly, carefully prying open the window that leads to Ryan's laundry room.

We've already quite literally cased the joint, jiggling every doorknob and window, even climbing the trellis in Ryan's back alley hoping to find unlocked upstairs access. Now Noah is just "removing the beading" from the window, which he assures me he can set right on our way out.

"Your call," he says. "I just thought you were the one concerned with feeding me inspiration. I thought you and the ex might have had a meet-cute."

"Are you insane?" I whisper. "You don't get to use my ex-meet-cute. Though, actually, it was a good one."

"Go on," Noah says, grunting a little as he levers the pane up from the frame.

In the quiet night, attempting criminal activities, I feel pressure to tell this story better than I ever have before. And so I do, in whispered segments, as the barred owl hoots in Ryan's maple tree. Noah listens closely, cocking his head when I reach the part about Ryan getting a ticket for riding without his helmet, telling the cop it was worth every penny because look at the woman he'd had to loan it to. I'm up to the detail about the dropped jaws of the Peony marketing department, who all saw me get off Ryan's bike at the doors of the convention center, when Noah frees the pane from the window, turns to me, and grins.

He gestures inside with a wave of his arm. "After you."

If he were anyone else, I'd fling my arms around him in gratitude. Instead, I keep my enthusiasm inside as I climb through. Once I'm on top of Ryan's washing machine, he passes me Javier Bardem in his kennel, and then we wait for Noah to climb in, too.

It's strange and thrilling to creep through Ryan's empty brownstone. I know it well enough that I can navigate in the dark, but since Noah doesn't, I put on my phone's flashlight as we move through the kitchen, to the dining room, through the swinging door into the living room.

"So then what happened?" Noah asks.

"With Ryan?" I say, surprised. I'd ended the story where I usually end it. Most people assume that after Ryan dropped me off, we swapped numbers and started dating. But there was one more thing that happened that first day.

"Well, I thanked him for the ride," I say, pausing at the foot of Ryan's staircase, memories flooding my mind. "And then he said, 'I'm going to marry you.'"

Noah is quiet. I can't see his expression in the dark.

"And I said, 'You don't even know me.' And he said, 'I can just tell we'll be great together.' And then he got down on one knee. I shut him up before he could actually propose. . . ." I trail off, remembering that feeling, how magical it all seemed, like the beginning of something amazing. Like this was the love story I'd been waiting for all my life.

It's hard to think about that now.

Luckily, just then, the beam of my flashlight falls on a box near the front door.

"There it is!" I drop to my knees. I see BD's robe at the top. I feel my mother's award. I'm so relieved.

"Thank you, Noah," I say, turning to look up him. "It was really generous and slightly crazy of you to help me."

"It's the least I can do."

He's standing very still, his hands clasped behind his back. He never looks comfortable, but in Ryan's darkened foyer, he looks even more uncomfortable than usual. We should get out of here.

"Hey," I say, hefting the box into my arms. "Wanna celebrate?"

❧

When Noah said he knew of a place nearby, I was not expecting a cash-only dive called Poe's and two cold cans of Natty Boh. But it turns out, a snug booth at the back of this crowded bar is the perfect place for Noah, Javier Bardem, and me to revel in my reclaimed possessions.

"You never told me what you're doing in D.C.," I say, still high on our achievement, and a little loose from the beer.

"I'm visiting my mom."

"She lives here? I don't know why I thought you grew up in New York."

"I did. I grew up on West Eighty-Fourth. My mom moved down here about ten years ago. I've been trying to get her back to New York but . . . it's complicated."

"Oh," I say, thinking back to the day I saw Noah showing Javier Bardem a building on the Upper West Side. Was that his old apartment? Also, why didn't he mention he was visiting his mother earlier? Now I feel guilty I've taken too much of his time. And what does he mean, complicated?

"Do you need to call her? Is she expecting you for dinner or anything tonight?"

"No," he says, busying himself with sorting through some loose change from his pocket. I realize he's searching for quarters for the mini jukebox on our table. And also that he's not going to tell me anything more about his mom. So, I turn my focus to the jukebox, too.

The machine is old, the glass too scratched, the labels too faded to make out any of the song listings.

"How do you know what you're selecting?" I ask, as he slips coins into the slot.

"I don't," he says, "but it's a chance I'm willing to take." He points at my box. "So what's in there anyway?"

I sift through my old things. In between a bunch of clothes, my hand hits the smooth wood of the Ninety-Nine Things list I gave Ryan for Valentine's Day.

Half of me feels indignant that he returned my gift; the other half feels extremely committed to hiding this artifact from Noah Ross. I don't want him to know this about me, that I was once a girl who made such a list, that I clung to it . . . up until about a week ago. I'm also not sure I can discuss this with Noah without blaming him, just a little, for my breakup. For everything. I shove it to the bottom of the box, as Noah points at BD's robe.

"Let me guess," he says, "your grandma's?"

This time, it doesn't feel hostile, not like it did at our first meeting in the park.

I finger the robe. "My grandfather gave it to her on their honeymoon. It's a little threadbare in a few places, but it's still awesome."

"Very," he says. "Where'd they honeymoon?"

"Positano," I say, smiling and meeting his eyes. "So I was thrilled when you set *Two-Hundred and Sixty-Six Vows* there. I've always wanted to visit."

"You should," he says. "I think you'd like it. It's hard *not* to like the Amalfi Coast, but I think you'd . . . get it."

I'm not sure what he means, or from where he gleaned this knowledge of my travel tastes, but it sounds like he intends it as a compliment, so I leave his logic alone.

"When I was a kid," I say, reaching back into the box, "my mom used to talk about taking me to Positano. She was conceived there." I glance at him. "Sorry, TMI?"

"I assume your mother had to be conceived somewhere," Noah says. "Positano's a good place for it."

I don't know why this makes me blush. We're both adults.

We have pored, professionally, over dozens of sex scenes he wrote into seven bestselling novels. Maybe Noah had great sex in Positano; it couldn't be less my business.

I need to change the subject. After a moment's hesitation, I take out my mother's award from the box. I set the plaque on the table. "This is the main thing I didn't want to lose."

Noah picks it up to get a closer look. He meets my eyes across the table. "Your mom's?"

I nod and sip my beer.

"She must have been an impressive woman."

"How did you know she died?"

"Because you told me and I remembered?" He gives me a funny look. "Did you forget that we've been friends for seven years?"

"I'm sorry . . . sometimes . . . a little . . ."

"It's okay. I know meeting me was a shock to your system."

We're quiet for a moment, because I don't know what to say to this, and he's basically the worst at filling awkward silences. Javier Bardem shifts around in his crate.

That's when the high guitar notes of ELO's "Strange Magic" reach through the jukebox speaker. "I love this song."

Noah smiles. "Tonight, we got lucky."

"We really did."

Noah sets my mom's award back gently in the box. "It's pretty shitty of Ryan to get rid of this. It's not like your late mother's lifetime achievement award is a half-empty shampoo bottle."

"Ryan's a good guy. It's just his mom . . ." I start to say.

"Wait, why am I defending him? It *is* shitty. And I am hereby adding it to the growing list of shitty things he did. Do you know he sold his motorcycle without telling me? That might sound trite, but—"

"He sold the motorcycle he was riding when you two met?" Noah shakes his head. "The motorcycle that was the origin of your story?"

"That's exactly what I said!" I say. "I loved our rides. Then Ryan just got rid of it and acted like I was crazy for caring."

Noah toys with the tab on his beer can. "After my ex and I split up, a long time passed before I let myself get angry. I guess, subconsciously, I knew it was a slippery slope. I had this idea that I should be better at relationships than the average guy, because of what I write. Which, I learned, is false. Just because I can write love stories, doesn't mean I can live them." He lets out a self-deprecating laugh, and through it, I see a tenderer part of Noah Ross. "Once I let myself accept that, I realized our relationship was pretty toxic from the start."

"When did you break up?" I say. Who was this woman? What did she do? Where was she from? What did she look like? How serious were they?

"About a year and half ago," he says, looking away.

My brain accidentally does some math, and I realize this would have been right after he finished writing *Two Hundred and Sixty-Six Vows*. That is, the last thing Noa Callaway wrote.

"Oh, don't do that," he says, reading my mind. "She is not the reason I've been blocked."

"Keep telling yourself that," I say, letting him know with my eyes that I'm teasing.

"Maybe she was a tiny contributing factor. At first." He shakes his head. "What am I doing? You're the last person who wants to hear this."

"It's okay—"

"It's not. I don't want to worry you. You came up with this grand plan to get me writing again, and I'm up for it. I think . . . it'll work out. I know your job is on the line and everything. So please, Lanie, don't worry."

"Sure." I nod. I'm surprisingly not worried. Inside, I feel reassured. For the first time, I can see the human heart that's written Noa Callaway's books.

Suddenly, I don't just want this next book for my career, or for Peony's bottom line. I want it for Noah, too.

"You want to see something that will make you laugh?" I say.

When he looks up at me, glad for the change of subject, I reach into my box and gather the courage to show him my Ninety-Nine Things.

Chapter Twelve

From: elainebloom@peonypress.com
To: noacallaway@protonmail.com
Date: Monday, March 9, 10:06 a.m.
Subject: a toast

Dear Noah,

A few months ago, I was the maid of honor at a friend's wedding. The best man was a Buddhist monk. My speech was first, and it was brilliant, if I may say so— one funny anecdote, one tear-jerking one, one Anne Sexton poem, and one Gracie Allen insult. All done in a tight ten minutes.

Afterward, the monk approached the microphone. He looked into the eyes of the groom, then the bride, and said:

"Lower your expectations."

Then he dropped the mic and went back to his seat.

This depressed me. It sounded like he was encouraging the newlyweds to let each other down. But the more I thought about it, I realized that expectations are rarely rooted in reality, and maybe all the monk was talking about was acceptance. Maybe relationships truly begin with acceptance of who the other is.

I want people to expect much of me—and not to be disappointed, but that's not entirely *in* my control. I like thinking that to accept who someone is, you have to find out who they are. And that can take a lifetime.

At the bar on Friday night, you said you thought meeting you was a shock to my system. I wonder if meeting me was hard for you? I've been thinking about this because today I'm moving into Alix's old office. I'm curious about your expectations of your editor. You've always worked with Alix. You and I have corresponded for years, but in some ways, we're just starting out. So I wanted to offer us a little grace.

Lowered expectations don't invite disappointment. They expect the imperfect in all of us. Your characters do this for each other. Could you and I try to do it, too?

Lanie

This is the first email I send from my new office. I've been wanting to write it ever since Friday night. I keep thinking back to the moment when I showed Noah my Ninety-Nine

Things. I expected him to laugh. I thought if he'd laugh, then I could, too, and my entire failed view on love might feel a little less grave. I thought maybe he could help me lighten up.

But he didn't laugh. He seemed humbled holding the wood panels. He read the whole list carefully, then looked up at me, his expression more serious than I'd ever seen it before.

"I'm sorry you didn't get your happy ending this time," he said. "But you're not like Cara from the book. She *needed* the list. Because she had no faith in love. You, on the other hand . . ."

"What about me?" I found myself leaning forward in the booth, like Noah was about to tell me an important secret.

He thought a moment, then said, "If faith in love were a source of energy, you could power a small planet."

It was the single most reassuring sentence anyone had said to me since my breakup with Ryan. Also, it felt true, and as if all I'd needed was for some kind soul to point it out.

✤

"Lanie?"

It's Sue in my doorway. Sue, who hardly ever leaves her office, who makes everyone come to her.

"I see you're all moved in. Sort of. Is now a good time for a chat?"

"Of course," I say, inviting her into my disaster of an office. "Did I miss a meeting?"

"Oh no," Sue says, closing my door then mazing through

my boxes. "I was just in your neck of the woods to see Emily."

Emily Hines is Peony's other editorial director. For years, she was Alix's low-key rival, due to her unconcealed jealousy of Noa Callaway's success. Every year Emily tries to acquire a knockoff Noa Callaway, and sometimes they're good enough to make the list for a minute. When Sue says if I can't deliver Noa's next book then she'll find someone who can—I know who that someone is.

"Emily's been raving about her new madeleine molds," Sue tells me. "I finally bought one over the weekend, and it's marvelous." She glances at me. "Do you bake?"

"Oh . . . sometimes," I lie, trying to think of a single successful thing I've pulled from my oven. "Brownies are . . . good."

"Yes." Sue nods slowly.

This is not going well. Do I have to start buying random crap at Sur la Table so I can stay on Sue's good side?

No. I just need a manuscript from Noa Callaway.

"I'm glad you're here," I say, taking control of the meeting. "Noa and I had a breakthrough the other day."

This is true—though our breakthrough was more personal than professional. Before Sue can ask for specifics, I push on, pulling confidence out of thin air.

"Noa wants to visit the Cloisters on Saturday to do some research," I say. "I have a feeling, soon after that, I'll be able to share the premise of the new book."

Sue nods, a hint of approval in her eyes. "The Cloisters is an interesting setting. But what's the hook?"

"It's still a bit inchoate, but we're getting there—"

"Get there by sales conference. Three weeks from tomorrow. And by 'there' I mean a title and some catalog copy. What about the manuscript deadline?"

"Still on track," I say, steadying my voice. "May fifteenth."

Ten weeks from now. It's in the outer limits of possible. *If he gets an idea incredibly soon, and then proceeds to write like the wind.*

"Good." Sue rises from my guest chair and makes her way out of my office. When she opens my door, she leans down and picks something up off the floor. A mason jar brimming with dusky purple tulips. "How nice. Your fiancé sent you flowers."

I force a smile and take the vase from her, walking it back to my desk. An envelope from Flowers of the World winks from beneath the ribbon.

As soon as I'm alone, I tear open the card.

Today's expectations: That these will make your move less hellish.

—Noah

P.S. I know the monk only had to stand up and deliver three words, but I'm willing to bet you were a tough act to follow.

I stare at the card. An image of Noah Ross dictating this message to a florist fills my mind. Was he in his penthouse, feet up on his desk, looking out at Central Park? Did he come up with the message on the fly, or did he labor over it the way I labor over my words to him? Was he wondering what I might think when I got the tulips? Because I don't know what to think. The more I try to understand my relationship with Noah Ross, the more indefinable it becomes.

Friends over email. Antagonists in person. Then, out of nowhere: people who break into brownstones together, enjoy ELO on the jukebox, and eat obnoxious foods on trains.

One thing I've always loved about Noa's characters is how they grapple with contradictory impulses. This makes for great fiction, but in real life, it's confusing.

"Excuse us," Meg says, slipping in with Rufus and closing the door. "Nice digs, by the way." She looks around and nods approval. "Rufus thought he heard Sue say something about Ryan sending you—" She breaks off, pointing at the tulips. "Whoa . . . what *happened* Friday night?"

Someday, I'd love to tell Meg what happened Friday night.

"Funny," Rufus says, picking up the mason jar. "I always took Ryan for more of a red roses kind of guy."

"Why is your ex-fiancé buying you flowers when my husband doesn't seem to know what they are?" Meg says. "Do you know what Tommy got me for Valentine's Day this year? A case of unscented dryer sheets. I kid you not."

"Meg, that *is* romantic!" I say, happy to steer the subject away from the tulips.

"Don't patronize me."

"You love to shop in bulk!" I remind her. "You guys got banned from Costco back when you were dating for heavy petting in the freezer section! Plus, unscented? He was thinking about your eczema."

"He was thinking about static cling. That's what our marriage is: static cling."

"So the flowers . . ." Rufus prompts me.

"Don't worry," I say. "They aren't from Ryan."

"Good," Meg says, "because that would have thrown a real wrench in Operation Get Lanie Laid this Friday."

I won't disappoint Meg by explaining that the odds of me getting laid on Friday are slim for many reasons. Not the least of which is that I need to be bushy-tailed on Saturday morning to escort Noah around the Cloisters. If you'd asked me a week ago, I probably couldn't have thought of anything worse than having a hangover while hanging out with Noah Ross. But the truth is, since our escapade last Friday, I've been looking forward to our visit to the uptown cousin of the Met. Or at least, not dreading it. It feels possible now that he'll actually get an idea for the book.

"Noa Callaway sent them," I say casually, looking at the tulips.

Meg raises an eyebrow. Rufus plops down on a box of books.

"Noa Callaway sends flowers?" Meg says.

"The transition must be going well," Rufus says.

"My mother had a tulip garden," I say, fingering the flowers' waxy leaves. "I've always loved them."

After a minute I realize they're both staring at me.

"You okay there, Lanie?" Meg says.

"Of course."

"Good," Meg says. "Stay that way. Because Rufus has chosen Subject on Suffolk as our venue for Friday night. Dress to impress."

"Come on, Meglicist," Rufus says, using his pet name for her. "You can do better than that."

"Okay . . ." she says, "dress to undress."

I laugh, because I know my friends well enough to hear in the cadence of their voices that this is a laugh line, but the truth is, I haven't heard the past couple exchanges. My mind went back to my mother, to a memory I have of pulling weeds together when I was a little girl.

As soon as Meg and Rufus leave, I write to Noah.

From: elainebloom@peonypress.com
To: noacallaway@protonmail.com
Date: March 9, 11:45 a.m.
Subject: wondering

Thanks for the flowers. They're beautiful. I've never seen tulips this color. My new office—which feels enormous and sort of like I'm squatting—needed them.

Can I ask you something? Why do you send tulips, over any other flower? They've always been my favorite, and I'm wondering what they mean to you.

From: noacallaway@protonmail.com
To: elainebloom@peonypress.com

Date: March 10, 11:53 a.m.

Subject: re: wondering

You told me once your middle name is Drenthe. I assumed it was a family name and guessed that you
were Dutch. Was I wrong?

   See you Saturday. It'll be fun.

❧

"What's this?" BD asks in a happy singsong over FaceTime
Friday night. She's been checking in on me each day since
Ryan and I broke up. "Is that eyeliner I see? And a hint of
bosom! Are you in a Lyft?"

"Indeed, I am going out tonight," I say as my driver turns
down Second Avenue toward the Lower East Side cocktail
spot Rufus claims I'll love.

The night is cool and a little damp, but I did go with one
of my more low-cut dresses and heeled boots. Mostly because I knew Rufus and Meg would have been aghast if I'd
shown up in what I really wanted to wear, a very comfortable
tan thrift store turtleneck.

"You know," BD says with a wink, "sex with a stranger is
a double mitzvah on Shabbat!"

"I'm not sure the 'stranger' part is actually in the Torah,"
I say. "Hey, can I ask you something?"

"You can always ask me about sex toys—"

"No, BD . . . my middle name—I know it's a city in Holland, but we're not Dutch. You and Grandpa were both born in Poland."

"Before the war," she says, "your grandfather lived in the Netherlands. He was born in Drenthe. Your mother must have told you that?"

"Maybe," I say, but when it comes to conversations with my mother, too much predates my memory. And I remember as a child that BD seemed so pained, so un-BD when she talked about what she'd left in Europe, that eventually, I stopped asking. I'm glad my grandfather lives on in my middle name. "So, Mom's tulip garden . . ."

"An homage," BD says, with a flourish of her hand. "She grew up gardening with your grandfather." BD looks away from the camera. She's in her kitchen, making popcorn, which she burns at each attempt. Her voice changes, and I wish I were there with her instead of having this conversation on the phone. "He lost all his family in the war. He never went back to Drenthe, but he wrote about it."

"In his poetry? Do you still have it? Can I read it?"

"Elaine," she says, "I'm going to ship you the biggest sack of poems you've ever seen."

"Thanks, BD. I'd love that."

"What about our other project?" She drops her voice to a whisper. "The Noa Callaway situation. Any breakthroughs?"

BD quirks her brow and I realize that I'm smiling. I try to wipe my expression clean, but it's BD, and she knows my feelings anyway.

"Check back with me tomorrow," I say. "I'm taking him

to the Cloisters for inspiration. I probably shouldn't tempt fate by saying this, but I have a good feeling about it."

I glance out the window as my Lyft driver slows to a stop. We've arrived in front of a crowded bar at the corner of Houston and Suffolk. Through the windows, I see high ceilings, dim chandelier light . . . and Meg on top of the bar, taking a shot with one fist in the air.

"BD," I say, "I've got to go walk in to a real hot mess now."

"Have a wonderful time, dear." She air-kisses the camera. "And don't be afraid to lead with your bosom!"

As soon as I step into Subject, Rufus spots me through the crowd. He waves me over and gives me a hug. "You just missed Meg's *Coyote Ugly* moment."

"I think I caught the finale through the window." I squeeze Meg's shoulders.

"Don't worry, it was amazing," she says, sipping the new drink the bartender has placed before her. "You know I took Irish dancing in college. And, well, people wanted to see."

"*People.*" Rufus air-quotes.

"I didn't realize this was a dancing-on-top-of-the-bar kind of place," I tease Meg, as Rufus shakes his head. "You are aware that your cocktail has an actual shiso leaf in it."

"I suppose most people stay off the bar until approximately midnight here," Meg acknowledges, her face falling a little. "But I can't stay up that late anymore!" Her voice cracks and I give her a hug.

"Well, your eyebrows are one hundred percent," I say, admiring her threading job.

Rufus plants a martini glass full of something pink and salt-rimmed in my hand.

"And your overalls are straight fire, Ruf," I say.

"Not as much as your *hint of bosom*," he says, laughing wickedly and clinking his glass to mine.

"Have you been texting with my grandmother?"

"I'll never tell!"

"All right," Meg says, drawing the two of us into a corner from which we can see most of the bar. "Let's get to work."

I let her scan the room on my behalf. That's what friends are for, and it gives me time to focus on my cocktail.

Meg lifts her chin in the direction of a guy down the bar. "He's gorgeous."

"He looks like Ryan," Rufus says.

"Pass!" I shout into my drink.

"Okay, what about the brawny blondie coming this way, oooh," Rufus says, nodding at an approaching man who is trying to get the bartender's attention.

He is good-looking, the kind of good-looking that never comes without a chin cleft. Meg and Rufus make a choreographed retreat from the bar, leaving an open space for him to sidle up next to me.

He signals the bartender for another beer, then looks at me and smiles.

"Hi!" I shout over the noise of the bar, feeling rusty as fuck at flirting.

"What?" he shouts back, leaning in, hand on the small of my back.

I step away. His eyes are so blue that it sort of hurts to look at him. "I just said . . . never mind . . ."

He shouts something I can't hear, and I realize how pointless this is. I'm not interested in this guy. Even on Shabbat. I start to back away, but he follows, fresh beer in hand.

"It's quieter away from the bar," he shouts, nodding toward a window. I glance at Meg whose wide eyes and frantic hand motions let me know that I'm not welcome back in their corner just yet.

And so, a moment later, I find myself pressed against a window, staring deep into this stranger's chin cleft, and wondering what the hell to say.

"So what do you do?" he asks, after we've been through the thrilling topics of our names and whether we've been to this bar before.

(His is Phil, and the answer is yes.)

"I'm a book editor," I shout.

"That's AMAZING!" he shouts back with so much enthusiasm I wonder whether I've written Phil off too quickly. Then the other shoe drops. "I read a book last year!"

"Was it . . . good?" It's the best I can do.

"So good." He winks at me. "You wanna get out of here? My hotel is just around the corner. Minibar . . . balcony . . ."

I just can't double mitzvah with this guy. "You know what, Phil? I've got an early meeting tomorrow. . . ."

"It's Saturday."

"Also, I just don't see it happening—you . . . me. . . ."

Phil nods and doesn't take it too hard. His eyes are already scanning the bar for another lady who'd love to hit that hotel balcony. I make my goodbyes and hurry back to my friends. But on the way, I catch eyes with a tall man nursing a Guinness at the bar.

He's cute and clean-cut, wearing tailored pin-striped suitpants with a white French-cuffed oxford shirt. His vibe is grown-up yet playful—both of which I like—especially when combined with the wry look in his eyes.

"Not a winner?" Pinstripes says in a British accent.

"In Phil's defense," I say, drawing closer, "he did read a book last year."

Pinstripes laughs. I put my drink down on the bar and see Meg and Rufus chest bump in celebration out of the corner of my eye.

"Are those ampersand cuff links?" I ask, admiring the flash of gold at his wrists.

He nods. "The ampersand has a fascinating history. I wrote my PhD thesis on their use in Shakespearean paratext." He pauses, stares at me.

"What?"

"It's just that you're still awake. Usually those words are verbal Ambien."

"Just don't slip your thesis topic in my drink."

We both laugh, then both drink, and I'm thinking: handsome, brilliant, witty in a British way. Operation Get Lanie Laid has entered the theater of engagement.

"Have you met my fiancé?" a woman's voice says behind me, and then I watch as arms slink around Pinstripes' shoulders. One hand at the end of those arms bears a simple, gorgeous diamond ring. I wince as Pinstripes is swiveled into a conversation with a cluster of fashionable, attractive Brits. He meets my eyes before he commits and mouths the words *good luck*.

I turn away and down the rest of my cocktail, then make a beeline for Rufus, who's got a second drink waiting for me. Or should I say, second drinks.

"Clearly, it's time to move on to Kate Mosses," he says.

I take the drinks from his hands and we all down our Kate Mosses. My eyes water. "I've got about one more teeth-puller in me before I turn into a pumpkin."

"We could mosey down the street," he says. "Go dancing?"

"Dancing, yes," Meg says, bouncing on her heels, arms stiff at her sides. "Preferably Irish."

"I like it here," I say. "It's just . . . would it be okay if we put Operation Get Lanie Laid to rest for the night? I'm more in a *sip-my-drink-and-try-to-keep-Meg-off-the-bar* kind of mood."

"Say no more," Meg says, and loops an arm around me. "We'll just pretend we're the only ones here—"

"Wait a minute," I say. "Is that . . ."

I rise on my toes, because a dead ringer for Noah Ross has just walked into the bar. Which would be three times the man has stumbled into my life in a single week. Surely some sort of world record.

But then, when he turns, I see it isn't him. Not by a long shot. Just some dark, curly-headed stranger in a pea coat. I'm surprised to feel disappointed.

Meg is studying me, following my gaze. "You like that guy

over there because he looks like your Man of the Year. What is your deal with him?"

"What do you mean? I have no deal."

"Lanie. You hid from him at brunch."

"You don't think he's attractive?"

I did not mean to ask that. I'm not sure why it would matter to me whether Meg thinks Noah is cute. Still . . . does she?

"His attractiveness is not in question," Meg says. "Your awkwardness is. You like him. You should go for it—"

"It's a nonstarter!" I say, more forcefully than intended. But it is true, even if I can't explain in more detail to Meg. Even if I can't explain to myself why a tiny part of me feels disappointed.

Chapter Thirteen

"DID YOU KNOW," I SAY TO NOAH AS WE ENTER THE castle-like museum the next morning, "that this place was built out of the reassembled pieces of five legitimately medieval French cloisters?"

He stops walking and turns to me, a smile held in his eyes. "All right, here's what we're going to do." He presses his palms together. "We're going to stand right here, and you're going to unleash all your museum docent facts. Every single one. Just nail me with them. Purge your system, Lanie. After that? We're going to walk around like regular people and enjoy our time at this place."

I roll my eyes. "Fine. I'll shut up. I can take a hint. Even a very overt one."

We start walking again, our footsteps echoing through the gray stone arches of the abbey. "You know, two weeks ago you would have reamed me for ribbing you like that," he says.

"Two weeks ago, you hadn't broken into my ex-fiancé's

brownstone," I tell him as we pause before a series of elaborate unicorn tapestries. I read that they were dyed with the
same plants cultivated in the garden outside, but I am keeping that fascinating tidbit to myself.

He smiles. "It's rare that I get to put those skills to use."

We stop before an apse, whose recessed walls are all
stained glass. Noah studies a panel of a Madonna and child.
He takes out his phone and snaps a picture. "This place is
really special."

I'm tempted to take a stab at pronouncing the Austrian
city where I read these windows came from, but I can tell
Noah is absorbing the atmosphere, and so, I leave a tender
moment alone.

I can't help sneaking glances at him. Things I've noticed
about Noah without realizing I was noticing: His curly hair is
always wet when he shows up someplace. His eyes are this
dark, mysterious green, which matches the cool ivy print on
his button-down today. His smile is slow—like it really wants
to be sure about things before committing—but once it's
there, it holds you close.

He's nothing like Ryan, who was inarguably handsome in
a *People*'s-Sexiest-Man-Alive kind of way. There's nothing inarguably *anything* about Noah, and I'm beginning to realize
that's the root of his appeal. For starters, he's a fashion cha-
meleon. He dresses one day like an indie rocker, one day like
an Italian film producer, one day like a hipster on vacation.
Even his physique—long and lean—is a body type that defies
classification into a single sporty build—does he do triath-
lons to stay fit? A combination of basketball and yoga?

The man is an enigma—one minute reserved, the next, totally game to commit a felony in the spirit of doing some-one a favor. You'd never know how successful he is from a glance or a casual conversation. But when he opens up, his spark is bright. He is full of complexities one wants to know more about.

That is, if one weren't wagering their entire future on get-ting a book out of him.

"Let's see the gardens," he suggests, and I'm down.

We step outside, walking along a colonnaded loggia that opens to a garden so charming it borders on the miraculous. Neat stone paths divide it into quadrants. A fountain burbles at the center. The air is fragrant with herbs and small red flowers, swaying on the boughs of pomegranate trees. It's transporting. Standing in this oasis, I feel as if we haven't only left Manhattan, but have journeyed back in time to medieval Europe. I want to linger, to make the most of this respite from my everyday concerns.

"Is that wanderlust in your eyes?" Noah asks, surprising me. I hadn't felt him looking at me, didn't know he could read my thoughts.

"Guilty," I say, adding lightly, "Wanderlust, tranquility-lust, go-back-in-time-and-make-different-choices-lust. Sort of a mixed-bag-lust."

Stop saying lust.

"If you know of any great destinations for people whose lives are imploding," I say, wrapping up my rambling, "let me know."

I'm not sure why Noah's grinning at me.

"What?" I say as we stop at the garden's center.

"As a matter of fact," he says, "I do."

"You do what?"

"Know of a great destination for you." He reaches into his coat pocket and pulls out a thick, cream colored envelope. It's addressed to Noa Callaway, but he hands it to me.

I slide the card out. It's written in Italian. "What is this?"

"An invitation to the Italian launch party of *Two Hundred and Sixty-Six Vows,*" he says. "Apparently, a video of you making that speech at the New York launch was posted online. Did you know it went viral in Italy?"

"You're kidding." This is news to me.

"My publisher in Milan asked if you'd consider going and making a speech. It's in May. They're having the party at the Bacio hotel, which is . . ."

He meets my eyes, and we both say it at the same time: "In Positano."

"Seriously?" I say. "That's the hotel where *Vows* is set."

"And," he says, a smile hiding in the corners of his mouth, "if memory serves, the city where your mother was conceived?"

"I would say I wish I'd never told you that . . . except . . ." I look at him. "Are you offering me a trip to Italy?"

"Technically, my Italian publisher is offering it. I won't be there, of course. But I'd be cheering you on from here."

The way he says this, a hint of bittersweetness in his voice, makes me wonder. Any other author would accept this invitation themselves. Noah can't. Does he ever wish things were different, that he could go to Italy himself and celebrate his work with his readers in the open?

I stare at the invitation, still trying to wrap my mind around it. What are the odds that an invitation to my dream destination would come—all expenses paid—at the moment I can't say yes?

"This party is on May eighteenth," I say. "Three days after your deadline for the book we have no concept for."

Noah looks unfazed. "If I promise to get you the draft before you leave," he says, "will you go?"

"I will go to Mars if you get me a draft before I leave. But realistically, Noah, we don't even have a premise yet." I press the invitation back into his hands. "I'm honored that you asked me. And it's really generous of your Italian publisher, but until both our careers aren't teetering on the brink, I can't in good conscience accept."

Noah scratches his head. He looks stunned. "I didn't even get to lay out my conditions."

"You and your conditions," I say. But I'm curious. "Well, let's have them. Just in case."

"It's really only one condition," he says. "Payback for your list. My List."

"Your list of what?"

"I lived in Positano for two months to research *Vows*. I know the best place to buy the vintage designer souvenirs for your grandmother—and where you can get a great Piedirosso around the corner."

"I never say no to a glass of Peidirosso," I say, hoping I've guessed correctly that this is a type of wine. The idea of traveling around Italy with a list of Noa Callaway's favorite local haunts in my pocket fills me with a secret glee. People would bid on eBay for such a thing.

Not that I'm going to Italy.

And then I realize: This is the first time I've reconciled Noah Ross and Noa Callaway as the same entity. It happened without my noticing. I wonder, if I can get comfortable with the man behind the books, could the readers? Could the press?

I want to explore this with Sue, and with Noah. Once we have a manuscript.

"I accept your condition," I say, "on the condition that—"

"We have a book?"

"Exactly," I say, "so in the meantime . . ." I motion at the museum around us.

Noah catches my drift, and we turn our attention back to the Cloisters. I mentally put on my Noa Callaway glasses and try to see the gardens through their lens.

Across the fountain, there's an older woman in a wheelchair being pushed by a pretty young girl. Likely her granddaughter. I watch the girl excuse herself around a young gardener who's toting a giant bag of sod. I point them out to Noah and lean in to whisper.

"So, what if . . ." I say, "he's the caretaker of the garden. The horticulturist. And she's the caretaker of the lady in the wheelchair. Who wants to be brought to the Cloisters each week. They see each other a dozen times. I'm talking lingering glances, a couple of 'excuse me's.' Each is forming opinions—

all wrong!—about who the other is. And then one day . . ." I trail off, thinking. "What happens? Who would break the ice? Maybe it's the old lady. She wants to live to see her granddaughter find love, so she slips the gardener the girl's number?"

"I like it," Noah says, no trace of sarcasm in his voice.

"It could work, right?" My heart and confidence soar.

"Maybe you should write it," Noah says, crouching to study a medieval aloe plant. "Or offer it to another writer you work with?"

And . . . heart and confidence now plummeting down to the core of the earth. Invitation to Italy spontaneously combusting. "Why not you?"

Noah circles the fountain, arms crossed over his chest. "I'm not trying to make this harder. But recently, I'm finding myself less interested in the meet-cute as an engine."

Two weeks ago, I would have found this comment obnoxious, dismissive of the books I love and he claims to love, too. I would have fought back: The meet-cute is everything! All good love stories need one.

But today is not about me. It's about helping Noah get inspired.

"And you're finding yourself *more* interested in . . ." I offer.

He looks at me. His green eyes flash. "The full rhapsodic spectacle of life."

Well, he was ready for me there.

"Okay," I say slowly. "Yeah, that can be romantic, too."

He tips his head for me to follow him, and we walk out of the garden, toward an elevated stone walkway that overlooks the Hudson River. It's a gorgeous day, a spectacular view. I resist the urge to tell him this is one of the highest points in all of Manhattan.

"My mom is sick," Noah says, leaning his elbows on the railing by the river. "She has Alzheimer's. And recently, she's taken a turn."

I stand near him, feeling crushed on his behalf. "I'm so sorry."

"I'm not telling you to make excuses. I only want to explain. My mom is the reason I started writing."

"Really?" I've always wondered about the Noa Callaway origin story. Everyone at Peony has.

"Her first name is Calla," he says. "I wrote *Ninety-Nine Things* because of her. She likes love stories. She used to, anyway." He rubs his jaw, and gazes out across the water. Sorrow shimmers from him. I recognize it well.

I know the best that I can do is listen.

"If this book is the last book I write that she gets to read," he says, "I want it to speak to the scope of love, not just to its beginning."

"The epic of a heart," I say, as my skin pricks with goose bumps. It's not bad. It's very good.

He nods. "I don't know who the characters are, or what the circumstances would be. . . ."

For a few moments we say nothing, but it doesn't feel like one of those silences you look for ways to fill. It feels like we are letting this quiet upper reach of Manhattan take our hard conversation in its gentle hands.

"Tell me about your mom," I say. "You said you were raised by a house full of women?"

"After my dad left," he says, "Mom and I lived with two other ladies from her nursing school. Aunt Terry and Aunt B."

"Back up. Aunt . . . Terry?"

Noah smiles, enjoying my surprise. "We were this crazy, estrogen-rich, romance-loving household. My mom and my aunts' favorite thing to do was swap novels and argue over plots and characters. It was like a book club that never ended."

"And eventually," I say, "you got inducted?"

"I read *Clan of the Cave Bear* in first grade."

"Those books are so underrated!" I say. "Jondalar was my first fictional crush."

"Oh, is that your type?" he jokes and I turn red, thinking back on those notoriously steamy cave scenes that I read at least three thousand times.

"So when you started writing . . ." I say, putting a corner piece of the Noa Callaway puzzle into place.

He nods. "I'd fallen in love with love. Though, obviously, at twenty, I didn't know a thing about it."

I picture Noah at twenty, not knowing a thing about love. It's sort of cute.

"When I showed the first draft of *Ninety-Nine Things* to my mom," he says, "she didn't believe I'd written it. If my own mother couldn't see it, what reader would want to open the back flap and see me?"

I consider what his author photo might look like. Smoldering green eyes flirting with the camera. Dark curls just long enough to suggest untamed. Black turtleneck. No, a button-down showing a little bit of chest hair . . .

He's right. His author photo would give his readers a shock.

"Alix didn't know I was a man until after she'd bought the manuscript," he continues, another key piece falling into place. "We had no idea *Ninety-Nine Things* would take off the way it did. I never thought I'd make a career of it. Once upon a time . . ."

"It was just a love story?"

"Yes," he says, meeting my eyes. It feels as if this is the first time we've ever really looked at each other. "It was just a love story."

We keep walking along the river, the sun high and bright overhead, the view of the George Washington Bridge growing in the distance.

"It's your move," he says, catching me off guard.

"What?"

"In chess." He waves his phone. "It's been your turn for over a week. You're about to forfeit the game."

"Oh! I've been—"

"Paralyzed by my impending victory?"

"More like trying not to distract you with push notifications! Also, I don't want to completely crush your confidence in this delicate creative moment. You've lost—what?—the past six games in a row?"

"That's only because I can't use my intimidation tactics over the app."

"And those would be?"

Noah squares off to face me, crosses his arms, and raises one eyebrow dramatically with an exaggerated tilt of his head. All he needs is a monocle to complete the look of total lunatic. I burst out laughing.

"I'm scared now," I say.

"See?"

"Scared for you that you think that's an intimidation tactic. You look like an Angry Bird."

"Fine, but I am a better chess player in person. The game of kings needs human beings."

"Well, if only you hadn't pissed me off so much that day in Central Park," I say, feigning a sigh. "We could have already put this argument to rest."

"I'm afraid there's only one solution," he says.

"Are you challenging me to a game of chess?" I say, feeling my competitive spirit rise.

He nods. "And hoping you like sushi, because I'm starving, and Saturdays are for sushi." Then he does the thing with the eyebrow again until I crack up and agree.

❧

Noah tells the cab to stop at Ninety-Fifth and Broadway.

"What are we doing here?" I ask as he opens the door.

"This is where I live." He leads us toward a black iron gate tucked into the center of a two-story Tudor-style apartment building. The place looks out of time, dwarfed by taller and more modern buildings on all sides.

I've been here before, I realize. This is the entrance to Pomander Walk, the pedestrian enclave of row houses Meg brought me to once for a party. It had been on my list of Fifty Ways to Break Up Noah and His Writer's Block. He crossed it out.

"You don't live here," I say as Noah takes out a key and unlocks the gate. He leads me up a set of brick stairs, which open to a private garden the length of an avenue block. "You live in a penthouse on Fifth Avenue overlooking Central Park."

"I write in a penthouse on Fifth Avenue overlooking Central Park," he says. "I live in a studio, right there." He points to a quaint brick façade halfway down the walk, with the sweetest little apple tree out front. "It's tiny, and I rent, but"—he looks around at the garden, as if it's still a wonderful surprise to him—"I'll never give it up."

Which explains why he was walking around the Upper West Side with his bunny while I was at Emergency Brunch. *Recalibrate, Lanie*, I tell myself.

I was expecting a doorman, an elevator, expensive steel and glass. I was expecting to be annoyed by my envy of his wealth, which I assumed he spent in flashy, impersonal ways. But now . . . something about entering Noah's garden-level studio apartment is disorienting. It's so intimate. Maybe too intimate.

He's unlocking his door. I need to decide whether to call this off right now.

"There's the sushi," he says, glancing behind us at a figure bearing take-out bags, waiting at the garden gate. "I'll get it.

Go on in. Just close the door behind you so Javier Bardem doesn't get out?"

"Sure," I say, accidentally deciding not to call it off. I step inside Noah's apartment and close the door. "What is happening?" I whisper as I attempt to acclimate to my surroundings.

It must be said: It's a beautiful studio apartment. Polished wood floors, a working fireplace, low ceilings but lots of natural light. The furniture is elegant mid-century, the kitchen tiny but well appointed.

It's very nice, but it's not *so* much nicer than my own apartment. I have more square footage, and an actual wall between my bed and the front door—so where does he get off demanding that we never meet at my place again?

But then, I think about our day today—how nice it's been, our rapport so different than it was at my apartment. There is a chance that I misread something about Noah's attitude that day.

I tour his apartment cautiously. There are certainly more plants than I expected—succulents and baby palms, orchids and bamboo, all of them thriving and green. There's framed art on nearly every inch of wall space—including a masterful Kehinde Wiley that I recognize from his Ferguson series. There's a surfboard in the corner, a metal trashcan with pictures of all the presidents up to Reagan, which tells me Noah's probably had this since he was a little boy. There's a beer-making kit on the windowsill that looks like he took it out of the box but never actually brewed anything. There's a stack of old Playbills under a lamp—the one on top is from

Oh, Hello, the Broadway show Rufus and I laughed our asses off at a few years ago on his birthday. There's no bookshelf that I can see, only a short stack of poetry books on the coffee table. Lucille Clifton, Paul Celan, Heather Christle. I approve.

I open the Christle and sink onto a leather couch just as Noah comes in with the sushi. Javier Bardem hops in from out of nowhere and Noah scoops him up.

"I thought I'd find you by the books," he says, turning to me. "Is this okay? Are you comfortable?" His expression suggests that I am very uncomfortable.

"Sure," I say, holding up the Christle book. "She's really good."

"I have her other collections at my office," he says, moving into the kitchen where I hear the rustle of unpacking sushi. "Most of my books are there."

"It's funny," I say, "I just found out my grandfather wrote poetry."

He looks at me through the galley window of the kitchen, eyebrows raised. And so I find myself telling Noah Ross about Drenthe, and the war, and how BD had FedExed me a giant Ziploc bag of poetry this week. I tell him how, reading it, I'd felt a new kinship with my grandfather; I wasn't the only weirdo in my family of doctors to ever care about words on a page. Saying all this aloud feels meaningful, and I'm glad to have Noah here to listen.

"If you hadn't sent me those tulips," I say, "I wouldn't have understood that my mother planted tulips for her father. I wouldn't have looked this closely to find the reason

I've always loved the simple way they bloom. Because of her. Because of him."

"I think what you're talking about is the second draft effect," Noah calls from the kitchen.

I rise from the couch and go to the kitchen, where I find him plating sushi like a chef. "Explain."

"You know how the second draft is the point where things start to make sense?" he says, taking out real chopsticks from a drawer, tossing aside the disposable ones. "It's why I blaze through my first drafts so quickly—to get there."

I know what Noah means. Back in the garden with my mother, that was the first draft. Exploring the cool, damp soil between my toes. The curving yellow stripes of a caterpillar wriggling across a leaf. The weight of my mother's hands over mine as she showed me how to pack the bulbs into the earth. The sunny sound of her voice when we sang Lucinda Williams songs together, "Car Wheels on a Gravel Road." The pleasure of being with her overwhelmed my power to know what it all meant.

Time and space and losing her, emails with Noah, talks with BD, and the Ziploc bag of poems have given things a new perspective. I can shine a light on the meaning that was always there. It feels like getting a little more of my mother and my grandfather than I'd had before.

"Can I help?" I ask.

It's too late to help, and this is not accidental. Meg would have called me out—*Classic Lanie!* But Noah has done a far better job setting up this feast than I could have. There are little dishes for soy sauce and ponzu and ginger, ceramic chopstick holders. He's even transferred the miso soup to actual bowls. It looks elegant and delicious.

"I think we're ready," he says, carrying the sushi to a marble table by the fireplace. I find myself watching the way he walks, blushing when he looks back and catches me.

There's a carrot roll for Javier Bardem to enjoy at his own small table. For several moments, I fall into the cute vortex of watching a bunny eat sushi.

"I need to expand Alice's palate," I say, thinking of the iceberg lettuce she had for breakfast.

"Chessboard's by the window if you want to set it up," Noah says, heading back into the kitchen. "I can make green tea," he calls, "or open a bottle of sake?"

"Sake," I say, finding the board and moving it to the table. "We're celebrating."

"What are we celebrating?" he asks from the kitchen. I hear the smile in his voice.

"Future epics of the heart. Saying *fuck it* to the meet-cute. And also . . . surviving a day together."

"We still have time to ruin it," Noah says, returning with a chilled bottle of sake.

"Your choice of outing is up next, you know," I say as he pours sake into crystal cordial glasses. "But don't worry, no one expects it to compete with today."

He raises his glass to mine. "I'm not worried. My excursion is pure gold."

"You have one picked out?" I assumed I'd have to harass him into making any sort of plan.

"I'm in the final scheduling phase right now."

"What is it?"

"You'll see," he says as we sit down.

We dive into fresh sashimi, spicy tuna on crispy rice cakes, divine crab handrolls, and halibut carpaccio in spicy yuzu jelly that pairs perfectly with the sake.

"You do takeout really well," I say, sipping my miso soup.

"You should see what I do in restaurants."

I laugh. "Where does one even get all these little bowls? And the chopsticks—are they made of jade?"

Noah smiles, watching me mishandle them to seize a slice of halibut. "They're from a shop called Bo's. Whenever I go there, I find something special, something I've never seen before. It's not far from Peony. You should check it out. He has chopsticks in pink quartz, too."

"I will." I don't want to let Noah know that most of my sushi eating at home happens on my couch, glued to BBC America, using my hands to drag a spicy tuna roll through the soy sauce I've squirted into the lid of the plastic container.

He points at the chessboard between us. "Guests go first."

I steel myself, intent not to laugh when he debuts that freakish eyebrow tic. But to my surprise, Noah has shifted into serious game mode and clearly isn't messing around.

I move my pawn into the center quadrant. I watch him do the same.

Though we have never sat across the chessboard from each other quite like this, there is not the curious tension of playing the game for the first time with someone new. We're used to moving these pieces around each other.

We're not used to knowing where our real hands go in real life between real turns. Twice our fingers graze at the edges of the board.

I remember our first handshake. How it sent a bolt of lightning through me. His touch now, even accidental, still does the same.

I tell myself to pay closer attention to his hands so as to avoid grazing them, but that backfires, because then I pay too close attention to them and lose my knight. I've never noticed how strong they are.

Lanie. Remember your career on the line? The precarious balance you are in with this man? Stop gazing at his meet-cuticles. Win the game and go home.

I swig another glass of sake, because something needs to take the edge off. Because, is it just me or is it getting a little too *Thomas Crown Affair* in here?

I focus on my tactical approach. Noah's strategy is different IRL than it is online. He castles on his left and brings his queen out daringly early. I find this style familiar, though, and after half a dozen turns, I realize Noah plays chess like the character he wrote in the chess scenes of his novel, *Twenty-One Games with a Stranger.*

It tells me how to win—a one-two punch with my queen and my bishop.

I wonder whether Noah based that character on himself in other ways. Whether I might revisit the pages of that book to better know the man before me.

But maybe, to know Noah, all I need to do is pay attention. To the paintings he's chosen for his walls—bright and urgent, each full of its own story. To his generosity—Saturday sushi, second-draft-effect tulips, Swiss Army knife treatments of my ex's window pane. To his confession at the bar last weekend that, when it comes to romance off the page, Noah Ross is as lost as anyone who's ever searched for love.

"Checkmate," Noah says.

My jaw drops. He's got me pinned between his rooks. How did I let this happen?

I want to be a gracious loser, but I honestly can't believe this. The only thing that makes it bearable is looking up at him and confronting The Eyebrow.

We both start laughing. Noah reaches for the sake, and we're surprised to find the bottle drained.

"Guess I should go," I say, though my dignity wouldn't mind a rematch.

Noah rises and gets my coat. He walks me to the door, then down the walk, where two old-fashioned streetlights have come on and make the place look like we've dipped back in time a hundred years. It's cold and our breath clouds the air.

"Thank you," he says as I hail a cab on Broadway.

"For what?" I turn to say.

"It's been a long time since I've felt inspired."

"Me, too," I say before I can stop myself. Because even though my being inspired has nothing to do with our mission, it's true. The chess game, the Cloisters, Noah's surprising apartment, and the invitation to Positano—it all mingles in my mind and makes me feel a little dazzled as I wave good night to Noah through the window of the cab.

Chapter Fourteen

Meg: Last-minute stroke of genius. Meet me at Color Me Mine in Tribeca at 11 a.m. Yes, it's a kid birthday party. But it's hosted by our class's one and only Hot Dad. And he's single. Boom.

Rufus: And I'm on this text thread because…? It is a known fact that I do Pilates Saturday a.m.

Meg: Because if you vote that Lanie should go, and I vote that Lanie should go, then we out-vote her ass two-to-one. Ruf, you can meet us after Pilates for cake.

Rufus: Lanie, your resistance is preemptively overruled. See you ladies 12:15ish. That cake better not be gluten-free.

I see my friends' messages as I'm getting out of the shower. I'm running late to meet Noah in Brooklyn in an hour, so I dash off an apologetic response.

Me: Sorry, y'all. Plans today. Maybe I can catch Hot Dad at the next party.

Meg: That is not how Hot Dad–physics work. If you don't

move on him at this party, a wiser woman will. Come on, Lanie! Blow off your plans so you can blow Hot Dad. Someone needs to confirm our class's suspicions of his well-endowment. I'll throw in a ceramic unicorn. . . .

Me: I can't blow off my plans. They're with Noa Callaway. Remember—the book that's five months late . . . and that all our jobs depend on?

My phone rings with a FaceTime from Meg. When I pick up, Rufus is already on the call.

"You're wearing *that* to Noa Callaway?" Rufus says, taking in my jean jacket with the fleece lining through the screen. "I mean, you look fresh, but . . . it's Noa Callaway. I would have thought BD's Fendi suit?"

I laugh to myself because, great minds, but also—I can't tell Rufus that Noah has given me something of a dress code for today's mystery adventure in Red Hook. Jeans and a "sturdy jacket."

I know my friends assume that I'm having a regular, business style meeting with Noa Callaway. One where we sit in an office with two laptops between us, a gallon of coffee, and pencils behind our ears.

"What's the status of the book?" Meg says. "Is she writing yet? Can my kids go to college or what?"

"Not exactly," I say. "We're still circling the right concept. That's what today is about." I find that I don't have to inject optimism into my voice. I truly feel optimistic. I know Noah and I have next to nothing of an idea yet, but at the Cloisters, inspiration felt near.

"I can't believe Noa Callaway has writer's block!" Meg

says, shaking her head while flipping pancakes. "Maybe she's going through menopause and can't be bothered with sex scenes? My sister's libido during menopause just . . ." She whistles the sound of a plummeting bomb. "Oh, I *need* Noa Callaway's sex scenes. The world needs Noa Callaway's sex scenes!"

"You have to fix this, Lanie," Rufus says. "Send over a gigolo!" His handsome-devil smile spreads across his face. "You know it's been done. Back in the sixties, editors probably hired sex workers for all their authors who were *blocked*."

"I'm working on it, believe me," I say. "Not the gigolo, but the inspiration. And I'm late, so—"

"Hold on," Rufus says, squinting into his phone. "Did you get *laid* last night? You look all flushed and happy."

"OMG," Meg says. "And you *did* say no to meeting the hottest Hot Dad in Hot Dad Land! You got laid! Who is he? Is he still in your apartment?"

I roll my eyes, but when I take a last look in the mirror, I have to admit they're right. I do look flushed and happy.

"I'm just excited," I say. That's the right word, isn't it? "I have this funny sense that Noa and I are close to getting somewhere great. I'm . . . flushed and happy that a new love story is about to be born." I smile at them. "Gotta go!"

"Bullshit—" Meg is calling as I hang up the phone.

⁂

Noah's instructions said to meet him in Red Hook at ten a.m., at a double-wide trailer behind the Ikea.

When I get there, in my sturdy jacket, full of questions, a woman is sitting in a lawn chair in front of the trailer. She waves like she's been waiting for me.

"Lanie, I'm Bernadette," she says, standing and sticking out her hand. She is sixty, buxom, with long, windblown, blond hair, a smoky eye, big smile, and a patch on her leather jacket that reads IRON BUTT ASSOCIATION. "You can call me B."

"You're Aunt B!" I say, remembering Noah's story about the women who had raised him.

Her smile widens. "He told you about me?" she says, in a husky twang reminiscent of Dolly Parton. "I guess that's only fair, because I've heard all about you."

"You have?"

"You're the editor. The Magic One, he calls you. Oh dang, Bernadette." She slaps her tan cheek twice. "He'll kill me if he knows I said that."

I brighten. On my best days, editing does feel like channeling magic, and it feels good to know Noah said that.

"It'll be our secret," I tell Bernadette. "So, what are we doing today?" I glance around the Ikea loading dock at the eighteen-wheelers parked there. Does Noah want to write a book about star-crossed semi drivers?

"You don't know?" Bernadette tilts her head. "Well, I'll let him explain," she says and points over my shoulder where Noah is walking toward us across the lot.

He wears torn jeans, a white T-shirt, black boots. I don't know if it's the time we spent together last weekend, or the natural course of moving on after my breakup with Ryan, but Noah looks different to me today.

Maybe it's as simple as this: For the first time, I let myself fully enjoy the sight of him. The way he ambles. How his thin T-shirt ripples a bit in the wind, revealing an unexpectedly defined chest, lean and muscular. How his hair shines in the sun. When his eyes find mine, I don't look away. By the time he reaches me, I'm a little out of breath.

"Morning," he says, his green eyes bright. "Are you ready to ride?"

"Ride what?" I say, as Bernadette rumbles around from the back of the trailer on a vintage Moto Guzzi motorcycle.

"Are you serious?" I gasp.

Tears burn my eyes. I try and fail to fight them back.

Noah's face falls. "Was this a mistake? I thought . . . after that story about your ex, I hoped you could reclaim the motorcycle for yourself. I never meant—"

"No," I say, blinking maniacally, "this is a very cool idea. I'm in."

His smile is wide, relieved.

"Do you ride?" I ask, getting an interesting mental picture. He does wear the boots well.

"Once upon a time I did," he says, "but I could use a refresher. And B happens to teach a master class."

"There could definitely be a book in this," I say, remembering the reason we're here. Making sure Noah remembers, too.

"Yeah, of course," he says. "That's the point."

"Right." Somehow the conversation got awkward. It got too close to me. We're here for professional purposes, bonus points if I learn to do a thing I've long wanted to do.

Bernadette cuts the Moto Guzzi's engine and climbs off the bike. "I hear you've got a trip to Italy coming up, Lanie," she says.

"A possible trip to Italy," I clarify.

"Well, just in case, Noah asked if I could get you ready to ride the Amalfi Drive. Better safe than sorry."

We follow Bernadette inside the trailer, which is set up like a classroom, a few desks and a whiteboard at the front, posters of motorcycles on the walls. Bernadette hands us both a liability waiver and a thick packet titled *Motorcycle Safety for Beginners*.

"For our first couple of hours together," she says, "I'm legally obligated to bore the pants off you. But after that, I'm going to light a fire under your ass."

Our morning is fifty percent Bernadette plowing through the course material for the written exam—and fifty percent Noah and I locking eyes as she takes off on wild tangents and hilarious personal anecdotes.

"I learned the hard way," she says, looking at me, "that it's a bad idea to cry on a motorcycle. No free hands for tissues. So promise me, Lanie," she says, wagging a finger, "that you'll never board your bike in a sorrowful mood."

In the afternoon, we suit up: hard-knuckled gloves, helmets, goggles. I barely recognize Noah inside all his gear, and it's kind of a shame. We leave the trailer and walk to the far side of the lot where three customized motorcycles await.

I choose the red Honda because it's smaller, easier to handle. Bernadette keeps her black Moto Guzzi. That leaves Noah with a sleek Suzuki street bike.

I mount the bike, grip the handlebars, and lean forward. A strange vibration passes through me. I've ridden hundreds of times with Ryan, but the joy of wielding a motorcycle by myself is new.

We do practice drills with the engines off. I learn how to walk the bike in neutral, how to let out the clutch smoothly, how to brake with my right hand and foot.

"Ready to fire 'em up?" Bernadette finally says.

I grin at her, at Noah.

"We're going to ride in a smooth, straight line across the lot," Bernadette says. "Ease the clutch out. Pick your feet up when you've got your balance. When you're ready, roll that throttle."

My engine hums. I put the bike in neutral, press the start button, and ease the clutch out, but my arms are shaking, not relaxed. I lift my feet and roll the throttle, but I roll it too fast, and the bike lunges like a mechanical bull.

My heart catches. Out of my mouth come curses I can't decipher. I become aware that I've lost control, and in my panic, I grip at everything that can be gripped and slam on everything that can be slammed in hopes I'll somehow find the brakes. I do—but too fast. My back wheel locks. The bike jerks to a stop and twists to the left. It slides out from under me and I hit the ground with the engine grinding into my left ankle. The pain is a fiery pop that spreads all the way up my leg.

A moment later, the bike lifts off me, and I see Noah's face over mine.

"Are you all right?"

I'm so embarrassed, I'm in shock. "How do I know if I'm all right?"

He helps me up carefully, studies me from head to toe. "You shake it out, and see what hurts. Wounded pride or wounded hide."

I'm worried about my ankle, but when I stretch it, there's only a dull pain. My jeans are shredded and a scrape bleeds through. But he's right, my real injury is a sprained ego.

Bernadette appears with a first aid kit. I roll up my jeans and clean the scrape.

"I panicked," I say.

"Fear is enemy number one on a bike," Bernadette says as Noah hands me a bottle of water. "Noah would say that's a metaphor for something or other." She playfully punches his arm. "You want to talk about panic, you should have seen him at sixteen."

"No, B," Noah says, "Lanie doesn't need to hear about—"

"The boy didn't know a throttle from a thyroid," she goes on, turning her back to Noah so he can't shut her up. "Matter of fact, he's the reason I got my certification to teach."

"You were that inspiring?" I say to Noah.

"Hell no!" Bernadette cackles. "I figured if I could teach him, I could teach a rock. Three days after I gave him a lesson, he took off on some used piece of crap for Colorado. His mama almost killed me, but he made it!"

I try to imagine Noah at sixteen, riding through the Rocky Mountains. Something twists inside me. "Why did you go to Colorado?"

"Why does anyone do crazy things?" Bernadette says. "For love."

"Her name was Tanya," Noah says, wincing at the memory. "She played volleyball and was in Colorado for a tournament. Let's just say, neither she nor her coach was impressed when I rolled into town."

Bernadette hoots. "He came back with his tail between his legs." She sighs and rubs at a smudge on her windshield. "Ah, well. Loving a human is nowhere near as simple as loving a bike. That's why Noah sticks to fiction now, and I stick to porkin' torque."

I bite back a laugh then turn to Noah, expecting him to do the same. But when he meets my eyes . . . is it two hours of riding in the sun, or is he blushing? I feel my own cheeks getting warm as Noah turns away and starts fidgeting with his motorcycle gloves like they really need his attention.

Bernadette glances at Noah, then at me. "Why don't you two take the bikes for a spin around the neighborhood while I set up the course for your riding test? A little street practice wouldn't hurt you."

"Want to?" Noah says to me.

I'm already starting my engine.

We take it slow around the neighborhood, gliding through quiet streets and back alleys. Noah knows where to go to avoid the traffic, and soon I start to see Bernadette's wisdom: This is much better practice for Italy than making circles in a parking lot.

I like looking at Noah on the bike. His olive skin glows

against his white shirt. His hair is just long enough to peek below his helmet. As my eyes travel downward, I stop myself—

I'm still his editor, and we still need a book idea. So even if Noah looks distractingly good, and even if I am now single enough to notice, I need to try, for the sake of our careers, to rein it in.

The sky is gold with late-afternoon light by the time Bernadette gives us our tests.

"Remember," she says over the rumble of the engines, "your eyes should always be where you want to be twenty seconds from now. Don't look down at where you are, only out at where you're going."

"I think that's a metaphor for something or other," I say to Noah.

I keep my eyes ahead as I demonstrate how I've learned to turn, to weave, to smoothly shift gears, and to make a short stop. It's glorious. It's exhausting. It's more fun and more challenging than anything I've done in a long time.

I roll to a stop before Bernadette. She jumps up and hugs me to let me know I passed. When she goes inside to print out the certificate I'll take to the DMV, I stand before Noah, wondering, are we also going to hug . . . or?

"Nice weaves," he says. "Very smooth."

"Yours weren't so bad, either."

My eyes catch on his lips, and I notice that one of his bottom teeth is a little crooked. It's charming. So charming I start to wonder things I shouldn't wonder, like what it would be like to touch those lips, those teeth, with my own—

Bernadette comes out of the trailer, two certificates in

her hands. "Who wants to get a celebratory beer at the Ice House—"

"I don't know," Noah says quickly, using the clipped tone I haven't heard in weeks. "I've taken up enough of Lanie's time."

"Right," I say—though if Noah hadn't shut it down, I would have loved to grab a beer with Bernadette. She's fun. And I enjoyed the insight into teenage Noah's romantic lunges, maybe a little too much.

Did Noah see me staring at his lips a moment ago? Did I freak him out? Or maybe he has plans tonight?

"Yeah, I should get back," I say.

"Next time then," Bernadette says and hands me a card with her email address. "You'd better send me pictures from Italy."

☙

"I never said that!" I insist to Noah on the subway ride home.

"You absolutely said it!" Noah laughs, his smile big and open as he leans against a framed map of the MTA. "I remember it clearly—you were storming past the gates of the zoo. I was chasing after you. You spun on me. You had your hands on your hips, your cheeks were flushed"—he's acting all of this out, badly—"you glared, and then—oh no!"

"What's wrong?"

"Don't you live on Forty-Ninth Street?" Noah points at the open subway doors, at the sign, which reads Lexington and Sixty-Third.

No way. Not possible. *I missed my stop?* I, Lanie Bloom, who has never, not once in my seven years of living in New York, not even before I knew the difference between Amsterdam and Park Avenue, ever missed my stop?

The next time these doors open, we'll be on Roosevelt Island. After that we'll be all the way in Queens. I look at Noah. A silent verdict passes between us. We bolt off the train just before the doors slam shut, and land in the station at Sixty-Third and Lex, where we double over, laughing.

"I cannot believe I did that!" I say, trying to catch my breath. "It's your fault for distracting me with your terrible impression."

"I think it's a sign," Noah says. "I think you were meant to take a sunset stroll with me through Central Park tonight."

I meet his eyes, not laughing anymore. His smile quickens my pulse.

"But you said you didn't want to get a drink with Bernadette. I thought . . . Don't you have plans?"

"I didn't want to get a drink with Bernadette," he says, still looking at me. "But I'd love to take a walk with you."

We stare at each other for a supercharged few seconds, and that's when I feel it. It's not just attraction I have for Noah. There's something between us. He feels it, too.

I should not go for a walk with him right now. I should go home and . . . is cold showering really a thing that people do?

But what if this walk becomes the moment that inspiration strikes? What if I pass on the chance to be there, because I was worried I was starting to think about Noah in subway-fantasy-material ways?

"Can I show you my favorite place in New York?" I say, pretending la-di-da, that no part of me wants to jump his bones.

"Is it the Austrian Cultural Forum?" he asks, then ducks before I can smack him.

I lead him to the Gapstow Bridge. It's cold but not windy, a rare evening where I'm wearing the exact right amount of layers. It's dusk. The light is glowy pink and enchanting. I've walked this path hundreds of times, but it's never looked as pretty to me as it does tonight. We pause at the center of the bridge and gaze across the pond.

"This is your spot?" he says.

"I started coming here when I was twenty-two, before I got the job at Peony. I'd stop here and look out at the city, and entertain my wildest dreams."

"And when you stand here now," he says, "what do you dream of?"

"You getting a book idea," I say, half joking.

"Is that—" Noah says, leaning forward, his hand shielding his eyes from the last of the sun. I follow his gaze, and I see them. The couple walking toward the pond. They're bundled up. They're holding hands. They have their picnic basket and travel table in tow.

"Edward and Elizabeth," I whisper.

He turns to me, wide-eyed. "You know them?"

"After a fashion," I say, and then—

"They do this every week." We say the words at the same time. We stare at each other, astonishment in our eyes.

"I've been watching them for years!" I say.

"Me, too." Noah sounds bewildered. "They've probably had two thousand picnics in Central Park."

We turn our attention to the couple. They've set up their picnic, put the lantern on the table. They're holding hands, just talking, as they always do before they eat.

"This is the book," Noah whispers.

I'm so hung up on the coincidence that it takes me a moment to register his words.

"The book," I finally say. "Wait. *This* is the book? *They are the book?*"

He looks at me. He nods. I clap my hand over my mouth.

"This is the book!" I shout out gleefully, my head flung back and arms spread wide.

"When I look at them," he says, eagerly, pacing the bridge as he thinks, "I see nineteen-year-olds on their first date."

"Keep going," I say.

He speaks quickly, excited. "I see the proposal a year later, and then a breakup, and then a second proposal. A wedding one parent can't attend. Children underfoot. I see the kids grown up and moved away. I see betrayals, hailstorms, poems scrawled in birthday cards. Pets. Cold chicken. Trips to the in-laws', lean years, and Saturday matinees."

"In other words," I say, "the full rhapsodic spectacle of life."

He looks at me, his eyes a potent green. "Exactly."

A shiver passes through me.

"How do they meet?"

Noah tilts his head. "That's the question, isn't it?"

Our eyes lock again and I smile because I love this idea, because he can write it, because it will be beautiful. And worth the wait.

We did it. Against all odds, we found an idea. We should be celebrating—and yet . . . I feel an unexpected pang in my heart. Noah's words at my apartment come back to me—his final condition that, once we agreed on a concept, I'd leave him alone to write it.

Which means it's the end of our Fifty Ways adventures. The end of our newly enjoyable in-person hangs. Noah has eight weeks to write a book . . . and I have eight weeks to wait for it.

This is fine. This is good. This is what I wanted. Then why does it feel bittersweet?

"Isn't it funny?" I say. "We've both been watching them all these years. . . . Do you think we ever passed each other in the park? Maybe on this very bridge, without knowing it?"

"Well," he says, glancing over his shoulder toward the towering high-rise on Fifth Avenue.

And I get it. The Gapstow Bridge, the Pond, Edward and Elizabeth—each is a piece of Noah's penthouse view.

"Would you like to see my office?" he asks.

⚓

The elevator door opens onto the most beautiful library I have ever seen. The smell of books is musty sweet. Three walls are made entirely of mahogany bookshelves, displaying a dazzling array of books. The other wall is a giant, single-paned window that looks out on Central Park at night. It's the view I've always imagined for Noa Callaway. It's perfect.

"This is a little different from your studio," I say.

"I bought it after *Ninety-Nine Things* was published," he says. "Terry got it in her mind that I needed to invest in something, but I didn't want to move out of Pomander Walk. Buying this office was our compromise."

My eye is drawn to the massive wooden desk, upon which sits the only photograph in the room. In it, Noah's barely twenty, grinning as he sits on a floral-print couch surrounded by three middle-aged women. One is kissing his cheek, and I recognize her as a younger Bernadette. Another appears to be giving him a noogie. I'm amazed to realize it's Terry. I didn't recognize her at first, because she's actually smiling. A third woman sits next to him, holding his hand. She and Noah have the same eyes.

"Is that your mom?"

He nods, sadness coming into his expression. "That's Calla." Then he nods for me to follow him to the window.

We stand side by side before a telescope. I can see the Gapstow Bridge. The city sparkles with lights coming on across the park. The moon is rising over midtown. For as much time as I've spent down there on the ground, it's a completely different view up here.

"What do you think?" Noah says.

"It takes my breath away."

"I meant the book idea," he says with a smile.

I turn to him, my heart racing. "I meant the book idea, too."

It's true, but it's not the only thing leaving me breathless at the moment.

"I want to write something you're excited about," Noah says. "Something you'd want to read, even if it wasn't your job."

"I'll read anything you write," I tell him, putting my editor's voice back on. "But, if you can write this book in the next eight weeks, I'll have the added bonus of it still being my job to read it, too."

"I can," Noah says with such easy confidence, I let myself believe him. "And now you can say yes."

"Say yes?" I ask.

"To Italy. The launch. I'll get the manuscript to you before you leave. You can edit it in time to celebrate with a glass of champagne on the plane." He turns to me. We're standing very close.

"How will you celebrate?" I ask.

"I have my ways."

"But what if—"

"If the book falls apart," he says, "and you need to cancel, I'll take the blame for it with the Italians."

I know that should have been what I was thinking. But in the space of two seconds, I imagined planning this trip then canceling it, and it was my heart, not the Italians', that felt broken.

Don't break my heart, I want to tell him, but that would be weird, right?

"Can I ask why it matters to you that I go on this trip?" I say.

"Because Positano is part of your story," he says. "You should go see what it means. If this were a novel, Positano would change your life."

"If this were a novel, I'd edit that last line out," I say, our faces just inches apart. "The foreshadowing's too on the nose."

Noah smiles his slow, luxurious smile.

"And I would beg you to keep it in," he says, "at least until you read the last chapter."

"And I'd say, then you'd better get writing."

Chapter Fifteen

"NEXT UP IS OUR SUMMER NOA CALLAWAY TITLE," Patrisse, our marketing director, says into the microphone at Peony's April sales conference.

It's been three weeks since Noah and I took our fateful walk in Central Park, three weeks since we landed on the brilliant idea for his eleventh love story. Three weeks of intensely productive writing time—I hope. And three weeks since I started planning my trip to Positano.

My plane tickets are booked. I'm flying into Naples in just over a month. Noa's Italian publisher is treating me to a suite at Il Bacio hotel, and Bernadette has agreed to give me a few more riding lessons to prepare me for the Amalfi Coast highway.

Noah and I haven't talked or emailed or played online chess since I left his office that Saturday night, and the silence between us has felt *big*. But every time I've wanted to reach out to him, I've reminded myself of one simple fact: My livelihood relies on him turning in this book. We both need him to focus every ounce of his energy on writing fast and strong.

I also didn't tell him about today's sales conference. For years, I watched Alix tear her hair out over Noa Callaway's strong opinions on her presentations, the edits Terry would send—sometimes up until the moment the meeting began. Noa had dogmatic thoughts about everything, from the cover direction to the tagline on the ad campaign, from the distribution of advance reader copies to the phrasing of catalog copy. But until that manuscript is delivered, Noah needs to tunnel his vision on Edward and Elizabeth's love story.

In the meantime, I'll handle the rest.

Up at the podium, Patrisse's clicker isn't working, so the PowerPoint presentation stays stuck on the previous slide—the glossy, fully designed cover for a new book called *The Bed Trick*. It's one of Emily Hines's big summer titles, and the in-house buzz is buzzy.

When Patrisse finally advances the slideshow, the contrast is stark. All of Peony's upper management division now stares at a white screen with simple black font that reads only:

CALLAWAY TITLE AND COVER TO COME.

My stomach drops. My thinking had been that this is Noa's eleventh book with Peony. We are literally pros at publishing Noa Callaway by now. Our robust Callaway marketing and publicity plans are well-oiled machines, tweaked only slightly each year, based on the content or theme of the new book. I'd hoped I could ride on Noa's previous coattails today, even with little actual material to show the team.

That might have been true . . . if this book weren't already almost six months late. I see now the doubt in my colleagues' faces. I see they fear the worst—about the manuscript, and about my role in publishing it.

I feel them turning to look at me. Even Meg is grimacing. When Alix was editorial director, we always had a title, a fantastic cover, and an edited manuscript by the time sales conference rolled around.

I've delivered sales conference materials for all four of my other titles on our summer list. I've approved the plans for the books of my entire team. I am not an abject failure! Only a failure with the one book that everyone's actually counting on.

Aude had been horrified by the paucity of Noa Callaway materials I'd given her to distribute before today's meeting. She'd muttered in French for half the morning. I kept hearing the word *disgrâce*. Maybe Aude should have become Noa's editor—maybe she'd have excised the manuscript from him already.

"We know Lanie will get the manuscript out of Noa . . . eventually," Patrisse says at the podium, and the room laughs uneasily. "Until then, we're moving forward with our standard, successful plans for marketing Noa's books across all platforms. Let's consider this a developing story, shall we? Unless Lanie has news for us?"

My chair squeaks as I stand up. This wasn't planned, but I can't walk out of my first sales conference as an editorial director looking like I don't know what's going on with our company's biggest book. I've been running through my conversation with Noah on the Gapstow Bridge for weeks. I remember everything he said.

"We have a working title," I announce on a whim, locking

eyes with a suddenly perked-up Sue. *"Two Thousand Picnics in Central Park."*

I know as soon as it's passed my lips that it's a knockout title. There are murmurs in the conference room.

"I can run with that," Brandi, our cover designer, says, making notes in her tablet. "With Callaway's name on the cover, it sells itself."

"It's going to be a very special book," I promise the room. "It's a love story spanning fifty years. And the characters?" I smile, picturing Edward and Elizabeth holding hands across their picnic table. "They're incredible."

"When are we getting the manuscript?" Sue asks, knowing I can't dodge the question in front of the whole company.

"May fifteenth," I say as confidently as I can. *Just in time to keep my promotion.*

"You're certain?" she asks. "That's already pushing our production schedule to its limits. If we have to move to fall, that will change the budget considerably—"

"It would be a nightmare," Tony from finance calls at the back of the room.

"You'll have it," I vow. My heart is racing. I sit back down.

As Patrisse moves forward to the next slide, I pull out my phone under the conference table, and compose the email I've been reluctant to send.

From: elainebloom@peonypress.com
To: noacallaway@protonmail.com
Date: April 13, 11:51 a.m.
Subject: Edward and Elizabeth

Are they finding their way?

From: noacallaway@protonmail.com
To: elainebloom@peonypress.com
Date: April 13, 11:57 a.m.
Subject: re: Edward and Elizabeth

I was just about to write to you!
     They're coming to life.
     Could we talk through the character arcs? I'd love
your thoughts before I get too deep.

I pore over the twenty-seven words of Noah's email. Ex-
clamation point after the first sentence—always a good sign!
And he doesn't seem bothered that I breached our agreement
and made contact. But "before I get too deep," suggests that
he's not yet deep in the writing. Just how un-deep is he? Ten
thousand words? Two fifty? And the use of the word *love* . . .
     After sales conference adjourns, I race back to my desk,
pick up the phone, and dial Terry, telling myself I will *not* take
any of her guff today.
     "Hey . . ."
     It's Noah's voice. It sounds softer. Or is this just the way
he speaks on the phone? It's our first time.
     "Oh," I say. "Hi. I thought I'd have to go through Terry.
You've never answered this phone before."
     Is he in his office? At that desk? Looking out at that view
of Central Park? What's he wearing? What's he drinking?
Does he have writing snacks?

"Terry's at the dentist."

"Well, that's lucky. I mean, not for her dentist. I mean . . ." Is this what happens to me when I don't talk to Noah for three weeks? I turn into a nervous wreck? "You wanted to talk?"

"I do. I want your opinion. I was hoping we could meet, but then . . ." He pauses. "I got a call from my mom's doctor, and I need to go see her. I'm catching a train this afternoon. I'll be back Sunday, if that works for you—"

"Do you want company?"

There's a pause. "On the train?" Noah says.

He sounds surprised but not necessarily intruded upon, so I persevere.

"A train's as good a place as any for us to talk about your characters," I say. "Right?"

"You'd ride the train down to D.C. with me, just to talk about the book?"

Now I'm fairly certain that Noah Ross sounds a little bit touched.

"Well, you know," I say, "interesting things happened the last time we were on a train together." I smile at the memory of Noah pulling out that Swiss Army knife, breaking into Ryan's brownstone. "I could even throw in a tuna sandwich with onions, or something equally pungent?"

"If you meet me at Penn Station in two hours," Noah says, "I'll bring *you* the best egg drop wonton soup you've ever had."

"Well, I'm not going to tell my friend Meg's mother that you said that, but I will meet you at Penn Station."

I'm grinning as I hang up the phone.

❧

"Say goodbye to editing," Noah says as I open the soup. "Because these wontons are about to blow your mind."

We're pulling out of Penn Station with our laptops open on the table between us and way too much Chinese takeout for two people. Not surprisingly, the other passengers have given us a wide berth—empty seats abound. They're probably jealous.

I swirl the Styrofoam container, give it a deep sniff, and then a long, delicious slurp.

"I pronounce this soup . . . the second best in the land," I say solemnly.

Noah clutches his heart. "My world is shattered."

"Speaking of your world," I say, "what's your character conundrum?" I want to make sure we cover everything during the three hours we've got together before Noah gets off the train to see his mom. Then I'll turn around and take the three p.m. Acela back to New York. It's a little absurd, and that's what I like about it.

He sits up straighter, brings his fingers to rest on his keyboard. His dark hair falls over his eyes, and I bank the image of Noah Ross in work mode.

"Usually," he says, "I start by asking what my characters want, and then what stands in their way of getting it. That how I get to know them."

"Sure. Writing 101."

"But the structure of this book is so different," he says, "I can't rely on a single guiding desire to propel the characters for five decades. I know Elizabeth is a doctor. I know Edward is a poet. I know what they look like, and how they walk, and what they eat for breakfast—"

"Ooh, what's on the menu?"

"Cornflakes and a quartered orange," Noah says. "At least, until Edward turns fifty. Then he learns to cook."

"Took him long enough."

"My problem is," Noah says, "since they already have each other, what else do they want?"

I think about his question. In life and in fiction, most people come to be defined by their obstacles. What they overcome and what they don't. Summiting the mountain often reveals an unexpected world. It makes me think about my own obstacles recently—with Ryan, and with Noah—and how they're changing what I thought I wanted.

"Maybe you need to ask yourself how they imagine the rest of their life," I say. "Then you could explore the scenes where they get close to that life. And the scenes where they fall short. Their love story might be the opposite of what they planned," I say. "That would be the fun of it, proving themselves wrong. Finding beauty in their missteps."

"I like that," Noah says. "And it works, because I think he's mercurial. Someone who can still surprise his wife, even decades into their marriage."

"Learning to cook at fifty would surprise me, too," I say. "And if she's a doctor . . ." I trail off. I find myself thinking of my mother. "She's meticulous, ambitious, generous, and stubborn."

Noah looks up from his computer to me. "What does she

wish for? When she stands on the Gapstow Bridge and lets herself dream big?"

I close my eyes. What did my mother want? I used to think it was to set the bar high for everyone she loved, to give us something to reach for. Recently, I see it differently. I don't think her final words to me were a gauntlet, but an expression of her faith. I think my mom *already* believed that I could really, really love someone—because she'd shown me how, by loving me that way in the ten years we had together. I think her words were a parachute, tucked away but always there, ready to catch me when I'm ready to leap.

"More," is what I tell Noah. "She wants more time. More memories. More laughter. More little moments you don't think you'll remember but you do. She doesn't want it to end. She wants more of what she already has."

Noah's typing like Rachmaninoff. He types for several minutes without pause. "This is what I needed." When he looks up at me, his eyes are bright and excited. "I don't know how you did it, Lanie, but you got me writing again."

"Duh," I say. "It was my Fifty Ways list."

"That must be it." He gives me a look I can't quite decode.

I take a second egg roll. "These are phenomenal, by the way."

He smiles, and takes one, too, and we chew happily for a moment. The mood seems right to mention sales conference that morning.

"So . . . I floated a title to the team today. . . ."

Noah's brow furrows in alarm, a look I haven't seen on him since our early days.

"I'm sorry," I say, "I should have checked with you first, but I was in the hot seat at a meeting and, honestly, the room loved it. I think it's pretty good."

He shakes his head. "I already have a title."

I brace myself. It's been well established that Noa Callaway sucks at coming up with titles.

"It's *Two Thousand Picnics in Central Park*," he says.

I exhale, laugh, then make a mind-blown motion with my hands. Noah grins.

"Yours, too?" he asks. I nod. "Well, that's a first! With Alix, it was always war."

"I remember. One of my first acts as her assistant was to book her a weekend at some New Mexico retreat so should could eat peyote and come down after the *Fifty Ways* title showdown."

"*That's* where she went?" Noah laughs.

"Around that time, I started picturing you looking like a young Anjelica Huston," I say. "You had your gorgeous side. And your witchy side."

I expect him to laugh, but Noah looks down at his hands.

"Not an Anjelica Huston fan?" I ask.

"It isn't that," he says. "I wish you hadn't gone so long not knowing the real me. It would have saved us a few bumps."

"It's okay," I say. Because it is—now. But Noah's right, it was choppy there for a minute. "Though I have wondered . . . why are you so sealed off, even from people at Peony?"

"When Alix bought *Ninety-Nine Things*," he says, "she wanted to keep my gender in the background. We pulled it off because, back then, no one had heard of me. By the time I signed my second contract, there was so much money involved, Sue insisted on the NDAs."

I had always thought the anonymity was Noa Callaway's personal preference. But of course, it makes sense that it was Sue.

He looks at me. "I wanted to come clean to you at the first chance. Sue didn't like the idea, but—"

"You went over her head?"

He nods.

"Noah?" I say tentatively, feeling out my question like the first step into the ocean. "Is there a part of you that wants to come clean to your readers?"

"It's too late." He shakes his head. "I don't want to disappoint them. I also don't want to stop writing."

"No one wants you to stop writing—"

"I have a feeling some people would enjoy a public come-uppance," he says in a way that lets me know he's given this some thought.

"What if we got out ahead of them," I say. Meg has pulled off mightier miracles. "We could plan a campaign around revealing who you are. We could coordinate it with this book's release. . . ."

I trail off because my mind is whirling. This dilemma has a moral aspect, and it has a business aspect. In the grand scheme of things, a man publishing novels under a woman's name registers low on the evil scale. But these books have been so successful that maintaining the secret *feels* manipulative, like we're trading on a lie. I also have a fiduciary responsibility to my female-owned-and-operated publishing company. And I need a job to live. But what if I could bring the moral and the business aspects together? What if honesty proved to be profitable?

I realize then that Noah hasn't said anything, and his posture has grown rigid. I ease off, telling myself it is enough, for now, that Noah has a book idea. That he's writing rich, compelling characters. That he plans to finish a draft in a month.

We can take on his pseudonym and gender identity in the next breath.

But still, as the train speeds on toward Washington, I feel good to have planted this seed. And reassured to know that Noah doesn't relish the fortress of his pseudonym.

"Can I ask you something unrelated?" I say.

"Please," he says.

"How's your mom?"

He takes a moment to answer. "The disease is progressing faster than we hoped. The doctor and I need to revise our plans, to prepare. We could have done it over the phone, but I'm her only family. I need to do everything I can."

"I was ten when my mom died," I say. "I can't imagine being responsible for decisions about her care."

"Would you . . ." Noah's eyes meet mine and hold them. "Never mind."

"What?"

"I was going to ask if you'd like to meet my mother. I think she'd like you, and, to be honest, I could use a friend there with me. If not, I understand, you've already taken so much time today—"

"I'd love to," I say. I'm flattered that he thinks his mother would like me, and that he wants me there.

"Really?" He smiles. "It wouldn't take long. I'd get you back to Union Station for a later train. I don't know how she'll be today, of course. Some days are better than others."

"Yes," I tell Noah. "I'd be honored."

❧

Calla Ross's apartment at the Chevy Chase House is small and neat, roughly the size of Noah's studio in Pomander Walk. It smells like lemons and clean sheets. I wait there alone while Noah and his mother meet with the doctor in the care center down the hall.

There's a La-Z-Boy, a double bed, a TV tuned to reruns of *Jeopardy!*, and several half-completed knitting projects strewn across the couch. The most prominent feature in the room is a large white bookcase near the window. It is filled exclusively with Noa Callaway books. His mother has *all* the foreign editions—the Turkish *Ninety-Nine Things*; *Twenty-One Games with a Stranger* in Hebrew; even the brand-new Brazilian edition of *Two Hundred and Sixty-Six Vows*. I take it off the shelf and study the cover, so different from Peony's punchy graphic design. There aren't this many Noa Callaway titles in my office, or in Noah's library on Fifth Avenue.

A queasy feeling comes over me, and when I face it, I know it's envy. I'm envious of this simple presentation of a mother's pride. Of all the things I miss about my mother, a sense that she'd approve of me is what I crave the most.

There's a knock at the door. When I turn around, I see Noah pushing his mother in a wheelchair through the threshold. Calla is thin and frail, but the similarities between mother and son astonish me. She has Noah's eyes—not just the bright green color, but the same shape and twinkle and intensity. Her hair is curly like his, though long and a silvery gray. He got his nose from her, too, and the same slow, cautious smile, which she is giving me right now.

I put my hand in hers. "Mrs. Ross."

"Call me Calla, honey."

"It's nice to meet you, Calla."

Noah sits on the couch facing his mom. I put the Brazilian edition back on her shelf and join him.

Calla nods at the books. "My son loved these stories growing up."

I glance at Noah, unsure how to respond. His face gives away nothing, and my heart goes out to him. As much as I've lamented not getting an adult relationship with my mother, I can't imagine her forgetting me.

"I love them, too," I say.

Calla smiles at me more broadly now. "Which one is your favorite?"

I lean in closer, drop my voice. "I hear Noa Callaway is writing a new book. It's supposed to be the best one yet."

"Did you know that?" Calla asks Noah. "A new book from Noa Callaway!"

"I'll believe it when I see it," Noah says, his eyes on me.

"My tender boy," Calla says. "I worry for you. Love is never so easy as it is on the pages of a book."

"Mom," Noah says, his tone half tease, half earnest plea for her to stop. "Bernadette embarrassed me enough in front of Lanie last month. Let me keep a little dignity, if you can."

I look at Calla, but when I see the blankness in her expression, I understand she doesn't remember who Bernadette is. I think back to the picture in Noah's office, when they'd all been young and smiling and well. I look to Noah, wondering what he's thinking, but he's looking away.

"That's nice, dear," his mother finally says, her tone more distant now. "Have you had breakfast yet? I put the cornflakes on the table."

❧

An hour later, we're back at D.C.'s Union Station, and our rapport feels different, like we've come through something together. Noah will stay the night in D.C., but first he's walking me to my train. He signals for me to wait as he slips inside a newsstand. A moment later, he returns, a bottle of water and two peppermint patties in his hands. He tucks them in the tote bag slung over my shoulder.

"How did you know I love these?" I say as we walk down the stairs to the quay. The train's already boarding. I wish we had more time.

He scratches his chin. "I believe it was our email exchange on the afternoon of October twenty-third in the year twenty—"

"Okay, wise guy—"

"You told me once, and I remembered."

"Because we've been friends," I fill in what he'd been about to say, "for seven years."

"And counting."

We stop before the train. Noah turns to me and meets my eyes. We're standing close enough that I get a little dizzy.

"Thanks for today," he says. "I hope it wasn't weird for you?"

"Not at all." I want to thank him, too, but the words don't feel right. I enjoyed today. Meeting Calla Ross was unexpected and illuminating. It felt profound to see Noah with her, the intimate family they make.

He seems tired, and I understand. I remember how much I slept the year I lost my mom. He has a hard road ahead of him with Calla's care, and I want him to know I'm here.

I step toward him, put my arms around him. My face presses to his chest. I exhale when I feel his arms around me. He's warm and firm and somehow not at all what I expected. Maybe it's just the way he holds me back that takes me by surprise. Like it's natural. Like we've done all this before. It leaves me breathless, and I realize I don't want to get on that train.

What if I stayed? What if—

"All aboard," a voice calls from the train.

"Good night, Lanie," Noah says against my ear as the conductor blasts the horn. "Thanks again."

Our arms fall away from each other. I turn from him reluctantly, and board the train.

Chapter Sixteen

WHEN MEG COMES INTO HER OFFICE ON THE MORNING of May 15, she flips on the lights, then jumps at the sight of me, curled in the fetal position on her zebra-print love seat.

"Cool if I hide in here for the next six to eight hours?"

"Sure thing," she says, tossing down her raincoat and purse. "Who are you hiding from? Are Aude's sisters in town again?"

I shake my head.

"Oh, that's right!" Meg's eyes widen. "It's motherfucking D-day for Noa Callaway!"

"Every time I hear footsteps," I say, "I think it's the Brinks messenger coming at me with that metal briefcase. The suspense may literally kill me."

Meg powers up her computer, sipping a very large mocha from the café across the street. "Just think, by tonight at six o'clock, you'll be curled up with Alice, reading the manuscript, swooning with delight, all your worries dissolved. But you'd better read fast, because Mama's coming over after *Goodnight Moon* to drunk pack for Italy with you."

I sit up on her love seat. "Meg, I have a confession."

"You don't want to drunk pack together?"

"It's not that."

She's checking her email, not entirely focused on me. "Is it about Noa Callaway?"

I get up and close the door to her office. I come back to sit across from her, clasp my hands together on her desk. Now I have her attention.

"Uh-oh," Meg says. "Is she . . . not delivering a manuscript for summer?"

"She is not delivering a manuscript for summer."

Meg spits out her sip of mocha.

"*He* is delivering a manuscript for summer," I say.

Meg wipes her mouth. "Wut?"

"Noa Callaway is a man. Like, anatomically. Facial hair, Adam's apple, the works." I make some gestures with my hands. "And you can't tell *anyone* I told you."

Meg bursts out laughing, waves me off—then freezes. "Oh sweet lord, you're not kidding. How? What? When? *Who!*"

I stand up, pace the room. "His real name is Noah Ross. I only found out three months ago. Right after my promotion. Which Sue kept saying was provisional, so I couldn't tell you until I got the manuscript. But now, well, here I am. Assuming he does deliver, assuming it's good—I might want to explore what it would look like to tell his readers."

"I understand," she says, putting up a hand. "Complicity, the patriarchy, et cetera."

I nod. I feel increasingly committed to telling the truth, to showing Noah's readers what I've seen in him. "Can you help?"

I look at Meg, needing hardened, streetwise, Meg-like reassurance. But she is pressing her button in the hollow of her throat, trying to calm herself down.

"Should we take a cleansing breath together?" I ask.

"Let's do that."

We both inhale deeply. We let it out. We repeat. And soon, Meg gets a focused look in her eyes.

"Let's start with the publicist's first question," she says. "What is he actually like? Is the guy playing GTA in his mother's basement with a boa constrictor and a sack of Doritos? Is he a trench coat flasher? Does he torture dogs? Because my powers of spin are only so strong. . . ."

How to describe Noah Ross? How to sell him to Meg as an asset? Over the past three months, Noah has shown me so many surprising sides of himself, I don't even know where to begin. Should I tell her about the motorcycle lesson? Our co-felony in D.C.? Calla Ross's bookshelf in the assisted living home? Should I tell her about Javier Bardem eating sushi? Then I realize, Meg's met him before.

"He's Man of the Year."

"No. Way." Meg squeezes her eyes shut. "You are messing me up right now."

"I couldn't tell you. I *still* can't tell you."

She opens her eyes. "But everything is making much more

sense. *That's* why he was at the launch that night. *That's* why you hid from him at Emergency Brunch. You don't secretly want him—you secretly work with him!"

"Well, yes."

It's funny she put it that way, because it's not that I actively *don't* want Noah Ross. Especially this past month, when we've barely corresponded and haven't seen each other . . . let's just say I've had a couple of very stirring dreams. But I can't tell Meg this—not right now. Her throat button can only handle so many pushes per hour.

"Lanie, does *he* want to go public?"

"We're . . . in conversation about it," I say. There have been a couple of emails from Noah, feeling out the particulars. Would we leak it to the press? Would he write an editorial? Would the two of us give interviews? Together? How close to publication should such a thing take place? And with what tone? What would be the rip cord if everything went to hell?

I've played it casual, optimistic, and slightly vague in my responses to him. The truth is, I need Meg to brainstorm a strategy with me. And then there's Sue . . .

"What about Sue?" Meg asks.

I look away, do some thumb twiddling. "You know, I think she's sort of interested in keeping things status quo. . . ."

Meg snorts. "You'd need to leverage her with a killer manuscript."

I nod.

"And Noah needs to want this for himself. No equivocating. If that's the case, *and* you've convinced Sue not to fire us all, I think we could spin a story to the press." She raps her nails on her desk, thinking. "What we wouldn't want is the *Post* scooping it first—the headline would kill us."

"*'Dude Writes Like a Lady.'*"

"*New York* mag would be good, or we could see about Jacqueline covering it for the *Times*. We'd have to get Patrisse involved for marketing."

I give her a cross-desk hug. "Thank you, Meg."

"It will be a giant effing headache," she says, slurping her coffee with a shake of her head. "Let's just pray this book is good enough to ride it out."

My phone buzzes with a text from Aude: Guess what arrived? Attached is a picture of the metal Brinks briefcase sitting on my desk, with a mason jar of golden tulips atop it.

"I'll do more than pray," I say, and flash my phone at Meg before sprinting back to my desk.

❧

My calls are held. My door is locked. My email set to OOO. The rain out my window is a bonus, as my noise-canceling headphones pipe in soothing river sounds.

I light a Diptyque candle, dim my overhead lights, and pour a cup of rooibos tea from the giant pot I brewed. Altogether, my first-read setup is something close to bliss. I'm ready to leave this world, with all its anxieties, and enter Edward and Elizabeth's:

CHAPTER TWO THOUSAND

It was sunset, as it always was for them in Central Park. The caviar glistened in its tub as Edward skated a blini across the top and fed the first bite to his wife.

"Happy anniversary, Collins." His pet name for Eliza-beth was her maiden name; it was how they were first intro-duced, and over the years it had stuck. "Here's to fifty more."

"Do you believe your life passes before your eyes when you die?" Elizabeth asked, dabbing her napkin to her lips. They had been discussing their mortality since their first date. Her husband was a poet, after all. But recently the timbre of the conversations had changed. Her sister had died the month before. His oldest friend, Theo, had passed that spring.

"I hope it isn't only a flash," Edward said. "I'd want to taste the caviar." He leaned toward her. "And your lips."

How could fifty years of kissing the same man still evoke that stir within her? The answer was that it hadn't always, not every single time. There were kisses given for the children's benefit—see how steady Mommy and Daddy are? There were kisses on ballroom stages, after one of them gave a speech ac-cepting an award. There were kisses one whole summer when she might as well have spat in Edward's face. But that was decades ago by now. And today, at seventy-seven, the most surprising thing of all: He could still kiss her in Central Park and make her want to take him straight to bed.

"Which of our picnics would you most like to experience at the end? With all your senses."

"You want me to list my favorite of our picnics? We'll be here all night."

She sipped her wine and smiled at him. "I'll cancel my other plans."

He took another bite of blini and gazed across the Pond, where a lovely young woman jogged across the Gapstow Bridge. "All right, you want my favorites? We could start with last week's picnic."

"Is that because your memory is going?" Elizabeth teased.

He took her hand across the table. "It's because of the red dress you wore."

When I come to the end of the first scene, I let out the breath I didn't realize I'd been holding. I love how Noah chose to open the novel with this prologue set in the present before we zip back in time to how they met.

I'm also relieved by his characterizations. I'd been nervous he might turn *my* Edward and Elizabeth into a couple I didn't recognize. But from this opening scene, the lovers I've long admired feel true. They read like the people I'd hoped they would be, as vibrant on the page as they've always seemed to me when I've marveled at them from the Gapstow Bridge.

And, hold up . . . did he give me a cameo on page one?

I smile, reading on, expecting the next scene to deal with a much younger Edward and Elizabeth.

Instead, Chapter One Thousand Nine Hundred and Ninety-Nine takes place only a week before the previous chapter. It's brief and told from Edward's point of view, and he really does like that red dress. I read ahead quickly, curious about the structure. Soon I realize what Noah is doing.

He's writing their story backward.

As a reader, this thrills me. As an editor, it scares me. It will be one hell of an ambitious undertaking to get the story to hang together right. It's like diving backward off a cliff into the ocean. It requires faith—and deep enough water.

I read on, drawn into the story. Out my window, the light fades to evening as I experience Edward and Elizabeth's love in reverse. Grown children become pregnancies, then glimmers in the lovers' eyes. Notable careers give way to apprenticeships and amateur mistakes. There's a summer Edward and Elizabeth spend every picnic fighting. Reading this era from finish to start, I find such beauty in how they lean on love to forgive each other, even before I know the nature of the betrayal. Noah has included some of Edward's poetry, and I'm touched to find inspiration taken from my own grandfather's rhymes. There's a racy scene in the back of a taxi. Another—even hotter—in a beachfront hut in Mexico. I know I'm alone in my office, but I blush reading them, my mind unable to resist casting Noah in Edward's role.

Before I know it, my teapot is empty, my headphone batteries dead, and I have arrived at the last chapter. I'm almost sad to be here, but I can't wait to see how it ends—or rather, how it begins.

I turn the page.

CHAPTER ONE

The rest is blank.

Is this a typo? Did he send the wrong file? Or has Noah not written how Edward and Elizabeth met?

❧

I trek to three fancy grocery stores in the pouring rain that night before I find the red-and-white-checked picnic basket I had in mind. Now, at Zabar's, I pay dearly to fill the basket with fried chicken, dill pickles, cheddar biscuits, and a nice bottle of California zin à la Edward and Elizabeth's favorite meal in Noa's book. I throw in a bag of organic baby carrots for Javier Bardem.

A quick recap of my day: Since breakfast, I have violated my NDA a second time by confiding in Meg about Noah; I have edited the novel that may save my career, *and* fretted over the issue that may end it—Noah potentially putting his name on this book. I emailed Sue to let her know the manuscript is fabulous, and that I submitted it for ARCs. I got an immediate reply: *Congratulations, Editorial Director.* Now, instead of going home to pack for my transatlantic voyage tomorrow, I am packing a surprise picnic for Noah as a gesture of my love and gratitude for this book. The weather will ensure it's a living room picnic, but I've heard it's the thought that counts.

Huddled with my picnic offerings under my crappy umbrella, I ring his bell at the outer gate of Pomander Walk.

"Hello?" He sounds tinny through the speaker.

"It's Lanie!"

There's a pause. It feels long. Too long. Is he waiting for me to explain my presence? That would be understandable. But *how* do I explain my presence? Why didn't I call before I came?

Then, suddenly, the gate buzzes and unlocks. I dash inside and up the stairs. He meets me at ye olde streetlight in the middle of the garden. His feet are bare, his T-shirt getting wet. My mind goes back to our hug in the train station the last time we'd been together. I wouldn't say no to an encore . . .

"You're soaked," he says, and waves me to his stoop.

Once we're inside, and Noah closes the door on the storm, it's suddenly so quiet that I get the chills. All the nice things I was going to say about his book flee my mind.

"You're here about the last chapter," he says.

"I'm here because I *adore* the book!"

"You do?" He looks surprised.

"Here's a celebration." I hold out the basket. He trades me for a towel. As I dry off, I watch him open and examine the picnic. He smiles, but it's one of his cautious smiles, from our early days.

"Aren't you leaving for Italy tomorrow?"

He sounds so serious.

"I do have a packing party scheduled with some friends in about an hour," I say. "I was just . . . dropping this off—"

"I won't keep you." He's looking at his phone, typing something, which seems a little rude.

"Oh," I say. He wants me to leave. How obvious is it that

I want to stay? I should go. Right now. But—"I *was* also wondering about the last chapter . . ."

He pockets his phone, looks at me. I think I see guilt cross his face, but he's so hard to read, I can't be sure. "I'm working on it. I'll have it to you by the time you're back from Italy."

"That sounds . . . good."

I stand on his welcome mat, glancing over his shoulder at the marble table where we ate sushi and played chess like two not completely awkward human beings. It feels like an alternate reality. Where did I go wrong?

"I'll go," I say, "just . . . one more thing."

This time, when he looks at me, his eyes flash, drawing me in. The lightning bolt licks through me. The image of leaping into his arms, adding a low-key straddle of my legs, intrudes upon my saner thoughts.

"I think this could be *the one*," I tell him. "For you to go out with under your own name."

"I have a lot to think about, Lanie," Noah says, opening his front door. "Is it okay if I reach out to you when I'm ready?"

"Of course." *Tell me everything that's running through your mind. NOW.* "Totally. Take your time."

A notification sounds on his phone. He turns the screen so I can see. "I got you a Lyft," he says, taking my umbrella, holding it over me as he walks me out. "I don't want you to be late for your packing party."

"Thank you," I say. I guess he wasn't being rude on his phone before? I guess he was actually being nice. I would have absolutely stood out here in the rain like a dumbass before I remembered to call myself a Lyft. Still . . . why don't I want to leave?

Noah points out the car, helps me inside.

"Thanks for the picnic," he says. "Have a wonderful trip."

❧

"I have vodka, Veselka, and Vigo," Meg says when she shows up at my door at nine-thirty, after she's finally gotten her kids to sleep.

"A and B," I say, reaching for the booze and the bag of take-out pierogi from my favorite Ukranian greasy spoon.

"C." Rufus reaches over my shoulder to snap up the DVD of *The Lord of the Rings*. He'd arrived half an hour earlier so I could give him the lowdown on tortoise-sitting Alice while I'm out of town. And also, so he could shit-talk my packing strategy, which he called a packing tragedy. By now he's rolled up all my shirts into a tiny corner of the Louis Vuitton duffel bag BD bought in Paris in the seventies.

"Do you have your passport?" Meg asks. "Travel adapter? String bikini?"

"Locked and loaded," I say. "Right next to my new motor-cycle license."

"I am deeply concerned about this," Meg says. "It's sup-posed to be a vacation, not a stunt show. And where is the Tumi suitcase I made you buy at the sample sale?"

"Doesn't fit on a bike," I say, ignoring Meg's shudder. "But with this bungee cord, I should be able to strap the Louis

Vuitton to the Ducati's luggage rack." I give the cord a couple stretches.

"You have no idea how that works," Rufus says.

"Or that you'll need more than one," Meg adds.

"That's what adventures are for," I say and pour three shots of vodka.

"Launching your vintage Vuitton duffel into the Tyrrhenian Sea?" Rufus asks as he takes his glass.

"Trying new things," I say.

"Cheers to that," Meg says and raises her glass. "And to Noa Callaway, for turning in the book just in time for you to have a whole lot of reckless Italian sex."

"Let me get this straight," Rufus says to Meg as we clink. "You want Lanie to be careful on her motorcycle but careless in the sheets?"

"Risk/reward," Meg says and drains her glass. "Falling out of bed is only a two-foot drop."

I laugh and drink, but I find myself picturing the bed in Noah's apartment. I wish I were with him, that we were making our way through the zinfandel and fried chicken, and he was telling stories about his mom before she was sick. That we were playing chess and I was winning, or that we were both reading beside his fireplace—

I stop myself. Noah couldn't have gotten me out of his apartment faster with a can of Mace tonight. Our relationship is professional. I need to stay clear on that.

I meet Meg's eyes as we sip. We share a glance, but I can't tell if she's picking up on my cues. I want to find a chance to talk to her alone before she leaves tonight, to let her know I talked with Noah today about the pseudonym.

"Ladies," Rufus says, "*I know.*"

"You know what?" Meg says.

"I know Noa Callaway is that sexy guy Lanie was hiding from at Emergency Brunch."

"How did you know that?" I gasp.

"I didn't tell him!" Meg says.

"I've known since that day he sent you tulips. Your pheromones were glowing. So I put a few things together. I figured I'd wait for you to tell me, but I'm not going to sit here all night watching you two shoot meaningful glances over my head." He pours himself more vodka. "And people say men aren't perceptive."

"You've known all this time?" I ask. "It doesn't bother you he's a man?"

"What's the big fucking deal?" Rufus says.

"Wait a minute," Meg says. "*Pheromones?*"

"No." I wave my hands. "It's not—"

"Lanie," Rufus says in his life-coach voice. "Remember how bad you are at lying."

I scoop some cabbage onto a pierogi, take a steamy, stalling bite. "Fine," I say with my mouth full. "I want him."

Meg gasps.

"But it doesn't matter, because he does not reciprocate," I say. "I mean, we've touched exactly once. It was a hug— a good one—but it was under very particular circumstances. And then I didn't see him for a month. Tonight, when I stopped by to congratulate him on the book, it was a mistake.

He treated me like I was a door-to-door vacuum sales-person."

"Oh, you've got it bad," Meg says. "Maybe it's a rebound crush?"

"Or something. It'll fade. Italy will be good for me. I'll get some me-time, and I'll come back with my pheromones less . . . pronounced." I sigh. "Either that, or I'll die alone, and lose my job, and take all of Peony down with me."

"Oooh," Rufus says.

"What?"

"I was just thinking. The name. *Lanie Callaway.* It suits you."

"I would never change my name."

"Not even Lanie Bloom-Callaway?" Rufus says.

"Wouldn't it be Lanie Bloom-Callaway-Ross?" Meg asks.

"This is a moot conversation in so many ways!" I say as my phone rings with a FaceTime call from BD.

"What'd I miss?" BD is on her Peloton, a rainbow sweat-band around her head. "Meg told me you were meeting to-night, and then my Hinge date had to sit shiva for his ex-wife, so it turns out, I'm available."

My doorbell rings.

"That'll be Postmates," BD says. "I sent you some Van Leeuwen's vanilla. Meg told me about the *V* theme."

"What's the *V* theme about anyway, Meg?" Rufus calls over his shoulder as he goes to the door. A moment later, he returns with two pints of ice cream. "Is it to wish Lanie buon viaggio?"

Meg shrugs. "I was just craving Veselka."

"Totally pregnant," Rufus says, passing out spoons.

"Shut up," Meg says.

"So," BD says, "have we gotten to the part yet where Lanie is a free agent in southern Italy? Because those men . . . mamma mia! And we all know how she feels about chest hair. Lanie, honey, the Italian word for morning-after pill is *pillola del giorno dopo*. Say it with me—"

I bury my face in my couch pillow.

"You have two days in Italy all to yourself before the launch," Meg says. "I recommend a shit ton of room service. And maybe Pornhub."

"And journaling," Rufus says.

"And a big, fat—"

"No, BD!" we all shout.

"Swim!" my grandmother says. "There's a secret beach in Positano, a few coves south of the pier. I don't know if you know this, Rufus, Meg—but Lanie's grandfather and I stumbled upon it once, when we were young. Magic happened there."

"Maybe you should drop Lanie a pin so she can retrace your, uh . . . steps?" Meg says.

"Or thrusts?" Rufus says, snickering.

"Because if anyone could use some magic . . ." Meg says.

"Some secrets can't be told," BD says and winks at me. "Besides, Lanie's got to twirl her own linguine. Have a wonderful trip, my dear. Wear sunscreen. Drink a Campari on the rocks for me. And please, do us all a favor and don't come back without having at least one irresponsible Italian tryst!"

Chapter Seventeen

"I FELL IN LOVE WITH MOTORCYCLES ON THE BACK OF my ex-fiancé's bike," I say to Piero, my new friend from the Neapolitan motorcycle rental agency, when we meet outside of customs. "For years, I meant to get my own license, but life got in the way. Then my ex-fiancé sold his bike, which led to our breaking up, which led to me being like: What am I waiting for?"

It's eight a.m. in Italy, two a.m. back home. I had three cups of coffee as the plane was landing, and I fear it's beginning to show.

"I'm here to give this speech in Positano. But I'm also taking a few days to myself. To work through some other stuff. And I figure—what better way to do that than on a motorcycle on the Amalfi Coast?"

I pause and take a breath. Piero nods like he's only catching one out of every ten words, which is possibly why I'm finding it so easy to talk to him. He leads me out of the terminal, along the airport entrance's sunny circular drive. I pause to take my first gulp of Italian air.

It doesn't *not* smell like the arrivals drop-off at Newark, but it's also deliciously exotic. This moment marks the beginning of a long weekend of warm sunshine and winding roads, of panoramic sea views and unhealthy amounts of mozzarella. I turn my phone to Do Not Disturb so I can fully soak it up.

Piero hadn't waited while I paused to appreciate the moment. He's speed walked three lanes of traffic ahead, so I hurry to catch up. I weave between gridlocked Alfa Romeos and Vespas, around chic Italian women wielding chic Italian roller-bags. Soon I see the parking lot where my bike awaits.

"I don't have tons of riding experience," I call to Piero, "but Bernadette—she was my teacher—she said never look down at where you are. She said to keep your eyes on where you'll be. Don't you think that's good advice, metaphorically speaking?"

"May I please check the box for our most comprehensive insurance policy?" Piero asks, eyeing me over the top of his forms.

"That's a good idea."

He leads me to a carbon red Ducati Diavel. It's just what I wanted: a sleek and shiny 1260, with a hundred and sixty horsepower, ninety-five elegant pounds of torque, zero to sixty in two seconds—plus a Bluetooth sound system soon to be playing many hours of Prince's greatest hits.

"She's beautiful," I say.

"And all yours for the next three days," he says, handing me the keys. "Do you need directions? Where are you staying?"

"Il Bacio in Positano," I say and flash the portable GPS Meg slipped into my carry-on as a going-away present.

"Ah." Piero grins. "My girlfriend says that is the most beautiful hotel in all of Italy. A place for lovers."

"And self-lovers!" I clarify, mostly for myself. When he smirks at me, I add, "I didn't mean it like that. Not entirely, anyway."

Piero gives me a sidelong glance. He looks at my duffel bag and reaches into the pocket of his jeans. He pulls out a bungee cord. "Take this—"

"That's okay," I say. "I brought one."

"You need two," he says.

It takes me fifteen minutes after Piero leaves to attach the GPS to the windshield, ten more to secure my duffel bag to the luggage rack with the bungee cords, and another ten to capture a cute selfie to send BD and Meg and Rufus when I feel like coming back on the grid.

After that, it takes me ten more minutes of sitting astride the Ducati to work up the nerve to start the engine.

I tell myself that once I get on the road, I'll be fine. But when I look past the parking lot, to the sunny street leading out of the airport, I see all of Naples zipping along at a pace that puts my heart in my throat. Bernadette said never to cry on a motorcycle, but anxious tears prick my eyes.

When I said yes to Italy, I thought that by now all my problems would be solved. The manuscript is in, minus one forthcoming chapter. My promotion is official. Why do I still feel like something's missing?

I think of what Noah told me in his office the night we found the idea for *Two Thousand Picnics*. He'd said that coming here might change my life. He'd been teasing—I think—and I'd dismissed him, but don't I want it to be true? Isn't that why I'm here?

I want to touch my mother's origins. I want to feel the roots of my grandparents' love. And now I've traveled all this way, and I'm scared I won't find what I'm looking for. I'm scared I'll go home knowing nothing more about my mother or myself.

In Noa Callaway books, heroes always find their stories' meanings. But how do they actually do it? What would a Noa Callaway heroine do in my motorcycle boots today?

What would Noah Ross do?

I wish I could talk to him. I wish he hadn't been so inscrutable at his apartment the other night.

I wish that he were here.

Lanie, I tell myself, channeling Meg and Rufus, *you're in a parking lot at the threshold of the Amalfi Coast. You're scared. It's natural. Take it one step at a time.*

I put the key in the ignition. I close my eyes and think of BD. I think of my mother. I think of Elizabeth from *Two Thousand Picnics in Central Park*.

I start the engine.

The Ducati hums beneath me. I ease off the clutch and gently roll the throttle. The bike and I glide forward. There aren't many cars around, so I take my time getting acclimated, letting my heart rate slow. I make a few loops, learning how the bike responds. When I feel ready, I exit the lot—and feel a warm slap of sun on my skin.

I whoop as I merge with the traffic, keeping my eyes on the stretch of road where I want to be. I remind myself to breathe, to keep my chin up for balance, to release the tension in my shoulders. The bike wobbles as I come to my first stop in traffic. *I will not drop this bike*, I vow through clinched teeth as traffic moves again and I wobble back into motion.

I'm on a highway outside Naples. The road is long and straight. The wind is calm, the sky deep blue. I can take it easy. I don't have to be anywhere until the launch tomorrow night.

Twenty minutes in, I'm jubilant. The traffic has thinned, the Ducati corners beautifully, and I'm riding south on a winding sun-drenched road threading through some of Italy's most picturesque towns.

The air grows fragrant with springtime scents—lemon and honeysuckle, and every now and then a salty blast of sea. The hills become steep, with only an occasional guardrail. Ahead on my left, the sleeping giant Mount Vesuvius comes into view. I hadn't planned on any stops on the hour-long drive between the airport and Il Bacio. I thought I might be jet-lagged or struggling with the bike. But when I see the sign for the turnoff to the famous archeological site, I take it. I've never been one to let a good sign pass me by.

I park the bike in a dusty lot filled with white tour buses. I pay the entrance fee, grab a brochure, and wander through a maze of ancient streets.

I stand in the center of Pompeii's forum, invisible columns rising around me. I touch the stones and get goose bumps, imagining a future visitor to New York City, wandering an excavated Central Park. Could she put her hand on a remnant of the Gapstow Bridge, reach back through time, and touch my life? Could she feel what that site meant to me?

In the Garden of the Fugitives, I stop before the figure of a mother cradling her child. Her love glows from the past. When I read on a plaque that these remains were cast from the negative space left behind when the woman and her child decomposed in the volcanic ash, I press my hand against the glass. I know how much can be felt in an absence.

I pause again before two embracing lovers. The anguish in their limbs is clear. I think it's not just that they know they're dying. I think they also grieve that a third thing—their love—will die as well.

But did it die? Can't I feel it, here, right now?

I know life is ephemeral, and we only get to do it once, but some true things—like this embrace, like the best love stories—live on.

I carry this idea with me as I leave Pompeii, as I mount the Ducati again. The bike climbs along a sloping cypress-lined promenade, past terra-cotta church spires, and a vast, immemorial herb garden whose towering hedges of rosemary scent the air. A mist of fog settles over the road, so I slow down, inhaling clouds. I feel a part of everything. I feel as though the deep, disbanded past is reaching out to me with its wisdom.

It's early evening by the time I park in front of cherry red Il Bacio hotel on the gorgeous Amalfi Drive. The jet lag has begun to set in. I peel myself off the bike, give the seat a grateful pat, and exhume my duffel from the tangled bungee cords.

"Signora Bloom," the smiling young receptionist says. "We are very happy to host you for the launch of Noa Callaway's new book. I am a fan!" She flashes the Italian hardcover of *Two Hundred and Sixty-Six Vows* from the behind the desk. "Everything has been taken care of. I will show you to your room."

I follow her through an ivy-lined foyer, up a curved flight of marble steps, then a second, more private flight of stairs, which end at a large wooden door. Using a golden key shaped like a cresting wave, she opens the door to my suite.

It's heaven. I step into a living room whose opposite wall is all windows with full ocean views. There are lilies on the coffee table and a plate of plump, deep purple figs. Through a curtain of glass beads is a separate bedroom, also with ocean views, and big enough for a white tufted king bed to sit in the center of the room.

The receptionist moves around the suite, adjusting shades, turning off lamps, lighting candles, and ensuring that the prosecco, in its bucket of ice by the bed, is properly chilled.

Though she's probably accustomed to tips the size of my monthly salary, I give her ten euros and a smile. When the door clicks closed behind her, I let out my breath and pop the prosecco. I carry a glass into the world's best rain shower, then change into the silky peach hotel robe.

It's sunset, and the view out the windows is astonishing—a horizon of full blue ocean and pink-hued, endless sky. I wander out to the terrace. A warm breeze rustles by, carrying the scent of wisteria blossoming in a great urn on the terrace next door.

Two flights below, a woman in a black bikini swims leisurely laps in the hotel's infinity pool. Farther down, on the pebble beach, oversize umbrellas make multicolored rows. Bodies glisten on the sand. Sailboats dot the sea.

It's the kind of overwhelming beauty that makes me feel a little lonely. I turn on my phone to let BD and Meg and Rufus know that I've arrived.

I laugh at the selfies I'd taken earlier in the airport lot. There's one I thought was good, my face in the side mirror of the Ducati. But I see now how terrified I was. Half a day in Italy has already done wonders for my complexion, and my mental state. I'm about to snap a better photo of myself on the balcony now when an email appears on my screen.

To: elainebloom@peonypress.com
From: noacallaway@protonmail.com
Date: May 17, 7:06 p.m.
Subject: Three Things You've Been Waiting For

Dear Lanie,

I hope this finds you on a balcony at sunset, glass of prosecco in hand.

Please find herewith three things you've been waiting for. The first is an apology.

(Come on, you know you've been waiting for it.)

I'm sorry I was _____ the other night.

(I see you on that balcony, rolling your eyes. I spent twenty minutes searching for the most precise descriptor. Was I weird? Distant? Cold? Brusque? (Brusque was my top contender, and one you'd line-edit into oblivion.) Or perhaps, simply, blank? I defer to you.)

The truth is, when you came by my apartment, I was scared . . . about the other two things you've been waiting for from me. They are attached. Once you read them, I think you'll understand.

Yours,

Noah

P.S. Regardless of how things turn out, I hope someday I'll get to hear about your ride down the Amalfi Coast.

Regardless of how things turn out?

Then I read the names of the attachments. The first is titled "Chapter One." The second—"NYT Op-Ed, run date 5/18." I click on the second attachment.

BY ANY OTHER NAME
BY NOAH ROSS

You don't know me, but you or someone you love may have read one of my books. For the past ten years, I have been publishing love stories under the pseudonym Noa Callaway.

A pseudonymous writer never meets their readers. I've never had a book signing, nor bantered with a fan on social media. My publisher has managed all publicity on my books' behalf. Every six months they send me a sack of letters from Noa Callaway fans. I never read them. They're not for me. They were written to Noa Callaway, and I am only Noa Callaway when I'm writing, never anytime else.

This distance from the readers of my books has bought me an ignorance, one that I was wrong never to challenge. I thought my stories ended with their final pages; I thought it didn't matter who I was.

That changed this year when I met someone who saw through me. Who forced me to see through myself. And when I looked close at what I was doing, I couldn't sleep at night.

I am a cis white straight affluent male. My email address is noacallaway@protonmail.com. If you are reading this and you are outraged, I don't blame you. Feel free to let me know.

This op-ed and its aftermath may be the end of my career, but I can't hide behind a name any longer. I want to be honest with my readers, with whom I am finding I have more in common than I ever knew.

The other day, I sat down and read some of Noa Callaway's fan mail. I'm sorry for the slow responses, but it's only now that I know what to say:

To June: Like you, I also enjoy reading in the tub on rainy days. Thanks for your book recommendations; I'll check them out. The best thing I've read recently is a tie between Julie

Otsuka's Buddha in the Attic *and Heather Christle's* The Crying Book.

To Jennifer: It's hard to pin down what inspired Ninety-Nine Things. *I wrote my first novel out of hope, back before I ever expected to publish, or ever dreamed I'd use a pseudonym. I had never experienced the love I wrote for that character, but I wanted it to be true. I suppose I've been trying to write it into existence ever since.*

To MacKenzie: Fifteen publishers rejected my first novel before I found my home at Peony Press. Keep writing. Finish your stories. It only takes one person to say yes.

To Sharon: I'm so sorry about your husband. My mother suffers from the same disease. It's heartbreak in slow motion. You'll be in my thoughts.

And to Lanie: Your letter to me is a decade old. I'm sorry this took me so long. Wherever you are when you read this, I want you to know that I agree: I think we could become great friends, too.

With my heart in my throat, I close the email, scroll through my contacts, and press call.

"Lanie?" The voice on the other end sounds surprised. "How's Italy?"

"Meg," I breathe. "Check your email."

I forward her Noah's op-ed then wait on the phone as she reads it.

"Ohmigod," she says. "Ohmigod. OhmiGOD. Lanie, do you know what this means? *He likes you back!* That last line? That's . . . *wow.*"

"What?" I say. "*That's* your takeaway? Meg, put on your publicist sombrero. We need to make plans. ASAP. Besides, he explicitly said he thinks we could be *friends*. Has there ever been a clearer kiss-off in the history of unrequited romance?"

"Speaking as your friend," she says, "I'll agree to disagree. Speaking as Noa Callaway's publicist . . ." There's a long pause on the line. Then a sigh. "Well, as mea culpas go, it's not the worst. I'm not saying there won't be hell to pay, but ultimately, my prediction, after I do my job of course, is that there will be no *permanent* cancellation of Noa Callaway."

"Really?"

"Give me a few hours. Let me see what I can do."

"What about Sue? Should I—"

"*You* should enjoy the Amalfi Coast," she says firmly. "There's nothing more you can do from there. I'll meet with Sue today. We'll circle back later. I mean it, Lanie. Hit the pool, sip a cocktail, leave this to me."

"Thank you, Meg."

When we hang up, I'm shivery with nerves. How can I leave this alone? How can I not obsess over Sue's reaction when she reads this op-ed? How am I not going to be fired?

But . . . if anyone can handle this, it's Meg. And she's right, it *is* a good apology, as far as apologies go. I picture Noah writing it. I picture his hands on the keyboard. I picture—

Pool, I tell myself, gazing down over my balcony at its infinity in the moonlight. *Cocktail*.

Sure. But first, Chapter One.

CHAPTER ONE

Edward waited at the stone bench in Central Park, his stomach tied in knots. He had been longing for this day for two
years. He had been dreading it, too.

When he saw her—Dr. Elizabeth Collins, in her Fendi
suit, striding elegantly toward the chess house—he fought an
urge to run. If he could get out of here, he could perpetuate
the lie a little longer. But the reality of Elizabeth stopped him
cold. She was so similar to the photograph he carried. And yet
in life, the way she moved, like a ballet dancer, was so much
more vibrant than any fantasy.

He saw her looking around, for Corporal Richard Willows, of course. The tall, blond, handsome soldier whose chin
she had stitched after a bar fight two days before Willows
shipped out to Vietnam. The soldier she'd had one date with,
a walk in Central Park, two years ago. The soldier she believed she'd been corresponding with ever since. The soldier
who had died in Edward's arms during their first week of
combat.

As Richard slipped toward death—Edward would never
forget this—the man had produced a photograph and two letters from Dr. Elizabeth Collins of New York. As well as a
half-completed letter he was writing back to her.

"Tell her," he begged Edward. "Tell her if I'd had the
chance, I know I would have loved her."

Edward meant to do just that. He barely knew Willows;
they had shared a few beers over a game of chess, but that was

it. He had sat down at camp that night, shaking and filthy and starving, and attempted a letter breaking the news to Dr. Collins. He had pored over her own two letters to Willows. And that photograph. She was sitting on a picnic blanket. Smiling. Squinting into the sun.

Edward still couldn't believe what he'd done next.

He lied. He had no beautiful girl to write to back home. Had no hope of correspondence with a wit such as Dr. Elizabeth Collins. He was as lonely as any other soldier, young, and scared, and far too far from home.

He would tell her the truth in the next letter, but first, he'd try Richard Willows on. Just to see what it felt like to write to a woman like that.

Only, Edward never did tell her. And somehow two years passed, and what happened was he wrote to Elizabeth every single day he was at war. He wrote her poetry. He wrote of his childhood and his family. He told her things about himself he'd never told anyone else. He signed them Corporal Richard Willows, feeling sick with guilt—until her next letter came. And then he read her words, hungrily, and the cycle just continued. He was too amazed—by her sense of humor, her intelligence, and her spirit—to stop writing Elizabeth back.

They fell in love.

And now he had to break her heart.

"Dr. Collins," he said, rising from the table at the chess house. To be so near her after all this time—it made it hard to speak. It made it hard to breathe.

Her eyes settled on him for an instant, then passed on. Of course. She was looking for the man she loved. Not the shorter, dark-haired man before her. It crushed Edward, but he persevered.

"Dr. Collins," he said again. "You're here to meet Richard Willows?"

She turned to him again, her beauty overwhelming. "Yes. Who are you?"

"My name is Edward Velevis," he said, summoning all his courage. "Mr. Willows . . . can't be here today. He gave me a message for you. I have carried it too long. Will you please sit down?"

Elizabeth sat. She waited. She was quiet. Edward could tell she was alarmed. He must choose now or never to tell her every truth that he'd been hiding.

"Elizabeth, Richard is dead."

"No," she gasped. "He can't be."

"Richard Willows died on August eighteenth, 1968. I was with him at Camp Faulkner—"

"That's impossible! He wrote to me only last week. To arrange this meeting. Who are you? Why would you say such a thing?" Elizabeth stood up. She started walking quickly away.

Edward couldn't let her leave before he told her. "It was a land mine," he said, following her. "He died in my arms. He asked me to write to you. So I did."

Something in his tone had reached her, scared her. She turned to him. Each was on the brink of tears. He watched her understand his words. And when she did, her face twisted in horror. She started running.

He chased her like a lunatic. What else could he do? She shouted for him to leave her alone.

"*Please,*" *he begged. It stopped her running and she spun on him. He touched her wrist. A bolt of heat pulsed through him. She looked down as if she felt it, too. But when she met his eyes, hers were daggers.*

"*How dare you?*" *she whispered. It broke him in two.*

"*I know you must hate me. But please know I have loved you for two years. I love you now more than ever. And if you ever change your mind, and want to hear my side of this story, I will be here, right here.*" *He pointed at the earth beneath his feet.*

"*You're going to wait a long time.*"

"*That's all right,*" *he said, and meant it.* "*I will be here every week. At just this time. In just this place.*" *He looked down at his watch.* "*Five-thirty.*" *He gazed across the park.* "*At the north side of the Pond, right across from the Gapstow Bridge.*" *He met her eyes and tried to tell her through them that he loved her.*

"*However long it takes, Collins. If it means a chance to be with you, I'll be here every Saturday at sunset for the rest of my life.*"

The End

Chapter Eighteen

"I RECOMMEND THE OCTOPUS ALLA GRIGLIA TO BEGIN," says Noa Callaway's Italian editor when we meet for lunch the next day.

When I emailed Gabriella late last night and asked if we could talk before the launch, she suggested this open-air trattoria on Positano's sea-facing Via Marina Grande. We're sitting at a shady corner table with a prime view for people watching.

The scene along Via Marina Grande is the opposite of my hotel terrace vista. Down here, you get the sense of being nestled in the arms of Positano's craggy coastline, crammed with Technicolor houses stacked into the hills. It's the kind of cozy beach vibe I'd usually find charming—but today I'm so jittery, it's making me claustrophobic.

Gabriella studies her menu, unaware of my knees bobbing beneath the table. "And then, the smoked mozzarella tortellini con brodo di parmigiano," she says. "My six-year-old son calls it 'cheese soup of the gods.'"

I run my finger along the edge of my fork, dig my sandaled toes into the pebbly sand under our table, and listen to the bees buzzing around terra-cotta pots of sunflowers. Ever since last night, I've needed touchstones to confirm that this is not a dream, that what I read in Chapter One was real. Real words Noah Ross really typed onto a page. And really sent to me.

It was a code. A not very secret one. A writ large and gorgeous code, illuminating what our first meeting in Central Park had meant to him. And yet, if anyone else in the world had read it, they would think the scene was purely the start—or in this case, the end—of a grand and fictional love story.

I know it's more than that. It's a question: *Do you feel the way I do?*

"I do," I say aloud—then catch myself as Gabriella meets my eyes across the table.

"You do what?" she says.

"I do . . . want octopus. And cheese soup." I can't imagine eating anything, but I'm trying not to let it show. "I see a career in marketing for your son." I stop pretending to look at the menu and raise my glass of chilled Ravello bianco to clink with Gabriella's.

As the waiter sets down a tray of lemony tomato bruschetta, Gabriella stretches her long legs from beneath our table until her square-toed white sling backs nestle in the sand. She is bright and charming, with wavy red hair she constantly tucks behind her ears, a long string of black pearls around her neck, and a flowy midi dress the same turquoise as the sea. Under normal circumstances, we could be friends, but I know as soon as I tell her about Noah's op-ed, and that it's probably landing in people's *New York Times* notifications . . . right about now—our lunch will go from pleasant culinary lark to Fellini-esque firing squad.

"Now," she says, holding out the plate to offer me a slice of bruschetta, "you said there was something you wanted to discuss?"

I have to tell her. It's the decent thing to do.

The waiter sets down two plates of gorgeously charred octopus, giving me an excellent opportunity to stall. I stab an olive with my fork and look out at the beach as I chew. Everyone I see appears to be part of an amorous pair—holding hands, kissing, sharing a scoop of pink gelato, rubbing sunblock into someone else's bronzed shoulders.

If I'm hungry for anything, it's what those people out there have.

I called Noah twice last night, and both times his phone went straight to voicemail.

I remind myself that I am grappling with two (mostly) separate issues. One is the giant question of what will happen when I finally do talk to Noah. The other is my responsibility as his editor to prepare Gabriella for the op-ed.

I'll tackle the less scary one first.

"It has to do with the launch tonight," I say to Gabriella.

"Of course." She smiles, taking a tiny bite of octopus and chewing languorously. "I will tell you all about it. This is our biggest event to date. And we're very proud to pull it off. We were inspired by your version in New York, and have invited two hundred and sixty-six of Noa Callaway's biggest fans from all throughout Italy. There will be cocktails and caprese, millefoglie—which is our wedding cake, sugared almonds for good luck. A famous wedding DJ is coming down from Rome. And of course, the highlight of the evening will be you. Your speech. We were so moved by your words in the video, Lanie. We are honored to have you here to celebrate with us."

"Thank you, but—"

"In fact, there is much interest from the media, including many requests to speak to you."

"To me?"

"Of course! You are Noa Callaway's ambassador. You know all the secrets." She winks at me. "If you are comfortable, I would like to confirm some interviews with our biggest newspapers and TV stations. Everyone wants to know what Noa Callaway is really like behind the scenes. I have prepped the journalists—they know you cannot tell them, but they are Italian, so they will ask anyway! If you are happy to do the interviews, I can confirm for this afternoon, before the party?"

"Gabriella," I say as the waiter comes to whisk away our starters, setting down the most aromatic pasta. It smells like heaven in a bowl, and I wish I weren't too anxious to enjoy it. "There's something I need to tell you. Actually, it may be easiest to show you."

I take out my phone and pull up the op-ed. I place it on

the table near her wine. She takes out turquoise reading glasses from her purse and slides them on.

While she reads, I think of Noah. I think of Chapter One. The Fendi suit. The way Elizabeth shows up at the park, naïve and optimistic. The way the truth crushes her. The way she runs. And then—

If it means a chance to be with you, I'll be here every Saturday at sunset for the rest of my life.

When Gabriella looks up at me, I realize there are tears in my eyes. She puts her hand out, takes mine in it.

"Lanie."

"I'm so sorry. I think it's right that the truth come out about Noah, but I had no idea this piece was coming, that it would publish now. I didn't want to ruin your event."

"I understand," Gabriella says, swirling her wine thoughtfully. "Secrets have their own lives." She picks up her phone and types furiously. "But I'm canceling your interviews this afternoon."

I nod. Gabriella knows her market, and it may be for the best to distance myself from the Italian launch entirely—

"You'll need to save your strength for the party," she says.

"You still want me to speak at the launch?"

Gabriella sets her phone down, looks up at me, and crosses her arms. "I think you owe our readers an explanation."

"Yes. And I will do my best to give it to them." I sit up straighter in my chair. I square my shoulders. "I believe in the truth of Noa Callaway *and* in Noah Ross. I believe in this book, and the ones coming after it. I didn't come all this way to hide."

"Very well." Gabriella smiles at me, approving. "I don't think the guests will go so far as to *actually* run you into the sea, but just so you're prepared, they will expect catharsis."

⚓

With eight hours to go before a couple hundred Italian women eat me like an appetizer at an elegant party that will be livestreamed around the world, I rev the Ducati's engine and wonder which way to go. What does one do with a free afternoon on the Amalfi Coast, a yearning heart, a looming comeuppance, and a man on the other side of an ocean who won't pick up his phone?

When I see a sign on the side of the Amalfi Coast highway for the road to Castel San Giorgio, I recognize the name. I remember I'd read it's the launch site for hang gliders over the Amalfi Coast. I couldn't have planned this better if I'd tried. I wind the bike up the long medieval road and park in a pebble lot behind an ancient Greek temple.

I come upon a woman about my age, inspecting the parachutes of two gliders next to a tangle of harnesses and helmets. She has a kind face and a lime green bandana in her hair.

She waves when she sees me. "Ciao!" she calls, unleashing a torrent of Italian. Noticing my confusion, she points at me. "Mariana?"

"No." I shake my head. "I—"

"Sorry," she says in English, more slowly. "I thought you were my afternoon reservation. What can I do for you?"

"Do you take walk-ins?"

She clicks her tongue and looks down at her watch. "Usually, we are booked at least a month in advance. But today, my party is late. You are in luck. I'm Cecilia."

"Lanie."

She holds out a harness to me. "Are you ready?"

I hesitate for a moment and then step into the harness, let Cecilia tug and tighten a dozen different straps. I summon the hang-gliding scene in *Fifty Ways*, the commitment the characters make as they leap into the abyss.

They can't see where they're going, but it doesn't stop them. They have each other and the wings of love to lift them.

I look down at the wooden ramp under my feet. To call it rudimentary would be a compliment. Ten feet long, it starts in mud and ends in clouds. This is what we'll run off the edge of together.

Vertigo grips me, and I have to look away. It seems suddenly, urgently mad that anyone runs off this cliff with only a thin yellow sail between them and death.

"What do you think?" Cecilia asks me, bringing me back to the cliff. "Do you really want to do this?"

"'Life's greatest mystery,'" I say, "'is whether we shall die bravely.'"

"I love that scene," Cecilia says, securing my harness tightly at my hips. She hands me a helmet, makes sure I thread the strap through tightly. "I love all of Noa Callaway's books."

"Me too," I say. "I'm . . ." *In love with him!* "I'm Noa's editor in New York."

"No!" Cecilia squeals. "I would say I'm her biggest fan,

but my boyfriend is even more crazy for her books. Tell me what she's like in person?"

I'm relieved to know the op-ed hasn't made its way to every corner of the world yet. I think about how to answer Cecilia's question, and the words that come first feel right.

"One of my favorite people in the world," I say. I give myself goose bumps, but Cecilia doesn't notice.

"I'm in town for the launch of Noa's new book," I say. "It's tonight in Positano, at the Bacio hotel. You should come. Bring your boyfriend. I'll put you on the list."

"We will come!" she says, and tugs the last ropes tighter.

She takes my arm, leading me to the cliff's edge. Now she attaches both our harnesses to the metal inner frame of the glider.

"On the count of three, we will run together. All you have to do is not stop running. When you think you've reached the end, get braver," she explains.

"You make it sound easy."

"I don't know if it's easy," she says, "but it's worth it."

"How far is it to the bottom?"

"I'm not sure. Two thousand meters?"

There's a metal bar in front of us that Cecilia explains she'll use to steer. There's a triangular sail the color of the sun over our heads. There's ten feet of flat plank before us, and an unseen expanse of adventure beyond. Through the drape of clouds, there are mountains, villages, and sea. And the rest of my life. I can't see it yet, and I know it won't be easy, but I need to make it worth it.

I cry out as we start running, but the sound isn't terror; it's triumph. My feet pound against the wood for ten paces and then, though I feel nothing beneath me, I'm still running. On air. On faith.

A gust of wind catches our glider, and I feel both of my legs buoyed upward until my full body is parallel to the earth, like a bird's. We puncture the clouds and the glory of the coastline comes into view. A panoply of green and gold earth spreads beneath us, pastel villages and glittering blue water as far as I can see. We're flying. I have felt nothing so exhilarating in my life.

Mom, I think, *I did it. I can feel you.*

And now . . . I know what I have to do once my feet are back on the ground. I have to tell Noah. He's the one I really, really love.

"For you, Lanie," Cecilia says, turning the glider to the right with a pivot of the metal bar, "I present a special tour, of our most romantic allusions. Look to the right, and you will see Li Galli islands off the coast of Positano. This is where Odysseus resisted the sirens."

I turn to see the rocky shoreline in the distance, the waves crashing on it. It's breathtaking—and easy to imagine the sirens singing there. I think about Odysseus resisting the irresistible, lashing himself to his ship to keep from crashing, to live more life and have more joy. To make it to the place his epic meant to take him all along.

I want to tell Noah about all of this. About Li Galli islands. About lovely Cecilia and her boyfriend, the fan. About the Ducati, and the view from my hotel room, and his chic Italian editor. About how it feels to fly.

But it's more than that. I don't just want to tell Noah about these things. I want to share them with him. I want him here. I want Noah with me in the sky, where we can gaze out at the future—the golden, glorious, complicated balance of our lives.

∾

I'm halfway back to the Bacio when I spot the silver Moto Guzzi V7 motorcycle in my side-view mirror. It's a hot bike, sporty and refined—and with his vintage motorcycle boots, dark jeans, and suede bomber jacket, it's easy to imagine the driver is as sexy underneath his helmet. When I glance back over my shoulder, he revs his engine, flirting.

"Not today, signor," I mutter, wishing my life were so simple that I could lose an afternoon at a cliff-side café with an Italian stranger. But I'd be awful company, checking my phone every other minute, praying for Noah to call.

I try not to notice that the Moto Guzzi takes the same left turn I do onto Viale Pasitea. Or that he winds with me up the hillside growing steeper by the meter, and turns into the Bacio's tiny parking lot behind me.

We roll to a stop at the same time under a flowering bougainvillea vine, parking beneath the breezy archway of the hotel's street entrance.

Illicit tryst, I hear BD screaming from her Peloton back home, but that ship has sailed. I've got a speech to rewrite and careers to save. I've got a space in my heart crying out for just one man.

I climb off the bike, shake my hair loose from my helmet, fix my bangs. I'm trying to make it inside the hotel, through the lobby, and up the stairwell to my room, all without looking back at Mr. Moto Guzzi, when a familiar voice says—

"Nice weaves. Very smooth."

I stop walking. I stop breathing. I turn around slowly, trying to prepare myself for something that can't possibly be real. My heart is racing as Mr. Moto Guzzi climbs off the bike and takes his helmet off.

Noah gazes back at me, that mesmerizing look in his green eyes. The one that had me transfixed from the first time I saw him.

I feel everything at once—

Relieved to hear his voice. Bewildered that he's here. Overjoyed to see his face, his lips, his eyes, and all that shiny, tugable hair. Flushed with desire. Scared that we've messed everything up. Hungry to put my hands on him. And that lightning bolt that's always in me when Noah is around.

So this is it. This scary, inconvenient, exhilarating, stomach-tightening, I'll-do-anything-for-it feeling is finally, really, really love.

"Noah." I can barely breathe. "What are you doing here?"

He takes a step toward me. Still ten agonizing feet away. He looks so beautiful, squinting in the sunlight, shading his face with one hand.

"I forgot to tell you where to buy BD's souvenir," he says. "So I figured I'd come show you."

I drop my helmet, my keys, my purse. I run toward Noah and jump. He catches me in his arms. He holds me close. Our faces tip toward each other, our lips on the verge of what my body is screaming would become the most spectacular kiss of all time, including the Etruscan period.

"Is it us?" I whisper. "Chapter One?"

"That depends," he says. "How much of it did you want to edit?"

"Small changes here and there." I smile. "I think it might be more realistic if Dr. Collins slaps Edward after he tells her the truth."

Slowly, playfully, Noah turns his cheek to me. I lay my hand gently on his skin. It's warm and pleasantly rough where he hasn't shaved since New York. He leans into my touch. He presses his lips against the center of my palm and I shiver with how much I want those lips on mine.

"The scene is who I want us to be," he tells me. "The whole book is who I want us to be."

I rise on my toes. I move my hands around the back of Noah's neck. I press my lips to his. He meets me with tenderness, then with passion, cupping the back of my neck and pulling me closer. He tastes like cinnamon.

The seam between our bodies tightens, and it feels just like I fantasized it would—exhilarating, satiating, part-itch, part-scratch, brand new, and such a very long time coming.

"So," I say, "how'd you like to go to your first launch party tonight, Noa Callaway?"

"I'll go anywhere," he says, and kisses me again. "So long as you go with me."

Acknowledgments

With thanks to Tara Singh Carlson, who knew, among other things, that this book shouldn't be about the CIA. To Sally Kim, for the insight into Noa Callaway. To Alexis Welby, Ashley Hewlett, and the terrific team at Putnam. To Laura Rennert, strong and elegant. To Morgan Kazan and Randi Teplow-Phipps, for the party on Forty-Ninth Street. To Erica Sussman, for tortoise intel. To Maya Kulick, for The List. To Shivani Naidoo, Courtney Tomljanovic, and Lexa Hillyer, for a million city rambles. To J Minter, original pseudonym. To Alix Reid, original boss. To the Author Mail crew. To inspiring breakups. To my family, love's example. To Lhüwanda's chin. To Jason, my kosher ham, who kept after me to write this one. To Matilda and Venice, for giving me the love I write toward.

By Any Other Name

Lauren Kate

A CONVERSATION WITH LAUREN KATE

DISCUSSION GUIDE

BOOK
ENDS

PUTNAM
— EST. 1838 —

A Conversation with Lauren Kate

While you have written multiple books, *By Any Other Name* is your first romantic comedy. What inspired you to write this story?

In my twenties, I had a spectacular breakup during a cliff-side motorcycle ride on the Amalfi Coast. Friends and family have been asking me to write about it for years, but until recently I couldn't see beyond the heartbreak. I didn't want to write a book about eating Ben and Jerry's while Facebook-stalking my ex . . . delicious as that era was! So I started thinking about other aspects of this character's life—like her job in publishing—that might see her through the darkness.

When I found a professional crisis to echo her personal crisis, it made me laugh. I've never written a comedy before, but this story refused to take itself too seriously. I mean, being dumped on the most romantic trip of your life is pretty funny.

Do you feel you are like Lanie in certain ways? How did you come to craft her character?

To prepare for this book, I cringed my way through diaries from that decade of my life. The details—a woman working passionately in publishing, dating thrilling but all-wrong men, summoning friends to emergency brunches, and seeking advice from a well-dressed grandmother—were there to be lifted, but I didn't intend to make Lanie as deeply *me* as she became on the page.

Autobiography has never appealed to me. Fiction is making stuff up. But this story demanded it. Then again, if Lanie is me, she's me from a bygone era, not me now, with two kids and a mortgage. I was glad to go back and visit her.

New York City is such a presence in this story that it almost feels like a character in and of itself. Where did you pull inspiration when crafting this setting and all the specific places Noa and Lanie visit?

Like Lanie, I showed up in Manhattan with a duffel bag and a dream. I was young and broke, which cast a glamor on the city. When mere existence is hard-won, the places you visit, like the Gapstow Bridge, feel legitimately magical.

Living in a great city changes you; I've gone through a metamorphosis each time I've moved to one. Lanie is evolving because of changes in her life, yes, but also, more simply, because she's part of pulsing, vital place like New York.

What was your favorite scene in the novel, and why?

Lanie's first in-person meeting with Noa Callaway. She

goes into the scene so earnest and enthusiastic, wearing her grandmother's Fendi suit. She ends up having an existential crisis in public and throwing her career and personal life into chaos. It's IRL gone majorly awry. And after a long quarantine of online-only encounters, I can relate.

What do you feel lies at the heart of Lanie's and Noa's characters? What do you think is the true success to any relationship?
A successful relationship is at ease with the heavy and the light. I wanted to explore how Lanie and Noa(h) can have a stimulating intellectual argument one moment, burst out laughing the next, and share each other's grief in the third.

The idea of revision is also at the heart of their romance. I think for many relationships, when one or both people change, it can feel scary, undesired. But as a writer and an editor, Lanie and Noa(h) understand what's beautiful about change. They don't expect each other to stay the same as they were in the first draft. They welcome the different versions each of them will become.

Have you ever experienced writer's block like Noa? If so, how did you overcome it?
I've never not experienced writer's block, but my most profound confrontation with it came after my daughter was born. I remember driving in my car, listening to a story on the radio about a beekeeper, and weeping be-

cause I wished I could just be a beekeeper. Writing felt impossible that day. I see now that 70 percent of that was sleep deprivation, but the other 30 percent was struggling to acknowledge that I had become a new person when I became a mother.

I think this is similar to Noa(h)'s traumatic experiences. When a writer goes through a shift that apocalyptic, it can feel like you suddenly have to learn to write all over again.

Is there a certain trope in romance books that you just can't get enough of? Maybe even a guilty pleasure that never gets old?
The build-up to the first kiss always thrills me, the emotional foreplay of establishing chemistry with another person, and then seeing how long you can stretch it out before you get together. (The longer the better.) I still think about my extended flirtation with my husband—all the enchanting obstacles in our way, how we knocked them down month by month, one karaoke night or creek-side stroll at a time, until eventually it was just the two of us in front of a fireplace, leaning in for a kiss.

Lanie's dream is to travel to Positano, Italy. Have you ever been there, or is there a dream destination you're excited to visit in the future?
Positano was the site of my spectacular breakup—and in an early draft of the book, it was the site of Lanie's breakup, too. When I cleared away this failed relationship

from this story, there was space for Positano to take on a deeper meaning—for her mother, her career, and Noa(h).

What would you like readers to take away from By Any Other Name?
I hope it feels like meeting a friend for lunch, one you haven't seen in a while but with whom you can pick right up where you left off. I hope this friend makes you laugh and feel less alone, and that you leave with a little more faith in love.

What's next for you?
More novels—some in genres new to me, some in familiar modes, all where love and wonder are alive.

Discussion Guide

1. Discuss how Lanie's and Noa's childhood experiences shaped their trajectories in life. If they had different experiences, do you feel they would have chosen the paths they did? How has your upbringing helped shape your life—your passions, future goals, or even your values?

2. What are the top 5 characteristics on your Ninety-Nine Things list that you want in a partner?

3. While *By Any Other Name* is a romance, it also feels like an ode to New York City. Where is your favorite place to go in New York City, and if you've never been, where would you most like to visit?

4. Lanie goes above and beyond in order to help Noa(h) with his writer's block in order to secure a promotion. Have you ever similarly done something out of the ordinary for your job? If so, what and why did you do it?

5.   Create a title of your love life based on this Noa
     Callaway–inspired prompt: Ninety-Nine Things I
     _____ About_____.

6.   In your opinion, what about Noa speaks the most to
     Lanie? Inversely, what do you think draws Noa to
     Lanie's personality?

7.   What would be your perfect meet-cute with a poten-
     tial romantic interest? Were you able to carry out this
     dream in real life, and if so, was it everything you
     expected?

8.   What was your favorite scene in the novel, and why?

9.   Lanie has a type A personality, which at times can be
     both good and bad. Do you relate to this character
     trait? Why or why not?

10. What's your favorite book, and why? How has that
     book changed your life?

11. Before she passed, Lanie's mom said to her, "Prom-
     ise to find someone you'll really, really love." What
     does this mean to you? What is your definition of
     love?

12. Were you surprised by the ending?

Lauren Kate is the #1 *New York Times* and internationally bestselling author of nine novels for young adults, including *Fallen*, which was made into a major motion picture. Her books have been translated into more than thirty languages and have sold more than 10 million copies worldwide. She is also the author of *The Orphan's Song*, her debut adult novel. *By Any Other Name* is her second adult novel. Kate lives in Los Angeles with her family.

VISIT LAUREN KATE ONLINE

LaurenKateBooks.net

LaurenKateAuthor

LaurenKateBooks

LaurenKateBooks